The Thirty-Ninth Man

The Primary Dakota Missions and Dakota Villages of Minnesota

Extended Tail Feathers · Lac Qui Parle Mission, 1835 - 1854

MONTEVIDEO

Wakenmani
Sleepy Eyes
Mazomanie
Red Iron

GRANITE FALLS

Anawangmani
Imyangmani
Otherday
Inihah
Akipa

Hazelwood Mission, 1854 - 1862
Pajutazee Mission, 1852 - 1862

Upper Sioux Agency (Yellow Medicine)

Red Middle Voice

Shakpe

Big Eagle
Little Crow
Mahkato
Cloudman
Wacouta
Wabasha

Lower Sioux Agency (Redwood)

REDWOOD FALLS

Zoar Mission, 1860 - 1862
Red Logs

Mazasha (Red Iron)

Fort Ridgely

ST PETER

Ishtaba (Sleepy Eyes)

Traverse Des Sioux Mission, 1843 - 1853

NEW ULM

MINNESOTA

MANKATO

Mississippi

MINNEAPOLIS

Lake Calhoun/Lake Harriet Mission, 1834 - 1840

Cloudman

Oak Grove Mission, 1843 - 1852

BLOOMINGTON

Cloudman
Pinesha (Mahkato)

Prairieville Mission, 1847 - 1853

Mazomani
Shakpe

SHAKOPEE

Eagle Head

Fort Snelling

ST PAUL

Kaposia Mission, 1846 - 1852

Little Crow
Black Dog (Big Eagle)

HASTINGS

Red Wing Mission, 1848 - 1854

RED WING

Wacouta

Mississippi

Wabasha

Mississippi

Legend

✝ Dakota Missions, 1834 - 1862

Dakota Villages

⋏ Prior to 1851 Treaties: Lower MN/Upper Mississippi River sites

⋏ Following 1851 Treaties: Upper and Middle MN and relocated Lower Minnesota/ Upper Mississippi River sites

▬ U.S. Military Forts

▲ U.S. Government Indian Agencies

CITY Modern Day City Locations

▲ NORTH

The Thirty-Ninth Man

D.A. Swanson

North Star Press of St. Cloud, Inc.
St. Cloud, Minnesota

ISBN: 978-0-87839-683-2

First Edition: June 2013

Printed in the United States of America

Published by
North Star Press of St. Cloud, Inc.
P.O. Box 451
St. Cloud, MN 56302

www.northstarpress.com   Facebook - North Star Press   Twitter - North Star Press

Acknowledgements

Many thanks to Deborah Peterson, Mystic Lake Mdewakanton Tribal Librarian, and her capable assistant, Angie Danner, who together provided me with invaluable information regarding this most painful episode in the nation's history.

I also owe a debt of gratitude to Jennifer Quinlan, Historical Fiction Editor, whose expertise and gentle nudges helped keep me on track.

Most of all, thank you to my beautiful wife of forty-seven years, who allowed me the private space and encouragement to complete the task.

The map of Frontier Missions and Villages is the property of Bloomington, Minnesota, and is used with permission from the City of Bloomington.

Contents

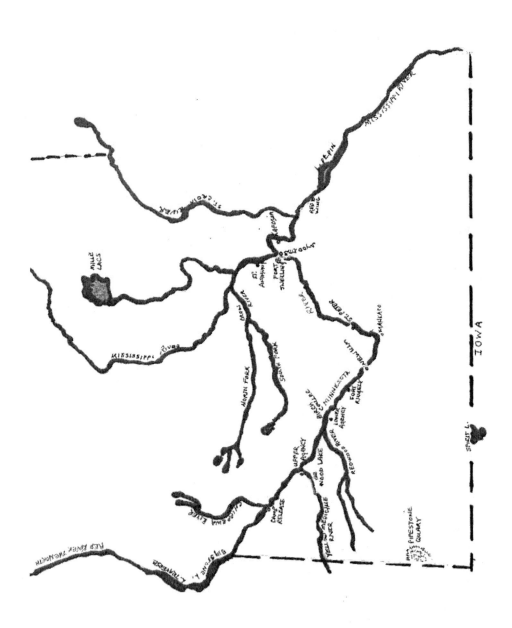

A Note to the Reader

THIS IS THE STORY OF A GREAT INJUSTICE and a handful of men and women who played a part.

At 10:00 a.m. on December 26, 1862, thirty-eight men were hanged in the largest mass execution in the history of the United States. It was said "three drumbeats signaled the moment of execution; a single ax stroke plummeted all through the gallows, the crowd cheered; bodies were buried in a single grave on the edge of town."

Thirty-nine were sentenced—thirty-eight died—one was pardoned at the last minute.

Sioux Legend

They were there from the beginning of time. There was one land base and one ocean. They began to fight and eventually began to hurt the earth. She gave out warnings. They didn't listen so she began to shake. The land divided into separate islands to isolate the people and give them a second chance.

They started over as separate people and as time went on they began killing again. The earth, again, sent out warnings to stop. Again they didn't listen.

This time, she shook and the land opened and swallowed the people. When she finished shaking, they were inside of her. A trickster lured the people back to the surface by turning himself into a buffalo to draw the people out. The place of their return is in the Black Hills of South Dakota. They are known, simply, as Oyate—The People.

Chapter One

Anton McAllister

DAMN IT, MAN . . . ya beat me again." McAllister threw down his cards with venom while the Indian seated opposite cackled in glee at the Scotsman's misfortune. It was the third hand in a row, and Jacob was wild-eyed, in part due to blathering intoxication.

In general, things came easily to Jacob McAllister. He enjoyed good looks and physical stature beyond most men, and women adored him—tall, handsome, a superb athlete—his failing centered on alcohol, a lazy disposition, and a total lack of moral character.

They'd been at the cards for seven hours, drinking cheap whiskey over the game that turned heavily in favor of the Indian, and Jacob's bile overflowed. As his left hand slammed the remainder of his stake on the table, his right reached to his side, and with purpose rose to bury the blade of his knife well into the planks serving as their gaming table. "One more hand, ya naked savage, and I slit yer blasted throat ear-t-ear."

The Indian, eyes placid under the influence of substantial amounts of alcohol, misunderstood the action. Instead of seeing it as a threat, he viewed it as a bet. Jacob's knife was of unusual beauty, with a keen edge that never dulled and was widely admired, and the Indian greatly desired to have it as his own. Thinking it of extreme value, he instructed his Algonquin mates, themselves weak of leg from too much drink, to retire to his lodge and fetch his most valuable possession. They soon returned, since his lodge was the closest to the emporium in which they sat, leading his reluctant daughter.

Through dull eyes, foggy mind, and heightened expectations, Jacob viewed the Indian's wager with carelessness and accepted the ante.

Cards were dealt and played, and Jacob stumbled from the saloon with his prize in tow while the poor Indian sat in incredulous dismay, watching his daughter dutifully exiting with the Scotsman.

Upon awakening the following afternoon, Jacob stared through painful eyes at his prize, and determining the folly of his actions, reasoned he would return her and demand restitution.

The makeshift camp in which the saloon was located was a conglomeration of diversity. This was a gathering place for immigrants with a desire for total independence and prosperity unavailable to them in their homelands. Among them were many with shady pasts, escaping to avoid prosecution for misdeeds back home. Most were French, some English, Scots, Swedes, and Irish—all there to try their hand at the fur trade and lusting for the fast track to wealth. Spread among the tents and half-built structures were pockets of Algonquin Indians seeking employment as guides to rich trapping areas known only to them.

With the woman in tow, McAllister stalked the camp looking for the man who had lost her. He found him on the backside of a wooden shed, sound asleep, leaning against the rough-cut planks that formed the shed wall. With careless ease, he placed his boot on the man's shoulder and pushed him over.

"What the hell ya mean, dumpin' the squaw on me?" Jacob said, yanking the woman by the wrist and propelling her toward the Indian who was now awake and trying to stand. She narrowly missed plowing into him before slamming into the shed wall.

The unfortunate Indian, not understanding a word, struggled to comprehend what was happening. His head hurt, his mouth was dry, and he had to throw up, and in front of him stood a very large, red-faced white man yelling and gesturing wildly while another person lay on the ground to his left.

Using the wall for support, he straightened and did his best to stop the world from spinning. He stood in an unsteady fashion for a short time before the spinning began anew, causing him to lose his balance and stagger in the direction of the invectives being hurtled his way. With arms outstretched, he reached for the white man to avoid falling on his face.

Jacob viewed the move as a threat. Stepping to one side, he drew his knife, and as the Indian fell forward, he plunged it into his chest.

Realizing the impact of his action, McAllister immediately lit out for the wild land to the south, figuring to make the White Mountains, where he could hook up with one of the logging outfits known to operate in the area.

On his third night out, the weather turned, and high winds drove frozen pellets of snow into the open sleeves and collar of his tattered Mackinaw. With fingers unable to grasp and feet numb from the cold, McAllister squatted beneath a large cedar and hugged its trunk, reconciled to his death.

The ethereal figure drifted among the blowing snow, closing the distance between them as Jacob struggled to fully open frozen eyelids. Then he had the sensation of floating toward the unnoticed opening in the rock wall . . . before he lost consciousness.

* * *

SHE WAS TALLER THAN MOST, thin and angular of body with a wide nose centered on a broad, impassive face that would have been more at home on a stodgy Indian woman. Her Algonquin name was Kanti—Woman Who Sings—and she had been on Jacob's tail the past three days, fearful of approaching him, yet unable to return to her people. The dishonor of her rejection by the white man ensured her outcast status and a life forever on the fringe of their encampment in virtual servitude. Her best chance was acceptance by the cruel Scotsman who had won her on a bet, so she dogged him, moving with the ease of a deer, following the unmistakable trail left by the man ahead of her.

The signs of a pending storm were evident, and seeing no attempt by the Scotsman to find shelter, she broke away, making a beeline for a promontory ahead, hoping to find a place to ride it out. As if by providence, she happened upon a substantial cave. Blackened rock around the entrance told her it had been used before, and inside was a heap of dead wood, unburned, awaiting the flame. There she huddled by the warmth of the fire for several hours while the wind packed the hard driven snow into exposed crevasses and made huge drifts on the leeward side of trees and boulders. She thought about the man outside, fearsome in countenance yet childlike in his inability to see the signs. She knew she must try to save him.

Leaving the warmth of the cave, the fierce wind slamming ice pellets against her skin, she found it necessary to hold her hand in front of her face, peering between slightly parted fingers to protect her eyes. Struggling forward through the blinding snow she was unable to see more than a few feet through the driven whiteness. The Great Spirit interceded, and a momentary calm fell about her, lifting the veil of white and exposing the figure hunkered in the stand of cedars twenty feet to her left. Approaching without hesitation, she clamped on to the neck of his Mackinaw and dragged him toward the shelter of the cave.

* * *

Whitehall, King George County, Virginia
1804

TEN-YEAR-OLD LAWRENCE TALIAFERRO inched along the branch extending nearly the width of the river. Twenty feet below, the water flowed deep and fast through the narrow opening cut between ten-foot vertical walls. He knew from experience if he dropped as near to the far side as possible, the current would deposit him safely into the small eddy pool created downstream. If he bailed too early and fell short, he would have to swim for his life to reach the opposite shore before entering the whitewater stretch beyond.

There were four of them, and they had been playing together most of the day. The new kid, Thomas Meredith, joined Lawrence, his best friend Timothy Overton, and young Davy Burroughs. Thomas had been nothing but trouble from the outset. This was the first time they let him hang with them, and as far as Lawrence was concerned, it would be the last.

Thomas, at thirteen, was the kind of kid who was difficult to like, full of brag and always with a quick answer. To top it off he seemed intent on throwing his weight around, challenging the other three every step of the way. He was especially focused on outdoing Larry Taliaferro, and an earlier provocation is what drove the ten-year-old to his current predicament twenty feet in the air.

It started with a dare from Thomas. "You ain't got the guts to do it."

"Shoot, I done a lot more than that before." Larry's three older brothers cut him little slack, so he was nonchalant and unfazed by the challenge, a fact that irritated Thomas to no end.

"Thomas . . . you have to know . . . Larry's the best swimmer I ever saw, and he ain't afraid of nothing." Timothy Overton knew from experience that Lawrence Taliaferro had never backed away from a reasonable challenge.

"I'll tell you what," Thomas, wanting to see Larry fail, sweetened the pot, "you do it, and I'll do it too."

That's all it took. The boys watched from safety on the bank as Lawrence worked his way along the branch.

"Don't you be slipping and falling, Lawrence. That water looks pretty bad to me." Thomas posed, confident that the younger boy would chicken out.

"Don't you worry about me, Thomas. You can start climbing any time now because I'm about ready to fly."

Thomas began to feel something he'd never before encountered. Always the instigator, seldom called on his cavalier dares, he was now expected to follow up for the first time in his life. A primal fear moved through his entire body one section at a time. It started in the pit of his stomach, moving down his legs. Every pore in his body constricted as his nerve endings tingled and shuddered with his building doubt. A chill spread upward, raising the hair on the back of his neck. As the fear rose, he could carry the bluff no further.

He turned to Timothy. "I ain't going up there. You think I'm as stupid as him?"

"Thomas . . . you have to go. You dared him to do it. Now you have to go." Timothy was appalled.

"Ain't no way I'm going up there. I ain't scared. I can't help it if he's stupid enough to do it. He ain't brave . . . he's stupid."

"Aw, Thomas. He's gonna want someone to do it."

"Then you go ahead and be as stupid as he is. Shit . . . you're probably scared to try it."

"Bullcrap. So, what if I am afraid? The only reason Larry did it was 'cause you said you'd do it too. Now you have to follow through and do it."

"You go right ahead, big shot. Show me how it's done. I ain't going."

Larry was as far out on the branch as he dared go. His concentration focused on the black water rushing through the cut gorge below. He shifted his weight, pulled his left leg upward and over the branch positioning for the jump, and in one smooth movement launched his body toward the exact spot he knew he must land. He entered the water feet first and began to back paddle with his arms the moment his head went under, having the effect of bobbing him to the surface. The current carried him forward, spinning his body, disorienting him, until he felt the bottom rise beneath. Crawling ashore, he flopped on his back gasping for air. As he had planned, his jump carried him into the eddy.

He lay on the sand bank, eyes closed, chest heaving, gasping for air. With his head clearing and his breathing under control, he opened his eyes, looked up to the extended branch, and was gripped with a sudden pang of apprehension.

A small figure worked his way along the branch. Timothy Overton was inching his way out over the river.

"Timmy . . . get off that tree! Go back! It's too fast! I almost drowned . . . go back!"

Timothy, hearing Larry's scream, stopped inching forward and locked his heels around the branch. Filled with trepidation after hearing the warning, he found himself unable to move as his body tensed.

From below Lawrence watched in horror as his friend slowly tipped to his right. Reaching forward to lock his arms around the branch, Timmy slipped and plummeted into the fastest part of the roiling water.

* * *

THE INVESTIGATION FOLLOWING the incident was a private, messy affair. The local constable assembled the boys in the Taliaferro sitting room. Timothy's parents were there—Julie Overton, his mother, sitting to the left of Jeremiah, his father. Timmy was their only child and Julie was wracked with sadness, shoulders hunched, white lace handkerchief pressed to her face.

Opposite the Overtons were Mr. and Mrs. Taliaferro, flanking their youngest son, who stared at the floor, unable to meet the gaze of those sitting opposite.

To the Overton's right sat Thomas Meredith and his father, Thomas, Sr., both with determined, unyielding looks. They had heard gossip about the tragedy and intended to defend the Meredith honor. Mrs. Meredith had stayed home with a debilitating headache, which had plagued her since the accident.

Lastly, sitting directly behind Thomas, were Clyde and Matilda Burroughs and their son Davy. A full year younger than Lawrence, Davy was a mess. With red eyes, a testament to bouts of unrelenting crying, he fought to maintain a fragile control over his emotions.

"All right . . . boys, we just need to learn what happened out there. We aren't here to place blame. This isn't an official proceeding, however, we are going to learn exactly what happened so Mr. and Mrs. Overton can start their recovery." The constable's delivery was directed to the boys, heartfelt, almost gentle, and intended to soften the proceedings for the sake of all present.

"Let's start with Lawrence."

His head was down. He knew what was coming. He'd faced his parents with answers that were painful memories. He looked up and said in a voice that was steady and so soft the constable had to lean in to hear him, "I guess it was my idea. We were playing and just talking and stuff. We got to talking about doing stupid things, and I said I could climb out on the limb and jump into the water. Then Thomas dared me to do it . . . so I did."

"Is that right? Is that what happened, boys?"

They nodded in agreement.

"Did you know that Timothy was going to do it too?"

"No. Thomas told me if I did it, he'd do it too. Thomas was supposed to do it."

The constable turned to face the older boy. "Is that right, Thomas?"

Thomas's eyes narrowed. In a clipped voice, he answered, "Yeah, and I'd a done it too, but Timmy told me he wanted to do it."

Davy Burroughs, who had been crying nearly nonstop since the accident, so distraught it was thought best not to hear his story until now, snapped his bowed head upright. "That ain't right, Thomas, and you know it."

Lawrence stared at Davy; mouth hanging slack. This was something new.

"Thomas called him a shithead."

"Ain't true, Davy. I done no such thing."

"Did too."

"Did not, you little runt."

"Okay, boys. That's enough." The constable stepped in to put an end to the bickering.

"Thomas told him he wasn't gonna do it."

"Did not! You lie, Davy!"

Davy had stopped crying and now stood in front of his chair. "Thomas, you're the liar. You told Timmy that Lawrence was stupid and that you weren't stupid. You weren't gonna do it, and Timmy said the only reason Larry did it was 'cause you said you'd do it too, and when you chickened out, Timmy said he'd do it, and you said he was too chicken to do it," his voice caught as he fought back tears, "and he said somebody had to do it 'cause you told Larry you would," he stood erect, knees shaking, tears beginning to stream down his face, tiny shoulders constricting as he fought for air, "and you said he was too chicken to do it . . . so he did."

Davy Burroughs wavered and his father caught him as he collapsed in a heap.

Thomas's face turned ashen at hearing the truth pour forth. His father cuffed him on the back of the head. "Thomas . . . you lied to me!"

Although Lawrence didn't like Thomas, he never considered that the older boy imposed his will on Timothy, in effect shaming him into doing something he knew was dangerous. Thomas's deceit and selfish nature made an imprint on Lawrence that was to stay with him for the rest of his life.

Somehow, no one knows for sure how, the story got out about what really happened, and the Meredith family packed up and left within a month. Rumors circulated that the family moved to Pennsylvania where the senior Thomas could ply his trade as a tinker among the populace of Philadelphia. According to reports, the young Thomas killed a neighbor's dog and spent a week in jail while his father earned enough to pay the fine and secure his release.

* * *

Northeast Wilderness
Late September 1804

THE BLIZZARD RAGED for three days, during which warm broth of juniper berries and bark brought him back from the dead. As Jacob recovered, his scurrilous nature resurfaced, and he made no attempt to conceal his distaste for the Indian woman who had saved his life. On the seventh day, with clear skies and warming temperature, he forced himself upon her with a roughness that left her bleeding and unconscious, gathered his belongings, and lit out for parts unknown.

Kanti survived, though bearing a wound on her soul that would not heal. After two weeks she left the cave, moving toward the river she knew flowed westward. Traveling slowly, she endured scattered bouts of poor weather, and in the manner of her people, built makeshift shelters for the worst of it. She came to a valley rich with game where she built her lodge and settled in to have the baby she knew was growing inside her womb.

On July 7, 1805, she gave birth and named the baby Annawon— Chief, in English, believing he would be a great warrior and leader of men. She fashioned a pouch from a lynx pelt and carried the child on her back whenever she left her lodge. Having killed many beavers by old methods, she ventured to the river where she bartered her skins for traps, kettles, and implements to improve her small encampment.

When Annawon was about a year old, she began carrying him in front, facing forward when she walked her trap line, and he learned the lessons of stealth and cunning required of a hunter. His father's genes were strong, and he inherited good looks and a solid frame, and was easily mistaken for one much older.

As he grew, Kanti continued to teach the ways of survival to her young son. He learned the various foods that were in abundance in the forest, learned, too, to read the signs of impending weather events and to trap, skin, and prepare hides for barter. Exhibiting a natural bent for conducting trade, he was blessed with an intuition for recognizing when to strike the deal, while in a convincing manner leaving the impression that he came out on the short end.

During his eighth year, the two of them nearly stumbled into a British patrol concealed near the mouth of a river Kanti called Rumble Creek. In actuality, it was the unofficial border between Canada and the United States, and the British were biding their time before launching an all out attack on an American outpost where Kanti and her son often traded pelts. Although the two of them knew that a state of war existed between the two countries, they had not seen a clash between them since it started the year prior, in 1812.

Sinking deeper into the woods, concealed by trees and heavy undergrowth, they worked their way to the top of a high knoll offering a view of the outpost and surrounding clearing, some 800 yards away. It was a breezy night with a full moon darting between drifting clouds, and Annawon was about to get his first lesson in battle strategy.

The post was an assortment of buildings surrounded on all sides by a wall of vertical timbers. The Americans had cleared trees for at least fifty yards on three sides of the outpost, leaving open ground and very little concealment for an adversary. The front gate to the compound faced the riverbank and lay about twenty yards from the water.

"Let us watch and see how the battle unfolds. There . . . to the right, at the tree line!" Kanti pointed to the flash of red she had seen.

Annawon carefully surveyed the area, seeing nothing unusual. Then his eyes were drawn to movement. A red uniform jacket, followed by another, and yet another passed the distant clearing. The British were positioning themselves for the fight. He shifted his vision to the walled outpost.

At each corner on the interior of the wall, a raised platform allowed anyone acting as a sentry to see all the way to the trees. Between the corners and lower than the corner platforms, a plank stretched around the inside perimeter, providing a shelf for men to stand on and shoot into the clearing. Annawon could see a man's silhouette at each of the lookout posts, and he wondered if they could see the red coats of the British uniforms just inside the trees.

Shifting his attention back to the trees at the edge of the cleared area, he saw that the British were positioning themselves to attack from two sides simultaneously.

Although the moon was full, the drifting clouds caused shadows to roll across the surface of the clearing, and Annawon sensed an eerie unpleasantness at the scene. Looking back toward the outpost, he saw a doubling of the guard at each corner of the wall. Just as a shadow passed over the gated portion of the wall, he saw several men leaving the protection of the fort and running toward the river, away from the approaching British.

"Look!" He touched his mother's arm and pointed to the figures. "They are running away. They are afraid to fight."

Kanti replied. "I think they may have something else in mind . . . just watch."

It seemed an awfully long time before anything happened and when it did, Annawon was speechless and a little afraid as the action unfolded. The British forces opened fire from the edge of the woods with a volley louder than anything he had ever heard. The firing came from the woods on two sides of the outpost, knocking bark and wood splinters off the wall. The bedlam was continuous, lasting for several minutes with only sporadic moments of gaping silence

Kanti explained, "They are coordinating their fire so many are always shooting while the others are reloading. That's the reason for the continuous barrage we hear."

"Why are the men of the fort not shooting back? Has everyone deserted the outpost?"

"I suspect those within are waiting to show their strength after the British charge. Those inside the walls need to get them to enter the cleared land to be effective with their shots."

The fusillade continued while return fire from the wall remained irregular and primarily focused from the corners. Then the British made their move.

Annawon saw movement in the tree line. As he watched the low-growing bushes turned autumn red as line after line of British soldiers came into the open and advanced on the outpost. Spaced about ten feet apart, the waves swept across the clearing, each step bringing them closer to the battered wall that, until then, had protected those inside.

Methodical in their approach, the first line would point and fire, and stop to reload while the second line stepped to the front, advancing three or four steps before they stopped to fire. Four such lines advanced across the cleared land on two sides of the outpost, each advance bringing them closer to the wall, each volley resulting in more damage to the upright timbers.

"Mother, they have killed those inside. There is no return fire. They are all dead."

Kanti replied, "Let us watch, son. The fight is not yet finished."

The troops were now at the midway point of the open clearing, and those in command now exited the trees, strutting left and right, yelling commands to their men.

As Annawon watched, each of the red coats seemingly in command of the troops crumpled and fell. As though on signal, rifle barrels appeared at the top of the fortification and opened up on the advancing soldiers, killing about a quarter of them. The British lines stopped moving forward, and all those with loaded muskets raised them and returned fire in the direction of the wall.

Annawon then saw something very peculiar. Without return fire from the Americans inside the fortification, British troops were falling dead on the cleared battlefield between the trees and heavy woods. It was several moments before he realized what was happening.

"There are Americans in the woods behind them!"

Mass confusion ensued as those caught in the open realized their situation. Again, rifles fired from the top of the wall, as simultaneous firing commenced from the heavy trees. The lines broke, red coats spreading in every direction trying to escape the trap.

Annawon had seen his first battle, and learned a tactical lesson. He realized the importance of ranging beyond a confined area to defeat an enemy with superior firepower. The Americans that had gotten behind the British had made the difference.

* * *

TWO MONTHS BEFORE HIS FOURTEENTH BIRTHDAY, Annawon and Kanti were mistaken for hostiles while flagging a steamboat. A shot was fired, hitting Kanti in the forehead and killing her instantly. For the first time in his life, Annawon was alone.

Grabbing their bundle of pelts, he vanished into the woods where he mourned and contemplated his future. With a strong distrust for the encroaching white population, he decided his best bet was to head for the wilderness to the west. Gathering his large store of beaver, wolf, and fox pelts, he made for the settlement he knew lay twenty miles to the south, where he sold the entire lot for cash and began his journey into parts unknown.

Witnesses to the exchange were Billy Bolden and Francis Glover, both of nefarious reputation and dangerous ways. Trailing the young man for the better part of two days, they made their move on the second night, intending to make his sleep one of eternity. Tying their horses, they crawled toward the encampment where Annawon, aware of their presence, lay in wait.

Billy was the first to die, catching a tomahawk full in the face. With the strike, Francis lunged toward the ghost that had delivered the blow, and with a single knife stroke lost his right ear. Screaming in agony, he ran from the scene in sheer panic while Annawon watched with satisfaction. The young man was now the owner of two stout horses and a Kentucky long rifle sporting gold inlay and a silver set-trigger.

Upon reaching the Ohio River, Annawon signed on with the American Fur Company as a hunter and scout for their expedition into the Northwest Frontier. Although only fourteen, his size and demeanor reflected one much older, and he quickly proved invaluable for his knowledge of the wilderness, earning the prestige of primary scout during the trek. During this time the other men, apparently unable to cope with his three-syllable name, simply began calling him Anton.

Impressed from the first day by the forthcoming nature of the young man, John Drury, a scientist traveling with the party, began counsel on rudiments of the English language, which were continuous during the journey. In the course of the next year, Anton proved to be a quick study, learning to read and write, as well as to speak as one with considerable schooling.

* * *

Whitehall, King George County, Virginia
1812

AFTER THE INCIDENT AT THE RIVER, Lawrence Taliaferro, never a great student, became a problem for his teachers, disrupting the class and often skipping classes altogether. His mother couldn't bear to see his keen intellect going to waste, so she hired the best tutors money could buy. The young man realized he actually liked learning, so he applied himself and began to blossom as a student, showing unusual insight in the areas of leadership and problem solving. In August of 1812, at the age of eighteen, his mother, the ultimate patriot, signed for him to join the fight for his country in what became known as the War of 1812.

"Lawrence, I want you and your brothers to do what this family has done for as long as anyone can remember. You fight for your country and show that the Taliaferro family supports this nation."

"Yes, Mother. Although, I'm not entirely sure I hate the British enough to enjoy killing them, I'm sure they're responsible for many American deaths."

"Lawrence, you don't have to hate them. We must fight for what's right and for what's best for the country without hate entering the picture."

With his mother's remarks etched firmly into his mind, he joined Captain Meriwether Taliaferro's volunteer company of light infantry. He was shortly appointed to the Thirty-Fifth Regular Infantry. During his subsequent three months of service, his animosity toward the British grew to the point that friends and superiors alike noticed it. After being told he needed to further his education to qualify for a commission, he jumped at the chance for more schooling. Eight months later he was appointed an ensign in the First Regiment United States Infantry and ordered to report to Belle Fontaine, Missouri.

"All I know, Mother, is that they ordered me to report to a fort in Missouri. I have no idea what my job will be."

"Remember this Lawrence . . . the nation needs people with a conscience. No matter the job, if you do the best you can, and you do it for the right reasons, you can make a difference. The Taliaferro name has a great history with great men in this nation since the settlement of Jamestown. They are big shoes to fill. I have no doubt you'll make your mark."

* * *

SHORTLY AFTER REPORTING TO HIS POST in Missouri, Lawrence was witness to the cold-blooded killing of an officer by a sergeant and three men in the company he had joined.

He was awakened by the sounds of a scuffle just outside the barracks. Rising off the military cot they called a bed, he walked outside to find the source of the noise. The terrible commotion came from someplace to his left.

It was a new moon, totally dark and so still a candle flame wouldn't waver, in spite of which he could make out three men beating on another. As he watched, a fourth ran into the melee swinging an ax handle and caught the unfortunate victim square in the face. He went down, and the three ran away while the fourth continued to hammer the prone body.

Lawrence, wearing nothing but his long-handles, charged the assailant.

"Hey, you there! Hey, stop that. You're going to kill him!"

The assailant looked up, making eye contact with Lawrence before dropping the weapon and fleeing in the direction the others had taken.

Lawrence raised half the post with his yells for help. Even the commander came to the scene in his bedclothes. That was when the dead body was identified as Ensign Carver.

"What did you see here, young man? What the hell happened?"

"I heard a ruckus. When I investigated, I saw three men beating this poor man. Then a fourth, a big man, charged in with that ax handle," he pointed to the weapon that lay a few feet away, "and finished the killing."

"Damn it! This marks the third officer I've lost in as many weeks. The first two deserted, this one got himself killed." His eyes moved over the scene, as though he were expecting an answer to his thought. *I wish I knew what was going on here.* Then he turned back to the matter at hand.

"Are you that new man . . . Taliaferro?"

"Yes, sir!"

"I want to see you in my quarters first thing in the morning."

"Yes, sir!"

Men were assigned to carry the body to another building and everyone left the scene. Lawrence headed back to his uncomfortable cot, his mind full of thoughts. He slipped under the single blanket, thankful for its warmth. It was a chilly night, cooler than most in Missouri during the month of June.

Just as his mind settled and sleep was about to overcome him, a calloused hand slapped over his mouth, and he felt cold steel against his throat.

"You keep quiet or you'll join him." The muffled voice was inches from his ear. "Take this towel off your eyes inside of a minute and you're a dead man."

* * *

LAWRENCE WAS AWAKE when the first man climbed from his cot. Feigning sleep, he peeked through shuttered eyes, watching every soldier as they prepared for the day. He was looking for the big man who did the killing, and he reasoned he came from within that barracks.

* * *

THE MEN WERE ASSEMBLED at the base of the flagpole on one end of the open parade ground inside the fort. Mid-morning, the commander was implementing the plan devised by the young ensign during their hour-long meeting. If successful, it would draw out the men who had a hand in killing Ensign Carver. The man who delivered the killing blows had been identified.

The commander stood twenty feet in front of the row of troopers.

"Attention!"

The command was delivered. The men, slow to react, eventually straightened to the posture required of the order.

"By now I know you've all heard about the murder committed last night."

A general murmur started among the ranks.

"I intend to get to the bottom of this. I'll only say this once . . . if you know anything about it, it will go easier for you if you come forward." He looked left and right along the ranks. "Think about it. This is the only chance you'll get to set yourself straight." As he talked, he clasped his hands behind his back and slowly advanced on the men. In the stillness that followed, he walked along the row of troopers, looking each man square in the eyes as he passed, then continued to walk behind them, passing silently.

The men were becoming increasingly uncomfortable, this being observed by the man in the commander's quarters.

The commander completed his circle and came to a stop in the same position he'd begun.

"Does anyone wish to come forward and tell me what you know?" There was only silence and determined looks.

"All right . . . suit yourself."

Turning to his quarters, which lay directly in front of the assembly he called out, "Ensign Taliaferro, front and center!"

The door opened to reveal the tall officer impeccably resplendent in his dress uniform. As he crossed the distance to the commander with brisk, measured steps, his brass reflected the morning sunlight, and his boots glinted with unblemished polish. Every eye was on the young ensign.

When he reached the commander, he came to an abrupt halt, slammed his heels together, and executed a perfect salute. The commander returned the gesture and pivoted to face the men.

"Men, I give you Ensign Lawrence Taliaferro. May the good Lord deliver the souls of the guilty from the perdition so richly deserved."

Lawrence stepped forward.

"At ease, men." Clasping his hands behind him, he began moving slowly to his right as he addressed the troopers.

"I can tell you with certainty that one man will die for this crime. Whether he is joined on the gallows is up to his three accomplices. You three will be given the opportunity to admit your involvement and have a chance to live beyond tomorrow."

He had walked to the end of the line of troopers and turned to begin his stroll toward the other end of the line.

"One of you threatened me last night after the affair," Ensign Taliaferro said. "You said if I didn't keep my mouth shut, I would join Carver in death." There was a murmur from the men. It was obvious they had not known of the threat.

Reaching the midpoint of the assembly, Lawrence pivoted away from the line of men, took the three paces that brought him to the commander's side, did an about face, and issued a command.

"Attention!"

Heads snapped up, eyes forward, and bodies straightened at the sound of the order.

Lawrence raised his right arm to shoulder height, pointed his forefinger, and moved his arm along the line, halting when it pointed directly at one man.

"Sergeant Pitt, you are under arrest for the murder of Ensign James Carver." As prearranged, troopers on either side grabbed Pitt's arms as another stepped behind and latched on to the collar of his jacket.

The sergeant's face showed no emotion, but his eyes blazed with a powerful hatred.

"Your first mistake was being seen, your second was to threaten me . . . take this man to the guardhouse."

Lawrence turned his attention to the rest of the troopers.

"That man will feel the noose. As for you other three, there's a faint hope you may escape the rope. I was there. I saw you kicking and punching Carver into submission. There's a slight chance a tribunal could find you innocent of murder." *This is it. It either works, or the three walk away scot-free.* "If you don't step forward now, before I call you out, that possibility vanishes. Take a couple of minutes to decide."

Lawrence turned to the commander and the two engaged in a brief conversation, and then he again faced the troops.

"Does anyone wish to step forward?" There was a barely perceptible movement as two men strained their peripheral vision trying to make eye contact. "Very well, as you wish."

He began to raise his arm as before, when a trooper stepped from the line and approached him. The two talked in hushed tones before being joined by the commander. Within minutes, all three accomplices had stepped forward and were placed under arrest.

"Bring these three to the guardhouse and place them as far away from Sergeant Pitt as possible."

Subsequent interrogation revealed that the sergeant had been stealing supplies from the storeroom, mainly tapping the supply of whiskey and selling it for his own profit, which he shared with his accomplices. They knew nothing of the earlier murders, intending only to scare Ensign Carver into silence after he learned of the misdeed.

By August, Lawrence Taliaferro had been promoted to lieutenant. Progressing ranks followed in rapid succession as he served in Ohio and Illinois. He was involved in the siege of Fort Erie during August and September 1814. In the spring of 1817, he led 130 recruits to Fort Howard, Green Bay, Wisconsin Territory, to fill the depleted Third Regiment. Then on to Detroit all the while earning notice for his intelligence and consistent devotion to fairness.

While on furlough in 1818, Lawrence was invited to visit President James Monroe, his patron friend, connection, and fellow Virginian.

* * *

Presidential Study, The Executive Mansion
1818

PRESIDENT MONROE WAS SEATED opposite Lawrence. On the small table between them was an open bottle of French wine. Monroe poured three fingers into a wine glass and placed it in front of his guest.

"Lawrence, I would like you to resign your position in the army."

Lawrence sat in stunned silence, finally finding his voice. "Mr. President, I have no idea what you may have heard about my service to the country. I can assure you it has been given with honor and a full commitment to the nation."

"Yes, yes. I'm sorry to have caused you concern. In fact . . . it is your exemplary service and considerable skills that I wish to put to use in a civil capacity."

"Sir, I'm at your disposal. May I ask what you have in mind?"

Monroe answered, "There'is a new frontier, wild and untamed. A new frontier that must be settled. You undoubtedly caught a glimpse of it when you were at Fort Howard, in the Wisconsin Territory. Places there are without civil authority of any kind. We have military posts in various locations to protect our people and provide a presence. We need someone who can regulate the fur trade and maintain peaceful coexistence with, and between, the indigenous people."

Lawrence listened with a building excitement as the president continued.

"Colonel Leavenworth is in the process of constructing a fort at the junction of the St. Peter and Mississippi rivers. There is need for an agent representing the U.S. Government to regulate matters."

Monroe continued, "Take your furlough. Go home to your mother. Wait until I contact you. Our expanding nation has a need for men of your caliber."

Chapter Two

Taliaferro on the Northwest Frontier

MOMENTS EARLIER, NEWLY APPOINTED Commissioner of Indian Affairs Lawrence Taliaferro, formerly of Whitehall, Virginia, had entered the camp of Chetanwakenmani, known as Little Crow. The Indian had assumed the mantle of leadership at the death of his father, who had gotten the position from his father before him, making Chetanwakanmani the third chief of the Little Crow Band of the Seven Fires of the Dakota Nation, and the third to carry the name Little Crow.

Lawrence now sat cross-legged opposite Little Crow, second in importance only to Wabasha.

"Your white father in Washington shows his concern for your welfare by sending his soldiers to ensure peace."

Little Crow responded with a brief nod.

"I have seen that the traders seem in direct opposition to the desires of the U.S. Government and the good will of the Indian nations."

Little Crow considered the words. After a long pause replied, "It is so. The traders stir trouble to their convenience."

"Although I am young in years, my heart is that of an old man, Taliaferro said. "My passion for fairness will be made evident to your people."

"My people hope it will be so."

Lawrence Taliaferro was in his element. Having been well briefed on the situation he was entering, he expected opposition from the agents in place with the fur companies, knowing they would see him as a threat. At the same time, it was necessary to create a peaceful coexistence between the Chippewa and Dakota Nations.

The fur companies, by their very nature, attracted hard men, men with wanderlust. With few exceptions, they gave no thought to the future unless it offered riches or new territory to be explored. They were opportunists to the core, transients with an eye to avoiding authority and often on the run from prior transgressions. Owners of these companies were interested in profits, and a few, like John Jacob Astor, of the American Fur Company, appeared to care little about how those profits were garnered.

* * *

Fort Snelling, Northwest Frontier
1819

THE AMERICAN FUR COMPANY party reached the confluence of the Mississippi and St. Peter rivers where a fort started by Colonel Leavenworth was now being constructed under the command of Colonel Josiah Snelling, who had assumed command upon Leavenworth's reassignment. Anton McAllister was with the fur company party.

Finding the topography similar to what he remembered from his childhood, Anton felt like he had come home. The skills learned from his mother had served him well, and he had proved himself to be the most accomplished trapper and hunter at the post.

Traveling widely with the fort as his base, he encountered native Dakota Indians and French trappers. Having learned the rudiments of the French language during the journey, he had no trouble striking up friendships.

During the thaw of 1822, he came upon a young Dakota whose leg had become entangled while crossing a stream swollen with spring rains. Nearly drowned, Anton pulled him from the water, and warmed him by his fire.

Only later did Anton learn that the young boy was the nephew of the Dakota chief Shakopee, when he was invited to the village for a celebration to honor his feat. Since that day, Anton traveled as a brother through all the Dakota Territory.

Colonel Josiah Snelling saw the benefit of having the young man serve as scout and interpreter for the new fort, and after a barter session, secured those services for the agreed price of one horse for every six months of service. On August 31, 1823, Anton McAllister became the voluntary property of the United States Army.

* * *

NO STRANGER TO HARSH WINTERS, Anton was about to get a cool welcome to the Northwest Frontier. His first winter was one for the record books. On New Year's Eve, it was cold enough to freeze a man's spit before it hit the ground.

His buckskins and wolf-pelt overcoat did little to allay the frigid temperatures. Nonetheless, on January 17 he left the fort in search of game. Entering Shakopee's camp, nearly stiff with cold, he was brought to the council tipi and warmed by the fire. There he stayed for three days, enjoying the hospitality of his Sioux friends. Upon his departure, he was gifted with a buffalo robe of superb quality. Anton no longer suffered under the icy winds or freezing rains that lasted into April.

Chapter Three

Tomawka's Dream

THE YOUNG MAN SAT CROSS-LEGGED and raised his arms toward the sliver of moon still visible behind the maples, oaks, and ash that grew to his west. Raising his face toward the heavens, he sang thanks for his delivery through the night, and then rose to his feet, turned to the east, and began his chant to the new day. Tall and thin, sinew and bone, his muscles were long. There was no other in the valley of his people taller than he, and he was widely known for his athletic skills. He loved this place and took every opportunity to visit the lake. It was holy. The unmistakable odors of lake and forest blended into a sweet perfume that filled his senses with absolute perfection. Gentle mornings like this whispered of the goodness of the earth and embraced all travelers within its warm cloak.

However, he had seen it angry. A time when the wind blew so ferociously that trees fell and the lake's surface was whipped into frenzy—the water, black as night, had waves so big they washed over the peninsula on which he now camped. It blew so hard that froth was driven from the white-capped waves and filled the air like fog on a warm spring morning. As much as he feared those times, he loved the peaceful feeling during mornings such as this.

His name was Tomawka and he had been sent by his leader to scout the area for sign of Chippewa war parties and to locate stands of wild rice and berries. The Chippewa were responsible for driving his people from their ancestral home to the north. They were his sworn enemy. Battles were not uncommon in this most special of places. An abundance of ancient burial mounds bore evidence to that fact. His village looked forward to trading and socializing with the other Dakota bands that gathered along the shores and islands of the lake each year, and a tribal war would not be welcome.

Tomawka traveled the shoreline around the entire one hundred plus miles of lakeshore and found no trace of the hated Chippewa. Today he would travel the final miles that would bring him to a place called Spirit Knob. Tomorrow he would return to the camp of his people.

He traveled light, his only possessions a knife given to him by the great leader Shakopee in recognition of his bravery in battle, and a flint securely held inside a leather pouch at his waist. His upper body was naked. He wore leather leggings and moccasins common to his people. A single eagle feather tied into his long black hair was a sign of his bravery. He had no fire to extinguish so he had very little to do to erase his presence from the small point of land. Tonight he would build a fire and cook fresh fish. It would be his first warm meal since leaving his village fifteen days earlier.

He left the peninsula, following the water's edge where it washed against a steep incline. As he walked, the terrain on his left slowly descended to water level, and he found himself on a narrow strip of dry ground running through a marsh. On both sides, the reeds opened to deep water. Behind him was the peninsula where he greeted the new day.

The large bay on his right would guide him to this evening's cooking fire. The journey, if undertaken directly, could be completed in less than half a day. Tomawka knew he would be lucky to arrive at the place called Spirit Knob before sundown.

* * *

THE CHIPPEWA WARRIOR WATCHED as the tall man approached the marsh. The Dakotas knew this Chippewa as Catka, a reference to his left-handedness. In truth, Catka was the fiercest of the Chippewa in his village, and many Dakota scalps hung on his lodge pole. He disdained spears and arrows, preferring the war club in combat. He liked the feel of breaking bones and shattered skulls at the head of his club. Catka fought for the love of battle, and he was well known and feared by the Dakotas. He had, deep within, a perverted love of killing. He now planned the death of the Dakota approaching through the marsh.

Catka had been raised like all the Chippewa children, however, by the time he was seven, he began to stand out from the others. He caught frogs, impaled them with a sharp stick, and roasted them over the fire while still alive. He was known to climb high into the trees and take baby birds from their nests, rip the heads from the bodies and throw them to the ground. While other children hunted for meat, Catka hunted for the killing, often mutilating animals beyond recognition. When he came of age to fight the enemy, he proved to be a natural combatant and gained instant recognition for his fearless embrace of battlefield chaos.

Seeing the tall Dakota warrior approaching, he knew his reputation would soon be bolstered.

As the Dakota knew Catka, the Chippewa knew Tomawka—what a gift he had been given! It was good he did not have his war club for it would have been difficult to leave the Dakota's face intact. He would not settle for the scalp, rather the entire head of this Dakota warrior would hang outside his lodge. All who walked near would whisper of his might. His enemies would fear speaking his name aloud. He would be as a God to his people. He would defeat the great Tomawka on the shores of this lake. His name would be sung by generations not yet born.

* * *

Tomawka moved steadily along the sandy high ground within the marsh. His head turned slightly from side to side, allowing his eyes to scan what lay ahead. Trained in the pursuit of wild game, he focused on nothing yet saw everything, allowing his peripheral vision to detect the flick of an ear or movement of a leg invisible to the focused eye.

Ahead, on the far side of the marsh where the ground rose around the open bay, seven wood ducks erupted and climbed, circling out over the water.

Strange, thought Tomawka. *All rose from the surface as one. Something disturbed them, something they are not used to.*

He continued walking without breaking pace and his head continued its side to side movement. Then he saw something even more disturbing. On the high ground and very near where he knew the trail passed, he detected a fleeting glimpse of color, unnatural for its surroundings. Then it was gone. Tomawka continued as though he saw nothing.

* * *

CATKA KNEW WHERE HE WOULD ENGAGE the Dakota. He reasoned the unsuspecting Tomawka would take the main trail unless alerted by sign of another person, or a branching trail that required inspection. There was no such trail between the two, and Catka had left no sign. The perfect place for engagement was where the trail crossed a gully created a decade earlier when a huge cottonwood uprooted during a storm. In the following hours, the rain fell so heavily it filled the root cavity and eventually washed over the side to flow toward the lake, taking surface soil with it. Subsequent rains continued to wash the ground away until the gully reached a depth of nine feet. The sides were steep, and roots from standing trees hung from the sides of the washed-out earth, the trees themselves threatening to crash into the open gully when sufficient ground washed from beneath them.

A natural slope led to the gully from both sides. Once at the bottom a traveler must walk several yards within the washout to reach the exit slope on the far side. This was where Catka would become a legend. He planned his attack at the place the Dakota would be most vulnerable. He decided to spring his trap as his enemy began his ascent from the depths of the gully.

Like Igmu Taka, the lion, Catka would pounce and slash the ankle tendons of his foe, leaving him helpless. He would bring death as slowly and painfully as possible. He had time. There was no hurry. If Tomawka was exceptionally strong and resisted death, he may strip the flesh from his arms and hear his screams.

They would sing of Catka the warrior.

They would sing of Catka the legend.

They would fear Catka the God.

He barely heard the red squirrel begin scolding him from above.

* * *

TOMAWKA LEFT THE MARSH and gained the slope to higher ground. His senses were attuned to everything around him. Something unsettled him about the flight of ducks. Even more unsettling was the glimpse of something through the dense leaves on the shore he now approached. Then he heard the squirrel, its agitated chatter commonplace in the forest. When coupled with the other warnings indicated danger ahead.

But where? He needed time to think, to prepare, to plan his response to the new threat. For the first time since he left the peninsula, he slowed. To an onlooker it was innocent, stopping to gather berries at the edge of the trail. To Tomawka it was time to prepare for battle.

He entered the bushes to conceal his movements, nonchalantly repositioning his knife so it could be withdrawn from its sheath in the natural motion of raising his arm from his side. His mind raced. He had walked this trail before. What lay ahead? Where was danger the greatest? If what waited was a Chippewa war party, they would already be upon him, which meant it was either a wild animal or a single human that prepared the ambush. Where would he position himself to improve his chances of taking a whitetail deer that walked this trail?

Then he knew. The ravine, of course.

There he must be most alert. There the ambush would take place, and that was where his instincts and reactions would be tested. To fail was to die. Tomawka had no intention of dying on this day.

* * *

CATKA WAITED IMPATIENTLY for the Dakota warrior to approach the gully. He had picked his position well—concealed by brush heavy enough to hide his movement, yet offering a natural opening through which he could launch his body noiselessly to drop upon his unsuspecting victim.

Tomawka approached the ravine as though he suspected nothing. As he walked the slope to the bottom, he shortened his steps and slowed his pace. With his weight riding on the balls of his feet, he was prepared for instant movement in any direction.

Catka watched the tall warrior descend into the gully.

Tomawka walked directly toward the concealed Chippewa. He approached the thick bushes to his right, and as he turned to exit the ravine bottom, he sensed movement behind him.

Catka launched himself feet first to deliver a blow to the middle of Tomawka's back, intended to break his spine. As his enemy lay helpless, he would slash the ankle tendons and quickly follow with a cut across the belly. In moments, this Dakota would be holding his own intestines in his hands.

Tomawka, with the sensation of movement, crouched and spun his body, right arm sliding upward, hand closing on the handle of the knife given to him by Shakopee, his leader. He dove to his left, twisting his body, and as his left shoulder hit the ground, his right arm swung in an arc. He felt the blade make contact as he rolled, struggling to maintain control. He spun to his feet, knife extended, ready to parry the expected thrust by his unseen opponent.

Catka was unable to stop his flight as he saw Tomawka spin away. He extended his left leg to place his heel into the kidney area and render his foe helpless long enough for him to recover and slash the injured body. As he saw the Dakota hit the ground, he felt a searing sensation inside his left thigh. He hit the ground hard and spun to face his enemy.

Tomawka's right arm was covered with blood as he faced the Chippewa. It dripped from his elbow, and he feared a deep wound, although he felt no pain.

Catka looked at the bloody arm and smiled, showing gleaming white teeth behind thin lips that refused to rise at the corners. As he stepped forward, his foot slipped from under him, and he went down hard. Strangely, the Dakota just stood there looking. What was wrong? Why was he not attacking? Then Catka noticed what kept Tomawka rooted in place. He, Catka, was lying in a pool of blood. He raised his left leg, and blood pumped forth with every beat of his heart. His eyes moved from his leg to his enemy's face, and he realized it was his blood on the warrior's arm. Catka's expression was flat, showing neither hate nor surprise. He was dying. He knew he was dying, and that knowledge was his last. As he lost consciousness, his lifeblood continued to spill on the ground in the ravine, and Tomawka looked on, feeling sorry that the death had not been nobler.

Every warrior wanted to die in battle, but none wanted to die from a single knife stroke.

Plucking the knife from the dead Chippewa's hand, Tomawka untied the rawhide strap affixed to the sheath, stood, and without looking back continued onward to Spirit Knob.

* * *

TOMAWKA WATCHED, TRANCELIKE, unable to take his eyes off the scene unfolding below him. He was deep into the big woods, trees so thick that sunlight could not penetrate their branches, and he was a vapor, floating above, without voice.

Below him, the naked Indian dodged the fusillade of crows, black and ferocious, and so great in number they couldn't be counted. They streaked through the branches and dove upon his naked body, hammering with beaks that dripped blood, stripping his flesh and penetrating to the bone. Singing the song of death, he raced to the precipice and launched his body to the rocks below.

Then Tomawka saw him transform into a grasshopper, and with great leaps, traverse the swollen stream on boulders, each popping to the surface as he was about to alight in the water to be carried away by the raging current. With each leap, the stream widened, and the shore that he sought moved farther into the distance. On the fourth leap, the grasshopper became the whitened bones of a skull, eyeless sockets staring skyward as it drifted through the air.

Tomawka awoke with a start, heart pounding as he sprang to his feet, knife in hand, ready to confront that which he did not know, only to face the silence of the night. Interminable moments passed before he realized it was a dream. Unnerved, he stalked the perimeter of his campsite before returning to his small fire, constructed with the certainty that there was no danger in the darkness surrounding him. Why now was he moved by the Great Spirit to see this vision, and what was its meaning?

Chapter Four

The Demise of the Three-Toed Wolf

LAWRENCE TALIAFERRO WAS FEELING SATISFIED. Since his arrival at the fort, he had faced stiff opposition from the trading post operatives and had deflected political arrows from all directions meant to remove him from his position. As a testament to his substantial connections in Washington was the fact that, in spite of these continued attacks, they failed to damage his character or place limits on his authority.

The confidence in his abilities was proving to be well placed by those in the top echelons of government. Great progress had been made with both the Chippewa and Dakota throughout the area. His fairness and ability to back his words with actions had resulted in a fragile trust between the agent and the two major nations—the Dakota Sioux and the Chippewa. In addition, he was attempting to instill the idea of boundaries to encourage peaceful coexistence between the two tribes. He was now seated across from Colonel Josiah Snelling, commandant of the fort.

"Colonel, it's my intention to gather representatives from the Dakota and Chippewa nations, bring them to Washington and present them to President Monroe."

Snelling had watched the progress made with the bands and separated himself from Agent Taliaferro, offering support when asked and allowing the man to go about his business, ignoring the many complaints from the traders in the area. He knew the respect Taliaferro had garnered from both tribes.

Lawrence continued, "I petitioned Washington for the opportunity to create boundaries setting tribal lands. This is absolutely necessary if we want to limit conflict between them."

Snelling answered. "You know, as does everyone in this godforsaken territory, they consider all land their birthright. Yet they have no concept of ownership and no concept of borders. The trouble between the Dakota and Chippewa nations is as natural as the trees and rivers."

"Yes, however, the country's changing. This fort's changed the dynamic of the area, drawing both tribes into this constricted space. Add to that the problem of the traders stirring trouble every chance they get, and you have increased tensions that must be dealt with." Lawrence spoke with passion for his red brothers.

Snelling paused before answering. "Well . . . I can control the traders. That's my job. I don't know if anyone can make the Indians coexist. It's obvious they respect your decisions, however to limit them to boundaries . . . I don't know if it can be done."

"It has to be done. We have no option if the nation is to move forward."

The men talked far into the night, sharing Snelling's private stock of excellent scotch whiskey while laying plans for Lawrence's excursion to Washington.

* * *

Nineteen miles west of Fort Snelling
July 30, 1824

THE THREE HORSEMEN watched from the shelter of a depression that stretched for nearly a mile along the route the Indian traveled.

"We been watchin' 'im damn near an hour, Anton. Ain't no sign o' the child. I say we jus' charge in and grab him. He be tellin' us soon enough where he stashed her."

"Just settle on down, Harvey. I'm thinking he ain't never seen the kid. That one looks familiar to me. I get the feeling I seen him afore. Give me a little time to put it together." Anton studied the rider from afar, lost in his mind's search for the familiar.

"I think I know where we seen him. Ain't he one of them from Shakopee's band over on the St. Peter?"

"Dang it, Earl . . . that's it! Good job!"

Earl Wheeler was a crack shot, and the fort's best tracker. Harvey Freeman was a fearless behemoth, touching 300 pounds. Both were selected by Anton to search out Rebecca Townsend, a ten-year-old girl who disappeared from her family while they were traveling from New Ulm to Snelling's garrison. On their way to the fort, the family stopped to gather wild berries. After loading their baskets to the brim, they realized the little girl was nowhere to be found. Their lathered horses charging through the gates, and the wild eyes of the wagon's occupants convinced Colonel Snelling to send a search party at once.

Anton and the two men were into their third day of searching when they happened upon Tomawka moving south of the big lake. Keeping their distance, sticking to the low ground, they followed undetected while the Indian traveled the edge of a stream.

"I'm thinking I should ride up peaceable-like and start a palaver with 'im. He likely can help us look for little Becca. You boys just stay here till I give the high sign, then ride in . . . nice 'n' easy."

Anton spurred his horse over the ridge to open ground. When he was sure his presence was known, he dismounted, and with a wave of his arm moved toward the Indian at the other side of the clearing two hundred yards distant.

* * *

THE SMALL FIRE CRACKLED, sending occasional embers skyward while the prairie chicken sizzled and steamed above the flame. Harvey and Earl reclined near the fire while Anton and Tomawka squatted some distance away. Anton had a passable understanding of the Siouan language, and the Dakota warrior spoke English, albeit touched by French influence, so they had no trouble communicating. Anton liked this Indian. For his part, the Indian had an immediate trust for the young man that spoke Dakota, and they talked far into the night.

Daylight found the party moving southeast, returning to the spot where the family stopped to pick berries four days prior. Using it as the hub, the four men scoured the ground with arcing sweeps in all directions. Earl Wheeler picked up the track. In a depression, now dusty dry from the July heat, the girl's footprint was unmistakable. Also unmistakable, was the wolf track obliterating her next footfall.

* * *

THE MEN KNEW THIS WOLF. The dusty impression clearly showed three toes on the right front paw, likely the result of a narrow escape from a steel trap intended for muskrat or fox. As time passed, the wolf grew more and more daring, and trappers around the garrison began to fear the animal that seemed to stalk their trap lines, stealing their livelihood before they could gather the valuable pelts. More than once, they teamed together, of a single mind to obliterate the menace, only to return empty-handed and discouraged.

One day Amos Baltree, out of Michigan, had decided he'd had enough and sequestered himself in sight of one of his traps baited with a fresh kill. After a sleepless night, he approached the trap, which held a ripening rabbit. The trap now gripped only the foreleg, chewed off at the joint. Unmistakable tracks clearly showed the wolf's visit, though Amos had never seen him. From that time, he was known as Wotehda WanaYi—The Hungry Ghost.

* * *

THE MEN GATHERED AROUND the last visible trace, faces showing the resignation that came with the discovery. The bloody clothing not yet crusted over told them the attack took place only hours earlier. All knew it unlikely that she was still breathing.

"Well, it don't look good for little Becca, does it?"

"No, it sure don't. It looks like they're headed for that clump." Anton raised his arm in the direction of a tangle of brambles.

Moving with haste, they searched the area, finding a gingham bonnet and shredded cloth. Both were bloody and told a grotesque story without speaking.

This was Harvey's second rendezvous with a wolf kill and his rage surfaced. "Damn it ta hell, that lil' gal didn't stand a chance. What the hell was her papa thinkin, lettin' her go like that?"

"Wasn't his fault, Harvey. Just one o' them things that happens. I'm wonderin' how we're gonna tell her mama." Earl was repulsed at the thought.

"Damn tellin' her mama. I'm a gonna fix her old man when we get back."

Anton, hearing the exchange, entered the fray with the logic demanded of a leader. "Listen boys, we're gonna look for whatever's left, and we're gonna bury the remains. Then we're gonna tell the family something besides what really happened. And, Harvey . . . you aren't going to say nothing to her pa. It'll be hard enough on him knowing she won't be coming home."

"Like hell I won't."

Anton's fist caught him flush on the temple, and the big man went down hard.

"Settle on down, Harvey. We ain't doing this."

Harvey sat in the prairie grass with glassy eyes and determined not to challenge the young Anton, perfectly willing to go along with any plan offered.

* * *

THEY CAMPED THAT NIGHT, and in the warm glow of the fire. Tomawka related his dream to the young leader, who listened intently.

Anton's mother often talked of visionary dreams, and Anton had great respect for those capable of prophecy, believing as the Dakota did, that dreams provided foreknowledge of future events. Several possibilities were offered for the dream's meaning. The two men agreed the grasshopper was surely meant to represent Tomawka. The boulders, they reasoned, symbolized four horses, or they represented years, or they might be Chippewa warriors. Whatever the meaning of the dream, both men thought it an important sign for something that lay in the future.

Talking throughout the night, Anton told of his Algonquin mother and his early years, relating her death and how it pushed him westward. He described the killing of Billy Bolden and how he came upon the Kentucky rifle he carried. Impressed with his new friend's openness, Tomawka explained the second knife on his waist and the death of Catka, the Chippewa. For the first time, Anton began to understand the hostility between the two great nations.

Then they planned for the coming day.

* * *

THEY WERE FANNED OUT, covering a swath of nearly two miles, moving south in the general direction that the tracks led from yesterday's grisly discovery of Rebecca's clothing. Earl Wheeler was assigned to one outside edge, Tomawka to the other, with the thought that the best trackers should be in position to pick up the signs if the wolf changed direction.

Their aim was to find and dispatch the predator turned man killer. The process was slow, with the high prairie grass hiding any visible trace of his passing. Each of them zigzagged their way through the heavy verdure, now crispy brown from the summer heat, paying particular attention to openings that once held puddles of water and the occasional thickets of low-growing bushes where they might discover hair or other evidence of his presence or passing.

Three hours passed when Anton, just inside of Tomawka's range, found the sign. Among a thicket of buckthorn on the outside of his arc, he discovered a tuft of fur from the undercoat of the killer they sought. Luckily, Tomawka was less than three hundred yards to the east of Anton's position, and he was summoned with a repeated lark call and waving of arms.

The two men hunkered outside the clump.

"What do you think? Got any idea where he might be heading?"

Tomawka had tracked this animal south of the river, always losing his trail after it crossed into the swampy bottomlands on the north side. He was never able to pick it up where it left the bottoms, but coupled with this new information his mind registered a spot that might offer a remote area, isolated enough to draw the animal.

"Yes. I've been in this area many times. If I'm right, he's headed to a gulch that lies east. Got enough space there to set up a den to support his damned ways o' killin and runnin'."

"How far?"

"Couple hours. Less, if we head straight out. What about the others?"

"Yeah, I been thinkin' about that. Harvey isn't exactly smart, but Earl will move this way in three or four hours wonderin' where we're at. If we leave sign, he's good enough to follow."

* * *

THEY APPROACHED FROM THE NORTHEAST to within several hundred yards of the jumble of rocks marking the north edge of the cut. Although dry now, the gorge had been sliced into the limestone by raging water over the centuries, and judging by the occasional track left by the Hungry Ghost, they were confident it was his destination. The final proof came with the discovery of fresh spoor, still warm. Anton dismounted, tethered his horse at the edge of a thicket, and joined the Indian on the rise.

"Well, what do you think, Tomawka? If we wait for Harvey and Earl. We'll be able to watch a lot more ground and get him anywhere he comes out. I'm sure he's seen us, likely watchin' us right now, but the last I knew wolves couldn't count. As long as one of us keeps his attention the other can get into position."

Tomawka favored spontaneous action. "I've been in that cut before. I know how it runs. I'll go in this end and you circle outta sight to the south. He isn't going over the edge. There's no place he can go except down the gap and out the other end. If we wait for the tracker and the big man, old Three-toes is likely to slip outta there before they get here."

"Yeah, makes sense. You hold tight here while I sneak around. Give me time . . . then go on in. If you hear my rifle, you'll know I got 'im."

Anton responded to Tomawka's nod with one of his own and dropped to his knees, leaving the Indian standing in plain view from the distant gorge as he scrambled out of sight.

Tomawka waited for a good forty-five minutes, moving back and forth on the ridge, staying in plain sight of the bouldered entry to the gorge. When he figured Anton had enough time to get into position, he ambled toward the gorge that ran about a quarter mile before dumping into the dry swamp at the far end. Being familiar with the lay of the land, he knew the Ghost would be there, and as savvy as this animal was, he suspected he'd drive it out the far end before he even entered the cut.

Working his way through the large boulders at the mouth, he entered a narrow notch that dropped sharply before taking a more gradual course, all the while winding toward the bottomlands that bordered the St. Peter River. The soil had been washed away by torrents of the past, leaving only fist-sized rocks that rolled underfoot and made walking difficult and stealth impossible. Ahead, where the river made an abrupt turn, sediment had accumulated behind a natural levee providing a foothold for vegetation to sprout. An impenetrable thicket of brambles and buckthorn grew there, reaching the edges of the steep walls of the canyon. Tomawka looked for an opening through which he could pass.

Without warning, a sudden impact sent him reeling. Unable to maintain his footing on the loose rock, he fought for balance as the wolf clamped his jaws into his shoulder, sinking fangs deep into his flesh, rear claws raking his left side as Tomawka stumbled under the weight of the beast. Instinctively he reached his right hand across his body and sank his thumb into the Ghost's eye socket. In desperation he pushed and gouged, yet the fangs held firm. As they hit the brambles, Tomawka was unaware of the thorns that cut through his leggings, breaking off in the skin. He felt no pain as they entered his back and arms.

The wolf shook his head violently, slashing a deep wound and opening the meat to exposed bone before tearing free. He lunged for another attack, and Tomawka raised his left arm to protect his face. As powerful jaws locked onto his forearm, he heard the bone snap. Anger more than pain filled his senses as he grasped his knife with his right hand and thrust it into the animal's chest. He heard a muffled growl and felt the air leave the wolf's lungs through the wound. Enraged, the huge animal whipped his head from side to side as Tomawka's arm flailed loosely beyond the crushing jaws. Again and again, the knife struck home as they struggled among the thorns.

Finally, thankfully, it ended. Exhausted, without pain, Tomawka pried the jaws off his arm and crawled from the awful thicket to lay his body on the comfort of the stony, dry streambed.

* * *

ANTON WAS GROWING RESTLESS sequestered on the high ground above the only exit from the deep ravine. He'd been there far longer than it should have taken the Indian to reach his position.

When they parted, Anton had circled wide, always out of sight of the ravine, making his way to its mouth. Moving fast, avoiding the thickets and clumps of small bushes, he left an unmistakable trail through the prairie grass, scraping the bare earth where spring puddles had drowned the vegetation leaving open ground, and breaking small branches on the infrequent trees that he happened upon. He reckoned that even Harvey could follow the trail.

The sun was at its zenith when Anton saw the two men approaching on the same trail he had taken to his overlook. Harvey's size was unmistakable so Anton picked up the rifle and walked to meet them.

"We found your horse tied in the thicket, so we picked him up and followed your track. Harvey here led the way. Pretty good job too."

Harvey puffed and his eyes glowed with satisfaction. Anton didn't bother telling him a blind man could have followed the trail he left.

Anton spoke with concern.

"I'm thinking the Indian might have run into some kind of trouble, maybe twisted an ankle on the rocks. It's been a few hours and I haven't seen the wolf. We figured he was holed up in the dry canyon, so Tomawka was going to spook him out this end. We better get up there and have a look."

Without further conversation, he swung into the saddle and the three of them cantered to the north end of the dry bed before dismounting. Leaving the horses tied to the bushes ringing the entrance, they followed the notch into the canyon.

About two hundred yards in, they found the body.

A pool of congealed redness surrounded Tomawka among the rocks, with a clear trail of darkening blood leading from the thicket, where, in the midst of fractured branches and bloody offshoots, lay the man killer.

"Damn . . . this must a been something. Look at the size of that animal." The wolf was a good six feet from nose to tail and had to weigh one hundred seventy pounds. The men were incredulous.

They used water from their canteens to wash Tomawka's body and reveal the terrible wounds he had suffered. His arm was crushed and flesh was torn from his shoulder. It was the wounds caused by the thorny trees that killed him. His tumble under the weight of the wolf landed him in the oldest section of the thicket where the buckthorn branches twisted together. Three-inch barbs acting like knife blades penetrated and ripped the skin. As man and wolf struggled, they tore horrifying wounds, cutting into veins and opening arteries. He was dead within fifteen minutes of crawling onto the rocks.

* * *

ANTON ENTERED SHAKOPEE'S VILLAGE under a deep sadness. He had met Tomawka only four days ago and knew him for only three. Three days . . . during which they had grown as close as lifelong friends.

Anton's bay mare was familiar to Shakopee's band, and the children ran ahead to tell of his approach. The murmurs that began when he passed the outer lodges turned to death wails as word spread that the travois the horse dragged held the body of a Sioux warrior.

As Anton was entering the camp, Earl and Harvey were approaching the fort with the wolf carcass dragging thirty feet behind, a necessary effort to keep the horses from bolting. They were under strict instructions to tell Rebecca's parents that her body had been recovered and buried on the plain. They were also to tell of the death of Tomawka and his single-handed dispatch of the three-toed wolf.

Lastly, they were instructed to hang the wolf carcass outside the fort, stretched to his full length, for all to see and marvel at the fact that it had been killed with a knife by a single Dakota warrior.

* * *

SHAKOPEE SAT CROSS-LEGGED inside his tipi, opposite the flap as he addressed Anton. Morning shadows dappled and danced across the tipi, entering through the open flap and painting the interior with morning light. Shakopee loved the dawn and made it a point to align the opening of his shelter to catch the rising sun.

"Again, I am indebted to Anton. Tomawka was a brave man, proving himself during many battles with the Chippewa."

Anton nodded.

"You have returned the knife I gave him, and you brought another. Did he have both knives?"

"Yes. The knife belonged to a Chippewa name of Catka. You know the name?"

"Catka is a fierce warrior, much respected by my braves. He has taken many Sioux lives. Do you know how Tomawka came upon Catka's knife?"

"Yeah, he killed Catka when he was scouting the big lake north of here. He said Catka jumped him, and he took one swipe with his knife . . . caught an artery. Said he bled out inside o' two minutes."

Satisfaction showed on Shakopee's face. "This night we will celebrate the death of a fearsome enemy. Tomawka's life will be honored. I will take personal responsibility for his family."

"You mean he has a family?"

"He has a fine son . . . born yesterday. He never knew he had a son. It will be hard . . . for her."

"Damn fine man. His family deserves better . . . he deserved better. I'd like to help if you'll permit it."

"I owe you much. You know you are welcome in my village. I will introduce you to Tomawka's woman."

They talked for a long time, and to show his respect for Anton, they smoked the Chanupa pipe, carved from Catlinite, a stone quarried three days ride to the west.

"Thank you for this honor, Great Chief. The pipe I now hold is of extreme beauty. Would you explain the symbols to me?"

Shakopee reached out with his right hand, and Anton carefully placed the pipe in his open palm.

"The bowl of the Sacred Pipe is made from red stone, a very special stone gathered from a sacred quarry, and represents Earth. The buffalo carved on the bowl represents all animals that have four legs, and the wooden stem, all growing things. The eagle feathers hanging from the pipe represent the winged nation of the Dakota." His voice was soft, reverent, and Anton understood.

After sharing the pipe, the two men stood, and Anton followed Shakopee from his tipi. The sky was overcast, the late morning air still, and a smoky fog from cooking fires hung as a cloak over the area.

Anton led his horse as the two of them walked through the center of the encampment. They exited, walking west toward the heavily treed area bordering the river. There was no talk between them, and Anton began to wonder how far they would walk before reaching Tomawka's camp. No sooner had the question come to mind than the woods opened to reveal a single tipi. A woman stood outside. Blood flowed off her fingers and down her shins from self-administered cuts to her arms and legs, and her hair was severed to uneven lengths according to the ritual demanded of her.

Her face was angular, with high cheekbones, and a thin, aquiline nose between almond eyes. Upon her forehead and chin, were tracks left from bloody fingers drawn across them. She was of average height, and even beneath the deerskin smock she wore, Anton sensed the well-proportioned body, in spite of the swollen midriff left over from the baby delivered less than a full day prior.

"Mr. Anton, thank you for returning my husband." Her voice was well modulated and composed, her diction flawless. "I am Star Woman. I would like you to see my son."

Chief Shakopee stood quietly as Anton was led beyond the open flap to the interior, where he was surprised by the amount of light inside the enclosure. She walked to the far edge and stooped to retrieve a bundle wrapped in a rough blanket.

She approached, the bundle cradled before her, the baby's round face visible among the blanket folds. "His name is Rising Eagle, and he was born yesterday. My husband chose the name. Will you please tell us how you met him and how he died?"

Anton was taken aback by her straightforward manner and felt an immediate and overwhelming responsibility for her welfare and that of her son. He told of his initial meeting with Tomawka, the subsequent discovery of the little girl's bloody clothing, their search for the Hungry Ghost, and what they knew of his final struggle with the beast.

Lastly, he told her about the death of Catka.

He stayed for a long time. Far longer than intended, and when he finally left her, Shakopee was gone, and Anton had determined to care for and protect the woman and child.

After sufficient mourning, Tomawka was brought to the high point on a bluff overlooking the Mississippi River opposite Fort Snelling. There, on a site called, Mendota, where spirits lived, his body, wrapped in a buffalo robe, was placed upon a scaffold raised six or seven feet, to remain there until time scattered the bones upon the ground, whereupon his family would gather and bury them.

Chapter Five

Treaty of 1825

AS SUMMER TURNED TO FALL, Anton spent more and more time in Shakopee's camp. Helped by lessons learned from his mother, he proved to be the most productive trapper in the village, trading valuable pelts at the fort, and adding to his already impressive reputation among the Indians.

The weather recorders at Fort Snelling noted that winter's descent upon the lower St. Peter was gradual in 1824, and the entire season was mild by Minnesota standards. The moderate weather permitted many troopers at Fort Snelling to travel beyond the walls to hunt game, and allowed Anton ample time to visit Shakopee's village.

The mild weather also encouraged trappers from Green Bay and lower on the Mississippi to visit the fort, bringing with them whiskey in quantities sufficient to become a problem for Colonel Snelling.

* * *

In December of that year, Anton traveled almost daily to Shakopee's camp, mostly to check on Star Woman and Rising Eagle. Beyond that, he was drawn by a growing respect for her people and a comfort he enjoyed while in the woman's company. Toward the end of the month, he entered the camp as he always did, and as he passed Shakopee's tipi, the flap was thrown aside. Through the opening stepped a tall white man followed closely by the great chief Little Crow. It had been some time since Anton had seen Little Crow, so he drew up, dismounted and approached the two men.

Little Crow spoke. "Anton, friend of the Dakota, I want you to meet the white chief Taliaferro, the White Father's agent for all the tribes from the great water to the north, to the land of the Winnebago in the south.

Anton reached forward to grasp the hand of the white man.

The agent said, "I've heard of you. You're the one who brought in Tomawka's body after he killed the three-toed wolf."

"Yes. I know you as well from the words spoken by my friend Shakopee. It is said you're the one who settles disputes between the Chippewa and Dakota peoples."

"I mostly employ common sense. I don't think I've settled any disputes of great import. It helps to understand the sensibilities of both nations."

Anton was impressed with the intelligence of the agent, and found it refreshing to speak with one as learned as Major Taliaferro, his manner of speaking not unlike that of John Drury, the scientist who tutored him during his initial trip to the frontier.

Taliaferro continued. "I wish there were more men like you at the fort. It seems the only kind attracted to this frontier are drunkards and those who wish to exploit the red man."

"Well, we sure do seem to have our share of them, although there are a few good men among the passel of bad. It seems like lately the whiskey's brought out the worst in them. If you ask me, the traders for the fur companies are the ones who stir the pot."

"Yeah, they stir the pot all right." Taliaferro looked around the camp. "I understand you're working at the fort as chief hunter for Snelling."

"Yes I am. It gives me plenty of opportunities to visit here, especially with the mild winter and the abundance of game."

"Well . . . keep something in the back of your mind. If you ever tire of working for Josiah Snelling, I can always use a good and honest man with your particular skills. Just file that away till the time comes."

Shakopee had joined the three men outside his tipi, and the conversation turned to small talk, the kind that transpires among close friends. They talked until the shadows were long before Anton excused himself, mounted his horse, and continued toward Star Woman's tipi.

* * *

Fort Snelling, Northwest Frontier
April 5, 1825

THE FORT BUZZED WITH EXCITEMENT. After an easy winter and an early thaw, word came from a rider that a provisioning boat was downriver and expected to arrive at the fort that day. Colonel Snelling had the troops fall out to meet the steamer *Rufus Putnam*, everyone in fresh uniforms and riding well-curried mounts. After the official welcoming ceremony, the ship's captain and first mate accompanied the colonel to his billet where they were treated to a superb meal of prairie chicken and wild rice prepared for the occasion while the ship's hands unloaded much-needed supplies. Unknown to those enjoying the meal, serious mischief was taking place on the *Rufus Putnam*.

As hard as Colonel Snelling and Agent Taliaferro tried to limit the delivery of whiskey, other high-ranking officers and fur traders schemed to bring in copious quantities of the stuff, having learned that drunken Indians made easy marks, allowing them to be bilked of trade goods, pelts, and large tracts of land. While the soldiers off-loaded provisions at the dock, the miscreants off-loaded whiskey on the opposite side of the boat, lowering kegs into large-bellied crafts for delivery to the American and Columbia Fur Companies, both with outposts farther up the St. Peter, not too far from the fort.

The flat land just west of the fort attracted Chippewa and Sioux alike. Camped in small groups, the nearness to the fort helped keep peace between them while their differences simmered just below the surface. With whiskey added to the mix, occasional conflict broke out between the two great nations, exacerbated by unscrupulous traders intent on personal gains.

On the second day after the arrival of the *Rufus Putnam*, Anton was returning to Fort Snelling after spending a week at Shakopee's camp. Approaching the fort wall, he heard a muffled cry from somewhere on his left. Reining in, senses heightened, he sat astride his bay mare and looked into the early morning shadows cast by the wall. He nudged his horse in the direction of the sound and heard a barely audible scream, as though from far off . . . or uttered beneath a hand firmly clamped over mouth and nose.

From his left came movement, a Chippewa brave was charging toward the shadows ahead and to his right. Vaulting from the mare, Anton hit the ground, legs pumping as he dashed toward the figures now visible at the edge of the fort. There were two men, one behind a struggling figure, a woman. The one holding the woman had an arm wrapped around her neck while the other hand clamped firmly over her nose and mouth. The second man was viciously clawing at her garments.

Anton and the Indian reached the threesome at the same time. Anton dove at the man in front, nearly missing him altogether as the man spun to meet the threat. His elbow slammed into Anton's left kidney and knocked the air out of his lungs. Rolling to escape the blows he knew would follow, he caught a heavy boot to the forehead and struggled to rise. The world spun, and echoing thunder filled his senses. Just before losing consciousness, he saw a shadowy figure fly over his body as the Chippewa charged Anton's aggressor.

* * *

WHEN ANTON AWOKE, THE WORLD was once again stationary. His head was filled with a cacophony of unrelated sounds and he felt like a horse had kicked him. After shaking his head to clear his senses, he rolled to his knees to see the Indian kneeling alongside a disheveled Indian woman who was hastily arranging torn clothing. The man he had confronted was nowhere to be seen. The other was in a heap, a creeping redness surrounding his body. Anton staggered to his feet, and when he turned toward the two Indians, they were gone. His mind reeled and the world spun once again. Staggering forward, he dropped to his knees, head down, the sand and pebbles in front of him blurring into a vortex as his arms collapsed and his face made contact with the ground. His last thought before succumbing to the spinning blackness closing around him was a niggling in the back of his mind. There was something familiar about the man he'd fought.

* * *

HIS EYES OPENED TO A COOL WETNESS on his forehead.

"What the hell happened to you? You look almost as bad as that Indian what kilt the wolf." Earl Wheeler, on his way back from an unsuccessful hunt, had discovered Anton lying in the shadow of the fort wall, and now cradled his head while swabbing water on his face with his moistened bandana.

"I figured I was gonna die, Earl."

"Well—ya dang near did it, by the looks of ya."

Anton's head pounded from the inside, threatening to push his eyes from their sockets with every heartbeat.

"Damn lucky you killed him before he killed you. He was a pretty big boy. Must a been a hell of a fight judging by that lump on your forehead."

Anton gained his knees as his stomach turned inside out and he vomited. Although he felt terrible, at least the ground was no longer moving. Again, he retched, his convulsions lasting several minutes before being able to recline and allow his insides to settle. After perhaps five minutes of silence, Earl's comment hit home.

"That isn't even the guy I was fighting. That Indian took care of this one." Anton motioned with his thumb to the body lying ten feet away. "I didn't see much of what happened. There were two of them. Looked to me like they were pretty intent on raping a squaw when we came along. The Indian and I got there at more or less the same time. Looks like he did better'n me. All I got was a boot to the head."

"I'd say you're lucky to be here. You got yourself a big knot for sure." Earl pointed to Anton's forehead.

"You ever see this guy around the fort?" Anton was examining the body.

"Nah, we got quite a few trappers came in on the steamer. I figure this was one of them."

Anton lightly fingered the immense bump on his forehead. "You know, I've got a feeling I've seen that other guy someplace. There was something familiar about him."

"Well, you oughta think about lying down on your own bunk till that swelling starts to go away. You want, I'll take care of your horse."

Anton was helped into the barracks where he gratefully reclined on his own bunk and was asleep before Earl made the door.

* * *

THERE WAS AN INQUIRY ABOUT THE KILLING, and much to his displeasure Anton could remember nothing of the fight that precipitated it, only that there were two men, one woman, and an Indian who had joined in the struggle, the latter likely saving his life.

The dead man indeed had been aboard the *Rufus Putnam* when she docked. The captain wasn't sure where he joined the crew, since records were slim in those regards. It seemed to trouble the captain not in the slightest that a crewman was now dead or that he had tried to rape an Indian woman.

Although unnecessary, Agent Taliaferro stood as witness to Anton's character. The provost determined by the tracks and marks in the dirt, and the fact that Anton's knife was clean, that he was telling the truth, and that was the end of it.

* * *

HEADACHES AND RINGING IN HIS EARS continued every time Anton stood, and he found it impossible to sit his horse without supreme discomfort. Finally, three weeks later, he felt good enough to ride, so he mounted up and headed for Shakopee's camp, a new blanket tied to the saddle, a gift for Star Woman.

The lad, Rising Eagle, approaching the age of one year, had jet-black hair and features considered European by the Mdewakanton band into which he was born. It seemed to Anton that Rising Eagle had been blessed with the best of both his parents. From his mother he inherited an oval face with high cheekbones separated by a thin, straight nose above a well-shaped mouth and a strong chin. His body was already showing signs of mimicking that of Tomawka's. Sturdy, well-proportioned, with broad shoulders and angular limbs that moved in graceful sweeps, unlike the herky-jerky movements of most children his age. Moreover, he never cried. His curiosity knew no bounds, crawling after beetles and prodding beneath loose sticks and rocks when his mother took him to the natural spring west of the camp. There, she dipped water for cooking while he was given the freedom to satisfy that curiosity.

The summer of 1825 found Anton in the Indian camp more than he was at the fort. Colonel Snelling, aware of his headaches, relied on others to do the hunting, offering Anton time to spend with his adopted family and to allow his body to recover fully from the beating received outside the fort.

During the summer, Star Woman began treating him for his headaches and dizzy spells with a warm poultice placed over his forehead and eyes, and she lightly massaged his temples with palm-sized stones worn smooth over time and cooled in the water of the spring. The headaches subsided, finally disappearing altogether, and Anton began to join other band members in hunting excursions north of the river.

At this point in time, Agent Taliaferro approached Anton, asking if he would join him in treaty negotiations with the Sioux, Chippewa, and other nations claiming portions of the territory for tribal hunting grounds.

"How'd you like to just sit in and listen to what goes on? Might give you some insight and help your understanding of the Indian situation. The government wants to press the issue of boundaries in an attempt to reduce the fighting between the various tribes." The agent knew this to be a partial truth.

"As much as I'd like to go with you, I figure to stick around here for a few more weeks." Although the thought interested him, Anton was relishing his time in the Indian camp and the hours spent with Star Woman.

The negotiations were to be held at a place called Prairie du Chien. Under the guise of trying to reduce tribal warfare between the Chippewa and Dakota, Taliaferro believed it was the necessary precursor to land cessions. Although he had an intense dislike for establishing boundary lines on a map, he knew they were important for the nation to grow.

He accepted Anton's refusal with a touch of envy at the hunter's independence.

* * *

ON JUNE 7, 1825, ANTON TURNED TWENTY. He spent the entire month as a guest of Shakopee, specifically with Star Woman and Rising Eagle, and was with them to celebrate the latter's first birthday on July 31. Anton found pleasure in being with the two of them and a heightening physical attraction to Star Woman that could not be denied. Although he still considered her to be Tomawka's woman, he couldn't refute his feelings, and it troubled him.

* * *

THE AFTERNOON OF AUGUST 19, 1825, in Prairie du Chien, representatives from nine Indian nations on the Upper Mississippi signed a treaty that would set the stage for land cessions and the end of a way of life for the sovereign Indian nations. Under the cloak of concern for the tribes, article one of the treaty stated, "There shall be a firm and perpetual peace between the Sioux and Chippewas; between the Sioux and the confederated tribes of Sacs and Foxes; and between the Ioways and the Sioux."

* * *

WELL INTO SEPTEMBER, ANTON was once again hunting meat for the fort and visiting Star Woman every chance he got.

The presence of new traders coming in from Green Bay and points south brought with it new problems for Colonel Snelling. The fort attracted an ever-growing number of Chippewa and Dakota Indians, all drawn by the opportunity to trade goods, and they set up camps outside the fort walls. With old enemies in close proximity to each other, keeping the peace became more difficult, and Agent Taliaferro spent a great deal of his time settling disputes.

Adding to the problem was the ever-increasing amount of whiskey being smuggled into the area by the trappers. Standards were posted by the fur companies regarding the consumption of alcohol inside their compounds, and although they stocked large quantities of whiskey, the overseers were aware of the dangers when men overindulged. A strict set of rules was in place regarding the serving, however, with barrels being smuggled into the area, they were ineffectual at best.

A day didn't go by that troopers weren't sent into the camps to break up fights between trappers arguing about claimed territories or infringement on established stretches of streams and prime pelt-producing areas. During the first seven months of 1825, there were fifty-seven murders and countless men disappeared without a trace.

After Colonel Snelling set up a military court and dealt with transgressors in typical military efficiency, with two hangings in a week, the killings between trappers stopped. In their place came trouble between the Dakota and Chippewa camped near the fort. Primed with bootleg liquor, and similarly priming the Indians, rabble traders instigated quarrels resulting in fatalities in both tribes. Snelling was forced to form a specialized unit to deal with the new threat to a peaceful coexistence between them. His task was made easier through the happenings on the day of September 23, 1825.

Chapter Six

Lightning on the Prairie

NTON WAS RETURNING from an unsuccessful hunt on the prairie west of the fort. Approaching the river, he was guiding his horse down a bluff, concentration focused on the uneven terrain in an area he had ridden many times, when a shot shattered the silence.

The man with the rifle lay hidden among the shale and low growing bushes above the route the rider had chosen. Since his arrival on the *Rufus Putnam* eighteen months earlier, the man had existed as a parasite, feeding off the labor of others. Friendless, a loner with a reputation of bad temper and short fuse, he was given a wide berth, partly due to his menacing appearance. Where his right ear had once been was only an ugly scar. Since he had been at the American Fur Company post, he had murdered twelve men, all of who simply vanished, never to be seen again. Knowing the failure of the authorities to recover a body would conceal the act, he became proficient at ensuring that none of his victims would be found. He traded their belongings with outlying Dakota and Chippewa villages, taking the pelts from the trades into the fort for barter.

This rider would be his thirteenth victim.

At the precise moment the man pulled the trigger, Anton shifted as his horse gathered to jump a small crevice. The result was a near miss taking the horn from his saddle and sending him reeling. To the man sequestered sixty yards away, it looked like number thirteen was assured. Nonetheless, he fired another round into the spot where the man fell, scrambled to his feet, and hurried to make sure the rider was dead, anxious to dismember the body and bury the clothes. The efficiency of nature to remove the scattered body parts was, he decided, a gift to his trade, and he thought it too bad others didn't have his insight.

Anton hit the ground, his reflexes allowing him to land uninjured. He lay for a moment gathering his senses before he realized what had happened. Rock fragments exploded on his left, stinging his face, and he dove behind a large boulder. The shot had come from above and to the right of where he now crouched.

Scampering higher on the slope while keeping behind a series of shale plateaus, he was able to reposition himself a good twenty yards from where he fell. Edging along the boulder he now used for cover, he saw the man who had fired at him cautiously approaching his old position. Something familiar about him struck a chord with Anton.

Before the killer took two more steps Anton recognized him as the man who had beaten him outside the fort, the man who'd been intending to rape the Indian woman. He was traversing the steep hillside, downhill from where Anton now crouched, his total attention directed to the spot twenty yards distant where Anton first fell.

As Anton aligned his rifle sights, the man stealing before him turned in his direction, and Anton recognized him as the one whose ear he had severed the night he'd killed Billy Bolden—the second of the two men who'd tried to kill him—the one who had escaped. At that exact moment, Francis Glover joined Billy in death.

* * *

THE GUARD AT THE FORT GATES took a menacing stance, blocking the entrance to the interior.

"You say this man tried to ambush you on your way in?" He nodded toward the dead man draped over the saddle of the horse Anton was leading. The trooper was a new man, having arrived with a detachment cut from the ranks of soldiers preparing for the following year's construction of Fort Leavenworth, in Kansas.

"That's right, now stand aside so I can report to Colonel Snelling."

"Like hell I will. Get down off that horse, or I'll pull ya off."
The young private edged closer.

"This doesn't have to be. I'm a scout for the fort and I report
to the colonel."

Mistaking Anton's reaction as conciliatory, the soldier reached
to grab the rifle, which lay across the remains of the shattered saddle
horn. With lightning speed, Anton thrust the stock squarely into the
man's forehead, and continued walking his horse into the fort, the unconscious trooper lying in a heap behind him.

After reporting the facts of the killing to the colonel, and somewhat hesitantly suggesting that it might be a good idea for Snelling to
send a couple of men to check on the young guard, Anton listened as
the fort commander brought up the problem that had recently surfaced,
namely, the trappers finding sport in stirring up trouble with the Indians.

Anton was offered command of a small group of men, all of his
own choosing, to monitor the trappers and put an end to the mischief.
Recognizing the limited capabilities of the army to maintain the peace,
he went to Little Crow and convinced him of the importance of peaceful
coexistence between the Chippewa and Sioux surrounding the fort.
With the help of the Dakota and honest trappers, Anton was provided
with information beyond that garnered by the soldiers. With that information, he was able to throw a scare into the scoundrels. Spending most
of his time outside the fort monitoring the trading posts and making
himself a general pest to those trappers who attempted to stir up trouble,
word spread, as did the fear of being caught with swift justice sure to
follow, and the mischief ceased. Relative peace returned.

* * *

Josiah Snelling's quarters
Early October 1825

SNELLING PACED THE ROOM while Anton was seated on the straight-
backed chair in front of the office desk. The smell of tobacco smoke
hung in the air. "I want you to lead a small contingent of troopers to

Lake Traverse with the sole purpose of studying the conduct of traders at the Columbia Fur Company and the organization of that post under the leadership of Joseph Renville."

Anton listened while the colonel explained himself.

"Renville is licensed to conduct the fur trade in the area of Lake Traverse and Lac qui Parle. He has a strong personality and natural leadership attributes that rankles a few who come up against him, none more than John Jacob Astor himself."

Snelling walked behind his desk and sat down before continuing. "Astor felt that Renville was costing him thousands of dollars by trading in the area that was controlled by the American Fur Company. The problem facing Astor's organization was one of poor leadership, so much so that Renville was approached to run the posts, sharing in profits as well as sharing any loss."

Anton commented, "Sounds like Renville's a pretty good leader."

"Somehow he's able to maintain order and discipline where no one else has been able to. I'm going to send some scribes into the area to learn all they can about his organization. I'd like you to take two men to Fort Washington and two others to Renville's post at Lac qui Parle."

Snelling tapped a well-used pipe against his desk, spreading cold tobacco ash on the floor, and then stuffed the bowl with fresh tobacco and laid it on the corner of his desk, unlit.

"Winter will soon wrap us in a blanket of snow, so I figure you should spend the season there. I calculate it'll take six months for my men to learn the ins and outs of how the posts are managed. While they do their work, I want you to move around the area. Get to know the bands and gain their trust. Most of all, learn their strengths and weaknesses."

"Colonel, I like these people. I relate to them. I'm not going to spy, looking for ways they may be defeated in battle." Anton liked talking to Snelling. He liked to speak in the proper manner taught to him by Drury, and the colonel was one of the few who spoke the educated tongue. There was a mutual respect, and each spoke their minds.

"Don't misunderstand me, Anton. The information you learn will help them when the area is opened up to settlers. The U.S. Government is making treaties with native people, and our Dakota friends will get a fair deal. There is no ill intent, only a desire to know what's important to them, the better to provide for their needs."

Anton knew that Snelling was a career officer, and as such strove for promotion and heightened authority. However, he also trusted the colonel's sense of fairness. Nevertheless, deeply troubled by the colonel's request, he sought council with a second white man, Indian agent for the western tribes, Major Lawrence Taliaferro, the man he first met at Shakopee's camp and for whom he had gained a great respect.

* * *

"ANNAWON, MY FRIEND."

Taliaferro often addressed Anton by his given name, and was likely the only living person to do so. "I fear for our red brothers. The Washington bureau concerned with affairs of the Indian is filled with scoundrels, unaware and uncaring. I fear for the future of these great people."

Anton responded, "Your high regard for them is felt by the Chippewa and Dakota. Your dealings have been fair and your words true."

"Last year, when I gathered the great chiefs from the Sioux, Chippewa, and Menominee people and traveled to Washington, I expected their stately bearing and outright openness to impress the powerful men there. In reality, they were a sideshow paraded from reception to reception in their finest dress, and treated as children. Oh, . . . great words were spoken and many promises made. Promises that have already been broken."

Anton was getting his first lesson in political reality and he was growing increasingly uncomfortable. "Surely the white father can see the ambition of these men, the men holding the power over the future of the great Indian nations."

With a chill in the late October air, Taliaferro rose to place another piece of wood on the fire. They were in the confines of his small office, and the fire crackled as the flame licked at the freshly split log, red-hot cinders popping and sending sparks streaming up the chimney.

"Annawon, you're a good man. Your concern for the people is evident. I believe we can forestall the inevitable if you are willing to help me."

Anton responded with a brief nod.

"The bureau has the power to grant licenses for trading in the territory. It's the agents' duty to fairly divide and issue those licenses in a prudent manner. A blanket license was issued to the American Fur Company through agents at Mackinac. One agent, George Boyd, issued blank sub-licenses. Trappers now roam the Indian country doing business wherever they please, neutralizing the law that designates points at which the trade should be conducted. My hands are tied until I receive specific authority to stop it."

Taliaferro leaned forward, elbows on knees, hands clasped. "Annawon . . . I would like you to go to the Big Stone area. Talk to people. If possible, contact Mazasha, Red Iron, and see if he's seen trouble brewing. Red Iron's one of the few who see the big picture. He is wise. I've got to control what's happening, and you can be a factor."

Anton again answered with a nod and the conversation deepened, revealing facts that were troubling, yet filling him with a positive energy for the future. A future that he could influence to a great degree by how he accomplished the dual tasks set before him by Snelling and Taliaferro—two men with their own agendas and visions.

* * *

FIVE DAYS LATER, ANTON SET OUT with four scribes and five troopers for Lake Traverse and Big Stone Lake, the source of the St. Peter River. Two trading posts lay upon their shores.

They traveled due west from the fort, electing to avoid the additional distance required by following the river. With the exception of the scribes assigned by Colonel Snelling, the others were hand picked by Anton and included Earl Weaver and Harvey Freeman, both of whom he trusted and had grown to rely on during his duties as chief scout and hunter for the fort.

* * *

THE MEN HADN'T EATEN for a full day so Anton left the party to search for wild game.

He felt more than heard the subtle click of the set trigger on his Kentucky rifle. Easing his index finger onto the main trigger, he aligned the front and rear sights on the shoulder of the whitetail buck, exactly ten inches above the point where the backside of the front leg intersected the lower body. Forcing a calmness he didn't feel, he sensed the pounding of his heart slowing to a manageable beat as the tension from his stalk subsided.

The shot reverberated off the granite wall opposite the falls as startled doves rose from the edge of the river, and the whitetail buck collapsed in instant death.

Knowing a storm was brewing, Anton wasted no time fording the river and eviscerating the deer. The rumble of thunder to his east prompted him to lay the carcass over the saddle and swing up behind. Knowing the weather was turning dangerous and knowing his party was caught in the open, his concern was building for their safety. Two loud claps of thunder in quick succession provoked a shudder up his spine, and he urged his mare forward, slogging through the marshy terrain through which he must ride to reach higher ground.

* * *

THE STORM FRONT MOVED IN, pelting men and horses alike in a late season rainstorm. Caught in the open on the prairie, they hunkered down and waited for it to pass.

"Damn . . . it's like we're under a pissin' cow. I've never seen it rain this hard." Harvey had his slicker pulled tightly around his ample body, trooper's hat planted firmly on his head. "You don't suppose this downpour's gonna last till sunset do you? I mean . . . I'm starvin'. We haven't had a thing to eat since that puny sage hen yesterday, and we had to split that between the nine of us. Damn . . . I'm hungry. I get a chance to close my eyes I'm afraid all I'll dream about is buffalo steak. Damn . . . I'm hungry."

"Give your jaw a rest, Harvey. Your yappin' is giving me a headache. If Anton don't get back pretty soon, your . . ."

The blinding flash was simultaneous with the deafening crack as lightning hammered the earth thirty yards to their right.

"Shit . . . that was close."

Earl didn't hear Harvey's comment. His eyes were fixed on the two horses that lay smoking on the charred ground where the lightning had hit.

"Everybody down—" Earl's scream was cut short by the next bolt. Earth, rock, and foliage exploded in all directions.

He bellowed, "Let's get out of here. Move your asses . . . now!"

Nine bodies scrambled from various spots, each scampering in random directions.

The dead horses were still smoking. While alive, they'd belonged to Harvey and Earl. They were now carrion, and the two men concentrated on vacating the area that seemed to attract death from above.

The scribes assigned by Snelling were running in fear as rocks splintered and earth erupted around them.

"Get your horses out of there!" Earl was running like he was being chased by the devil.

Anton had chosen his men well. As if rehearsed, the three remaining troopers—Cal Smith, Drain Cooper, and Sven Olson—charged to the hobbled steeds drawing their knives as they ran, and sprinting from one to the next, severed the hobbles, allowing the freed horses to race wide-eyed toward the open prairie.

* * *

THE FIRE CRACKLED AS THE MEN huddled together in an attempt to absorb the heat. The storm had ended as abruptly as it had started, and with its demise came a raw coldness, more typical for that time of year than the moderate temperatures they had seen until then. Anton had taken Harvey and Earl, mounted on fresh horses recovered after the onslaught, to retrieve those scattered during the storm. They now rode into camp trailing the strays, each tethered with a strong rope.

After dismounting, the two troopers joined the others while Anton secured the horses on the east edge of their campsite.

Harvey, distant and quiet until now, approached the squatting troopers.

"What the hell were you boys thinking? You scattered like quail leaving the horses to the hellfire. I'm gonna show you something to be afraid of." His hulking figure strode toward the four scribes.

"Hold up, Harvey!"

"Damn it to hell, Anton. These boys scattered like roaches."

"It wasn't their fault, Harvey. Those boys are fresh troops. They haven't been here for more than a month."

Much to his credit, the scribe closest to Harvey stood his ground. "Captain Anton's right. We're trained as military organizational specialists, not accustomed to the violence of the frontier."

Harvey's face reflected incomprehension. The revelation stopped him in his tracks.

"Leave them be, Harvey. Now you tell me . . . what the hell happened?"

"I'm not sure. All I know is all hell busted loose."

Earl offered his take on things. "It was like we were sitting on a lightning rod. The first one took the horses. I never seen anything like it, Anton." He calmly recounted the chaos. "I didn't see the strike, but I seen those horses lying there. They were actually smoking. The way I figure it, something in the ground was drawing that lightning."

"Yeah, I've heard of that happening. I don't know what does it, but I heard of that happening."

Silence grew among them as venison steaks were placed on rocks centered within the hot coals of the now mature fire.

"This is going to slow us down. We'll take turns walking. We've got another day's travel the way I figure it, two days at most. Those four guys are going to ride all the way." Anton gestured toward the four scribes assigned by Colonel Snelling, "Earl, you and I are gonna walk first."

Earl Freeman took the news as expected, a testament to Anton's faith in his durability . . . then he picked a steak off the fire and set about eating.

* * *

RED IRON'S HUNTING PARTY watched from a mile to the north as the soldiers in the distance darted to and fro among the lightning bolts. The first strike occurred as the Indians topped a low depression in the prairie. Cut Ear, the leader of the group and first to see the threat, watched the initial explosion launch two horses into the air. Incredulous, the party watched the distant men scramble for their lives. Even before the threat ended, Cut Ear sent one of his men to report the army's presence to Red Iron, whose temporary camp was seven miles west of there.

Red Iron and his party had just returned from a sacred quarry to the southwest where they went to gather Catlinite stone for their pipe maker. Red Iron, himself a friend of the white soldiers, set out with the messenger upon hearing the news, two fine horses in tow.

* * *

"I AM TRULY HONORED BY YOUR VISIT," Anton said. "How is it that you come to this place at this exact time?"

"My men, a hunting party, saw the lightning hit your camp. As soon as I heard of your misfortune I came directly to offer my help."

"I thank Red Iron for his kindness." Anton sat next to the Indian chief as his men busied themselves around the camp.

"Your name is well known to the Dakota. You are a friend." Red Iron's frank and open face was without guile.

"Colonel Snelling wishes to ensure that whiskey is not a problem for the Indians. He has sent me to view and study the conditions within the trading posts around Lake Traverse and Big Stone Lake. It's important that trappers aren't stirring trouble with the Dakota in the area."

"I have heard of trouble where the rivers meet. For the most part, things are stable with the bands near the Big Stone."

Anton knew Red Iron was making reference to Fort Snelling. "That is good to hear, my friend. I'm told the Great White Father in Washington is watching closely. I'm also told he knows the name Red Iron. The gift you have brought me seems to be directed by the Great Spirit. We are truly brothers."

"Yes, my brother. There is much to think about. I think the white man is like the grass in the meadow. It can be trampled beneath hooves, yet it sprouts again with the next growing season."

Anton, instincts paramount, felt a comfort in talking to this man and almost a compulsion toward sharing his innermost thoughts.

"I have seen their numbers grow from places many days beyond the sunrise. They spread like grasshoppers devouring everything they encounter. It is wise to be cautious, my friend."

This was the second time he had called Red Iron his friend, and he felt a comfort like when sitting at the fire with his first true Dakota friend, Tomawka.

"There have been treaties with Chippewa to the east, and Winnebago, Fox, and Sacs to the south. It's impossible to stop the flow of settlers to this area. It is hoped the treaties will keep peace and limit the settlement, allowing our red brothers to continue the old ways. Be cautious. I have seen their might and their great numbers cannot be controlled. There are good men, but also bad. It is the bad that we must be mindful of. They seek trouble between the red man and the white."

"It is no different in the bands of the Seven Fires. The young men wish to strike what they do not know."

Anton, making a mental note of Red Iron's statement, decided to move the conversation to a less volatile area. "How is it that you are on the trail?"

"I am returning from a quest for the sacred red stone used in our pipes. My carver will form a bowl to ensure the successful marriage of my daughter to a powerful warrior from another band."

Anton answered, "I have shared the pipe with Shakopee. I know the strength within the ceremony."

They continued to talk. As their comfort level grew, Anton again spoke of the influx of whiskey and how it was being used to cause problems between the Chippewa and Dakota around the fort. He felt it important that Red Iron understand the steps taken to punish violators, hoping to instill confidence that the soldiers were capable of controlling the situation. It was well after midnight before the two men concluded their visit, and the Indians left the encampment.

Late in the evening on the seventh day after leaving Fort Snelling, the soldiers reached Fort Washington. Leaving two scribes and the remainder of his command to enjoy the relative comfort provided by the fort, charging them to learn as much about the operation as possible, Anton, Harvey, and Earl accompanied the two remaining scribes to the American Fur Company post on Lake Traverse. There he met with Joseph Renville and acquired an instant connection to the man who was brother to the Dakota.

After settling his men into the routine business of the fur company post, a process that took three days, Anton set out alone for Hazen Mooers's post on the East side of Big Stone Lake to see how that operation differed from those with which he was familiar.

Chapter Seven

Red River of the North

SEVENTY MILES TO THE NORTH, fifteen men were moving south on the Red River. They were trappers, mostly French, hired by the Northwestern Fur Company, and they had traveled the Red River from Canada carefully mapping streams and lakes and searching out areas rich in beaver and otter, sometimes drifting as far as fifty miles from the river.

Rounding a bend, they'd come to the foot of a rapid where the water crashed down after rushing through a narrow neck. Boulders lined the edges of the constricted, fast-flowing deluge.

Their leader, Peter McCarin, used small trees as hand supports as he climbed out of the ravine, pulling as much with his arms as he was pushing with his legs. He had been scouting the east side of the river, not looking for tributaries or offshoots, rather a track for the men to follow during the long portage they were about to make.

"You men pull them canoes out and set up for a tote." His voice boomed over the cacophony of the rushing water. "I'm gonna find us a path to skirt this here rapids."

Since the start of their journey four months prior, they had been forced to portage off the mostly languid river no more than a dozen times, mostly because of impenetrable logjams. Prior treks were made arduous only because of fallen trees over which they had to pick their way. This was the first altitudinal change of consequence and the men grumbled as they drew the crafts ashore.

"Clacker! You and me are going to go and find us a path. The rest of you, empty them boats, set some packs, and get ready for the portage. You men there," pointing to the two men in the first canoe, "find the best way to get up this here slide while me an Jim-boy go ahead an see what we got."

Taking the shortest route to the top, Peter, and his best friend and second in command, James "Jim-boy" Clacker, scrambled over and under the large trees lying in a tangled mass alongside the coursing river. At the top of the slide, they saw that the entire river was strewn with timber. A large tree had wedged between boulders, effectively forming a bung at the top of the rapid. As more and more refuse floated downstream and the water rose behind it, there was scarcely a square yard that wasn't filled with dead wood.

"Damn, we're going to have to go past that bend to see how far we have to carry those boats. Shit, man, this could go a mile or more depending on how long this has been stacking up." Peter's mood was dark.

"Must have been some blow to take down all these trees . . . looks like it's been awhile too."

The two men moved a good hundred yards into the woods before the deadfalls separated enough to allow room to maneuver the twenty-foot canoes.

"Right here's the trail we're going to take, Jim-boy. Get on back and bring those boys this way. I'm gonna go around the bend and see how far this jam runs."

The portage required dragging their crafts and supplies nearly a quarter mile before the river opened enough to relaunch. Two hours later, they were once again paddling the river.

The relatively mild weather held as they continued south, allowing them to map a large number of streams while searching for good trapping grounds.

* * *

IN LATE FEBRUARY OF 1826 Peter decided it was time to set in for the winter. Using the knowledge and survival skills gleaned from spending the past seven years learning the ways of the northland from French trappers and the Chippewa, McCarin chose their winter camp location, a sheltered belt where the river had cut a gorge while making a sweeping eastward jog, with flat prairie on both sides. Four days later, they had erected lean-to shelters in a manner favored by French trappers, and within six days they received a Dakota hunting party drawn by the smoke from the camp's fires. Breaking out the trade goods, Clacker proved his ability to stretch a deal to his advantage, and the Indian party left with several thick wool blankets, albeit minus four good horses.

With mounts, the party could range far from the river for game. Peter McCarin's men could now take whatever the winter weather would bring.

* * *

ON MARCH 19, 1826, THE WEATHER, which had been below freezing and clear, turned nasty. Snow began to fall as the sky boiled. A relentless wind blew the falling snow horizontally across the prairie. Anton was riding to the north. He was of a firm mind to find a large camp of Sisseton Sioux that had set their tipis in a wooded valley where a river cut a gorge large enough to protect the band during the bitter winter. His senses on alert, knowing the danger present in the building blizzard, he traveled fast, urging his horse onward. To be caught in the open would result in freezing to death in spite of the heavy buffalo robe he wore.

Anton rode the flat prairie, sleet peppering his face with a wind-blown ferocity that limited his visibility to less than ten yards. His horse skidded to a stop, nearly toppling him from the saddle. Regaining his seat, he realized her instincts saved them from crashing down the steep cut that appeared before them. He knew the river lay below, and he knew he must reach the other side to take advantage of the shelter the bank would offer from the awful wind. Dismounting, he led the bay down the steep embankment to the edge of the river.

"Well, old girl, this looks like the best place to cross." Alone on the prairie, Anton had had countless conversations with the mare he rode. Through squinted eyes, he examined the lay of the land through the blowing snow and sleet. Between squalls, he could see solid ice stretching the width of the frozen water. "Looks like still water. It should be thick enough to support our weight. I'm gonna tie this rope to your halter, and you set here while I cross first." He knew better than to try to ride across the stretch of river ice. "If it's thick enough, I'll be back, and we'll cross together."

With great apprehension, he inched his way onto the solid water, each yard bolstering his confidence. Uncertain determination turned to relief as he approached the far shoreline. Sporadic calm between gusts softened the torrent of snow pelting his face, and he saw the outline of the far bank, now visible through the milky vista.

Without warning, the ice gave way, and he plunged into the frigid water. Only his grip on the rope kept him from being pulled completely under the ice. He gasped air before his head went beneath the surface, and he flailed his arms, fighting the swift current. Without thought, he released his grip on the rope and he watched as his only hope for survival blew beyond his reach across the icy expanse. Thankfully, the thick buffalo robe he wore gave him buoyancy, allowing him to surface and stretch his arms over the edge of the ice preventing him from being carried downstream.

* * *

PETER MCCARIN AND JAMES CLACKER picked their way along the bank, keeping a tight rein in the terrible wind. Caught in the open by the quick-forming storm, they had abandoned their hunt for food and were now approaching their camp.

"Lookit that, Jim-boy. Ain't that somebody in the river?"

Clacker drew even with Peter and followed his pointed finger, focusing his eyes on the dark blob barely visible in the blowing snow. "Sure is, boss. He'll end up dead if we don't hurry."

"You get down there. See if you can drag him out. I'm gonna ride downstream to the roils. In case he gets sucked under, it should be open there. Might give me a chance to grab 'im if he goes with the current."

Peter urged his horse forward as Clacker jumped to the ground and slid down the embankment. The snow was coming down so hard Clacker ran right past where Anton hung precariously to the ice sheet. A momentary lapse in the wind allowed him to relocate the man.

"Hang on, partner. I'm a-coming."

Clacker's foot hit the ice, breaking the surface, and he went down face first, smashing through the thin ice at the edge of the river. Picking himself up from the shallow water, he retreated to shore. "Can you hang on, partner? I've got to find a branch or something you can grab."

"I don't know . . . this damn coat's gonna drag me under." The buffalo robe, which had saved him earlier, was now water soaked and heavy, threatening to drag him under the ice. "I can't hang on much longer . . . cold . . . tired." The frigid water drained his strength and slowed his mind. It was all he could do to keep his head above the ice. He knew if the current caught the neck of the robe, it would suck him under the surface.

As in a dream, he heard the man on the shore shouting instructions, "Open below . . . big breath . . . go with it . . . grab you."

Then he slipped beneath the surface, managing one last intake of air before he disappeared. His face skidded on the underside of the ice before he tumbled and twisted as the current whisked him downward. A sharp pain to his left shoulder snapped his mind to awareness, and he realized the bottom was rapidly coming up, swirling, and bubbling . . . to an opening. Throwing his arms outward, he stopped somersaulting as he drew near the unexpected opening in the ice. The bottom came up sharply as he gathered his strength, placed his feet downstream, and uncoiled his legs against the gravel bottom. As his head shot through the opening, he felt hands gripping the back of his coat . . . lifting . . . lifting . . . blackness.

* * *

AS HE WATCHED, THE UNNAMED INDIAN was gesturing wildly, face elongated, thinly stretching from forehead to nose, lower jaw distorting terribly, first one direction then another. He was mid-air, screaming words without voice . . . as his head exploded. The skull floated upward, twisting, turning, finally morphing into swirls of vapor, dissolving into the surrounding blackness, itself all encompassing, until only a fearsome darkness remained.

* * *

UNBEARABLE COLD PENETRATED HIS SENSES, and he began to shake uncontrollably.

"By damn, I think he's going to make it." Peter squatted at Anton's side and nudged additional stones against the blanket in which he was wrapped. It had been nearly three hours since he was carried into the shelter, and the stones first warmed by the fire then placed on and around the blanket covering his naked body, seemed to deliver life to the inert figure. The next several hours found Anton lapsing in and out of consciousness.

On the second day after being pulled from the water, he was sitting up, taking food, and feeling strong enough to carry on a conversation with McCarin and Clacker. Not fully in control of his mental state, he shared stories of his mother with the two men responsible for saving his life. Things he had never told another human being.

Three days passed before the storm subsided. With the air still, the temperature dipped well below freezing. On the fifth day he ventured outside the shelter, pleased to find his mare well cared for, tack safely stored, and his personal items dry and clean.

* * *

THEY WERE SEATED AROUND THE COOKING FIRE. Jeremy Dokkins, Peter's cook, was putting the final turn to the rear quarter of an unknown animal that had been on the spit since early morning. The haunch was now blackened, outer layer cracked and arid, begging to be taken from the flame. Jeremy was a perpetual over-cooker. Although his culinary skills were atrocious, he was an eager participant in the cooking ritual and had proven himself up to the task of preparing meals for a passel of unkempt and outspoken curmudgeons over the years. Truth was, their uncaring and un-Christian attitude was caused, for the most part, by the marginal food they were served, each of them unwilling to offer criticism for fear of Dokkins' fierce temper and the surety of being forced to do the cooking honors until Dokkins figured his point had been made.

Anton chewed on the chunk of unknown meat handed him by Dokkins.

"By damn, Jeremy, if this ain't the toughest thing I ever ate."

The eyes of every man within earshot turned to the cantankerous cook. The last criticism of Dokkins resulted in a vicious verbal attack launched on the perpetrator and the cook's refusal to make a single meal for nearly a month. Now a guest had issued this challenge, and everyone secretly hoped Dokkins would take the criticism to heart.

"What're you bitching about? You're damn lucky to be alive to even taste the damn food. The captain should have let you drift on downstream. It would've saved us a passel of trouble. Damn half-breed."

Eyes snapped to the man dragged from the river five days earlier.

"You know . . . I think I'd watch my words, Mr. Dokkins. You're pushing me just about as far as I can tolerate. I'm just saying the meat's a little dry. Nothing to argue about, just an observation."

"Yeah . . . well you probably never tasted anything except muskrat and swamp coot before anyhow, what with a squaw bringing you up."

His earlier conversation with McCarin and Clacker had brought old memories to the surface, and he had since looked into his past to relive the few joyous moments he shared with his mother before her untimely death. The cook's words stung as though striking an exposed nerve.

Anton's reaction was instantaneous and extreme. With cat quickness, he pounced. Locking his fingers on the cook's throat, he gave a quick twist that forced the startled man to the ground, his eyes nearly bulging out of his head. As the others watched, unable to look away and unable to move, Anton raised his free hand in preparation for a killing blow meant to crush the larynx and cause death by suffocation.

"Hold on there, mister!" The command roared from the opening that served as the door.

Anton, a man accustomed to acting on impulse, gave pause.

"You smack him in the throat . . . who's gonna cook for me? I don't figure Jeremy ever had anyone call his bluff before. If you were to consider letting him take back those words, I'd be much obliged."

Anton slowly shifted his concentration from the man he was about to kill to the source of the words. Peter stood, casual attitude, relaxed stance, inside the opening to the makeshift cooking tent.

"I figure you for someone smart enough to grant a life for no other reason than it's the right thing to do. Unless you think it's okay to kill a fool what doesn't know words can hurt, go ahead . . . but know it'll cost me a cook."

Anton slowly lowered his arm as his rage subsided. Releasing his grip from the man's throat, he watched the cook slide to the ground, nearly unconscious and scared to death.

"Jeremy, you had no call to talk to me like that. Just so you know. I'm sorry I lost my temper. You better learn to curb that jerky hole of yours before somebody less forgiving takes exception . . . and you end up dead." Stepping over the prostrate form, Anton moved to address Peter McCarin, who remained at the kitchen shelter entrance.

"I'm sorry for the problem, and I thank you for putting yourself in the middle of it. It would've been a damn shame to have it end like that. I figure I'll just get my stuff and get along out of your hair." With that, Anton pushed through the flap and headed outside, already planning for his departure the following morning.

* * *

THE MORNING BROKE CLEAR. Snow squeaked underfoot as Anton approached the mare. Grabbing the horn, he swung into the saddle with confident ease, gathered the reins and urged her to move. She responded, springing forward, anxious to get started after so many days of inactivity.

He rode in deep thought. The gulf between Indian and white man seemed unbridgeable and widening. The attitude of the majority of trappers working the streams and rivers was unyielding toward recognizing traditional tribal lands, and uncaring about how their actions depleted game on which the Indians relied for their subsistence. The red man, up until now willing to share his land with the whites, was aware he was losing more than just his land. He was losing his way of life. It was clear to Anton the two sides were on a collision course.

The incident with Jeremy Dokkins and the talk of his mother struck deeply, and Anton felt an unfamiliar emptiness. For the first time since she died, he longed for her companionship. His mind returned to the years spent with her and to the lessons she taught him about natural things. Through the fog of time, memories of long ago began to filter into his mind. His earliest memories were of being carried while facing forward, and one memory rose to the surface as clear and distinct as though it had happened yesterday.

They were mid-stream, crossing where it was shallow, when suddenly, his mother fell forward pitching face first into the cold water. Before going under, Kanti cupped her hand across his face, effectively blocking his mouth and nose, preventing him from inhaling the water. She was up in an instant, and he was no worse for the experience. For some reason the memory never faded, often reappearing in dreams, comfoting dreams, those he awoke from with a peaceful ease enveloping his entire being.

With the sky clear, the sun served as a directional compass, and Anton kept it on his right side while giving the mare her head, ensuring only that she maintained the basic southeastern route that would take them home. They were on a prairie, flat and treeless, where the drifted snow seldom exceeded a foot in depth. As he rode, his thoughts turned to Shakopee's camp and the woman and child who waited there. His sense of responsibility was being augmented with a burgeoning affection for Star Woman.

"Well, old girl, I figure it'll take us a good while to get back to the camp. And guess what . . . I miss that woman." Anton spoke to the mare as though talking to a close friend. "And you know what? I miss the kid even more."

The bay mare raised her head and gave a few shakes, rattling the bridle hardware and causing Anton to chuckle.

"I don't think I've ever felt this way about another person. You don't think I've fallen in love, do you?" He knew the question was rhetorical, yet he wished his horse could answer. This was something new. His heart was surprisingly heavy with a hollowness he had never experienced before, while at the same time he was filled with an undeniable hope for the future. The combined feelings were confusing and unsettling.

"What say we talk about something different? Like what I'm going to say to Snelling and the agent . . . we've got to think this one through."

This was more familiar territory. As his thoughts turned inward. The conversation with his horse ended. His report to Colonel Snelling would praise the organizational structure put in place by Joseph Renville at the post at Lake Traverse. His three-day stay there impressed him with the order of the place. He would rely on the report generated by the two scribes left in place at Fort Washington, and those left at the fur company post, to reveal the details.

Much deeper thought would go into his reports regarding the status and mindset of the Indians and trappers in the territory. Unwilling to arm Colonel Snelling with information that he could use against the Dakota, he had to be careful what he passed on to the man. Although Anton liked and trusted the officer, he knew that beneath the surface was an ambitious person driven to improve his position in the army. At what cost, he did not know.

Taliaferro was a different story. Based on the trust shown by his Dakota friends, coupled with his personal knowledge of the man, Anton would hold nothing back from the agent.

Suddenly, he noticed the mare was standing still. Unsure of how long they'd been stopped he realized he had been lost in thought.

"What's going on, old girl?"

Surveying the area and judging by the tops of bushes just ahead, he figured they were on the edge of some kind of depression in the prairie. The snow, pushed by heavy winds, was now drifted to the level of the surrounding ground giving the appearance of flat land. Dismounting, Anton stepped ahead carefully, one hand on the reins. With his first step, the ground beneath the snow cover fell away sharply and he would have tumbled forward had he not had a firm grip on the rein leather.

"Well, ain't you something? You knew this was here didn't you? That's twice you saved us from a fall." He offered his face, and the bay nuzzled his neck.

Looking around, Anton realized they had stopped in an area where seeds had found purchase in the soil and small bushes had grown at the edge of the crevasse.

"This thing runs pretty much north and south, right across where we need to go to get home. Hold on here while I cut us a feeler pole. We're going to have to take it slow. No telling how deep this thing is, and I sure don't want to get stuck in it."

It didn't take long for him to select and cut a probe, about six feet long. Walking the undisturbed snow and pushing the probe into it, he found the edge of the ravine and led the mare parallel to the cut. As they progressed, the hollow became deeper and wider. Some spots devoid of drifted snow were a good twenty feet deep. As the sun approached the horizon with dusk soon to follow, they found themselves at the point where the ravine began to level out as it intersected a bluff overlooking the St. Peter River. Looking down upon the river valley, Anton saw that this side of the river was nearly snowless while the opposite bank was heavily covered with deep drifts.

"When we get us off this bluff and down by the river, we can make pretty good time."

Walking his horse and using his probe, he worked his way across and down the slope until they reached the river's edge.

"Look at this. There's even some grass for you to munch. We'll spend the night here and get started at sunrise. Won't take us long to get to the fort if we don't run into some deep drifts. Looks like the wind kept it to the other side."

* * *

The camp of Star Woman
1826

THE SUN PEEKED OVER THE HORIZON and shone upon a totally white landscape. Not a single patch of exposed ground, even the trees were painted white with blown snow. The storm had lasted three days. Three days during which Star Woman and Rising Eagle were confined to their tipi.

More a result of luck than planning, she had a sizable store of wood intended for the cooking fire when the blizzard hit, and it was more than enough to maintain warmth over the three days they had been inside. As long as the flap remained closed, the heat inside the tipi was constant. However, maintaining the life-sustaining heat forced them to empty their bladders and relieve themselves as close as they could to the outside wall opposite the door. Their diet over the past days had consisted of dried venison and water gleaned from melted snow.

This was the first time she had been outside since the storm, and she was intent on checking a trap set two days before it hit. She had discovered a trail with fresh cottontail sign, a place that begged for a snare. She'd found the spot while schooling Rising Eagle on identifying and following tracks of beaver, otter, mink, and muskrat. Rising Eagle was now approaching two years old, the age when children were introduced to the natural world.

For his part, Rising Eagle was developing more rapidly than most. He was already putting sentences together and responding to words spoken both in English and his native Dakota, a result of Star Woman's near fixation on his linguistic studies. She spent all her waking hours talking to him as though he were an adult, switching easily from English to the Dakota language.

Traveling the windward edge of the ridge-top where the snow was thinnest, she was able to jog. She had left Rising Eagle alone for short periods before. Never had she been this far from the tipi, and she was nervous. She reckoned he would do as told, he always had in the past, however, then she had made it a point to stay within sight of her camp. The decision to leave him alone was made with very little hesitation, but the further she got from him the more she questioned that decision.

She knew she was in the right area yet nothing looked familiar. Everything was buried in snow. Even the trees and bushes appeared foreign, as though she was in a place she had never been. The only constant was the river itself. Walking the edge, she finally came to a spot that resembled where she had made the snare, and she began to carve into the snowdrift that covered the spot. Twenty minutes later she retreated with a cottontail rabbit, frozen stiff as a board. Holding it by the rear legs, she literally sprinted for camp, swinging the frozen rabbit like a club as she pumped her arms.

Her mind conjured bad things, and by the time she reached the tipi, she was almost in a state of panic. She reached for the flap, finding comfort in the fact that it looked to be just as she left it. Clutching at the corner, she threw it open and dashed through. Flipping the rabbit toward the fire in the middle of the space, her eyes darted left and right looking for the child. Nothing. Bile rose in her throat. Her numbed mind failed to control her body, and her arms and legs began to shake uncontrollably as she fell to her knees. Rising Eagle was gone. Anguish filled her body as the air left her lungs.

"Ohhhhhh!"

"Mama . . . what's wrong?"

Spinning to her right, she saw the blanket begin to move, and the child crawled from beneath.

Immense relief filled her. She scrambled and gathered him in her arms.

"My big boy! I thought you were gone. I was so afraid."

"I go nowhere. I wait for you."

She held him close for a very long time, not willing to put him down. Her mind churned with emotion, and for the first time in a long time she thought of Tomawka. She realized how much she had relied on his strength, how much his touch had comforted her. Seamlessly her mind transitioned to Anton and his apparent growing commitment toward her welfare and that of her son. She wondered where he was at that precise moment. Was he on his way home? She hoped so.

* * *

Fort Snelling,
Two days later

SNELLING SAT IN HIS QUARTERS, chair near the hearth upon which a fire crackled, while Anton preferred to sit cross-legged nearer the fire.

"Damn nasty storm, eh, Anton?"

"For sure. If it weren't for a group of trappers following the Red south out of Canada, I'd likely be frozen into the rocks of that river right now." Anton continued telling of his near death experience and the men that had saved his life by pulling him from beneath the ice.

Snelling listened in fascination while Anton related the story of his return journey to the fort.

"Riding back here alone doesn't sound like the smartest thing you've ever done," the colonel responded. "This storm killed most of a band of Sisseton trying to move to a new hunting ground. Thirty lodges with about seventy-five men, women, and children got caught in the open." He paused to take a pull from the whiskey tumbler at his side. The action troubled Anton. He had noticed that the colonel seemed to enjoy the amber liquid a little too much.

Snelling continued, "The strongest strapped on what snow-shoes they had and went for help. The nearest trading post was almost a hundred miles away, so by the time the rescue party got there most of them were dead, and those that weren't survived by eating them that already died."

Anton looked aghast. "You're kidding me. Cannibalism?" The news was astonishing. His Algonquin mother, familiar with sudden onslaughts of life-threatening weather, taught him the secrets of survival. He wondered how it was that the Dakota were caught in the open without shelter. Almost at the same moment the question formed in his mind, he remembered how the storm had overtaken him, and he realized the helplessness of the unfortunate band.

"That's what the advance rider says. We're waiting for what's left of the party to be brought in here." Snelling doubled over, and a bout of coughing ensued that lasted for a good two minutes. "Damn, this has been a hell of a winter. It seems like I've been sick since you left. Now . . . what did you learn?"

"I met Red Iron on the prairie. He talked of friendship toward the white man, while warning of ever-present troublemakers on both sides. As do you, I believe him to be a man of peace, trustworthy and honorable, and a friend. He's aware of young men within the bands of the Seven Fires that talk of striking out against the whites, but says things are stable around the Lac qui Parle area." Anton paused. "You're going to have problems with the trappers. All I met consider the Northwest Frontier open ground, aware yet uncaring that they tread on land used for centuries by the native people for subsistence." This was as far as Anton intended to go in explaining what he learned to the fort commander, however, he had one more thing to report.

"The biggest problem you will face is not with the Dakota or Chippewa. It is with the bastard traders that ply with whiskey, cheat the unwary, and steal from the Indians. They are a band of scoundrels that must be controlled."

"As I figured. Thanks for your openness. I'll be watching them closely, and I'll do all I can to eliminate the whiskey problem. I know I can control it within the posts. It's another matter trying to control the trappers who smuggle the damn stuff in."

They talked in general terms, comparing thoughts on everything from military rifles to favorite foods while in the field. They both recognized that there were as many good men as bad, but the worst of the bad seemed to outnumber the best of the good. Both knew the situation was a powder keg waiting to blow . . . and the fuse was lit.

Leaving Snelling's quarters, Anton went to Taliaferro's office and found it empty. Rather than wait for his return, he headed directly to Shakopee's village and Star Woman's tipi.

* * *

IT WAS EARLY APRIL AND THE DAY was overcast, one of the few without rain or snow. Anton was walking the trail with Rising Eagle on his shoulders. He learned from Star Woman that Taliaferro had been called to quell a building dispute between Dakota and Chippewa villages someplace to the north. She wasn't sure how far north or how long he would be gone.

Star Woman walked with lightness to her step and a joy in her heart not experienced since before Tomawka's death. Anton's return the day prior buoyed her spirits, and she realized how much she had missed him. They were now walking adjacent to an oak ridge thicket where she had found shed whitetail antlers every year since her fifteenth birthday. Her father, Burning with Rage, had shown her the place, where he had found sheds for eleven years running. His streak ended when he was killed during a raid on a Chippewa village.

"Oh, look!" She bent and retrieved a sizable shed, seven distinct branches protruding along its curved length. "This is the largest I've ever found."

Rising Eagle, from atop Anton's shoulders, bounced and moved his arms in circles while chattering, "Mama find. Good find, good find."

Anton, with a satisfied smile, took it all in. The empty feeling he'd had while on the prairie was a distant memory.

* * *

A FEW DAYS LATER, A YOUNG MAN from Shakopee's band approached him while he was with Star Woman and Rising Eagle. Major Taliaferro wished to see him at his quarters at Anton's earliest convenience. That evening found the two men together in the agent's office.

They shared a pot of tea and visited, as old friends were apt, interjecting small talk into Anton's report on things to the west. Anton concluded with a final statement. "I'd bet my best rifle that corrupt agents are gonna drive a wedge that'll split everything wide open."

"Yeah, it won't surprise me. There are lots that would take advantage of the Indian." Lawrence knew it was time his friend was told about an administrative change bound to affect the future of the frontier. "There is a new agent who is supposed to administer to the Chippewa up north."

"You mean you're not agent for both nations anymore?"

"That's right. President Adams appointed Henry Schoolcraft as agent over the Chippewa in the Northwest Frontier and left me as agent for the Sioux."

"How long has this been in place?"

"It's been coming for a while. The last time I was in Washington with the tribal leaders, I was told it would happen. Now that it has happened, I'm having trouble convincing the Chippewa to work with Schoolcraft." There was a pause as the agent breathed deeply. "I need a favor. These constant raids taking place between Chippewa and Sioux are affecting the whole territory."

Anton stated what he thought to be the obvious. "I can't see any other way for it. The fort draws them like a magnet, and it brings them close to the trading posts. Both nations are taking advantage of this proximity."

Taliaferro answered, "I need someone I trust, someone to spend a little time with the Chippewa to get a perspective on their take on things. I need to figure out what it might take to have peace between the two nations. Things are getting serious. I'm afraid Colonel Snelling is close to doing something foolish if they don't stop their warring. "

Had Colonel Snelling requested the favor, he would have turned him down flat. Major Taliaferro had asked for help and Anton immediately agreed. His respect for the agent grew with every meeting.

The plan was to head cross country to pick up the Rum River, and then follow it north toward Lake Mille Lacs. If he kept his eyes open and paid attention to what he heard, he reckoned he could get a good fix on the Chippewa perspective.

As recommended by Taliaferro, he would wear the uniform coat of a cavalryman and carry paper identifying him as a representative of the agent. As near as he could figure, the trip would take upward of two weeks to complete. The next morning Anton mounted up and headed north.

Chapter Eight

The Gauntlet

RACING THROUGH THE GATES of the fort, Anton rode at a full gallop between the hospital and officers' quarters and on to the parade grounds, reining in twenty feet before the commandant's quarters. The mare was skidding to a stop, rear end touching the ground, front legs locked with hooves digging into the packed earth, as he leaped from the saddle. He was at the door to Snelling's quarters at about the time she came to a stop in front of the hitch rail.

For the first time in his life he neither stopped nor knocked. Hitting the latch, he pushed through the opening.

"What the hell's goin' on, Colonel?" He was three steps into the room before realizing Snelling wasn't there. "Colonel!" He strode toward the door leading to the adjacent room, grabbed the handle, depressed the latch, and pushed it open. The shutters were closed and the room was in semi-darkness although it was near midday.

"Colonel, you in here?" Anton scanned the interior, eyes coming to rest on the rocking chair facing the fireplace hearth. There, slouched to one side and apparently sound asleep, was Colonel Snelling. An unmistakable odor, reminiscent of the pungent smell of pickles, nudged Anton's nostrils. To the right of the chair lay an empty whiskey bottle. On the table to the left, within arms reach, sat an opium pipe with all its accoutrements, the source of the odor. "Colonel . . . c'mon, snap out of it. We've got a problem."

There was no response.

"Colonel Snelling! What the hell's happening here?" Anton grabbed him by the shoulders, and none too gently gave him a shake. The only response was a barely discernable groan. Turning to the door, he marched through the outer office and on to the grounds outside, and headed to the officers' quarters. There he meant to find the post surgeon.

* * *

"ALL I CAN SAY IS, IT'S THE RECOMMENDED way to treat the colonel's illness. You don't realize . . . he's been sick, I mean really sick, since before you left with the scribes."

"There isn't a better way to deal with it?"

"None that I know of. Limited use of opium and controlled use of brandy will reduce apprehension and encourage rest, exactly what he needs to shake whatever he's picked up."

"Not exactly what he needs if he intends to maintain control." Anton was having trouble relating to the logic.

Clearly agitated, the medical officer put an end to the meeting. "Look. You might be the best scout in the territory, but you don't know shit about the medical profession. Just leave me alone. The colonel and I will be just fine. Now, if you don't mind, I've got things to do."

Anton turned on his heel and headed for the door. Reaching the threshold, he turned and spoke. "Just answer a question for me. Why is Shakopee in the guard house?"

"All's I know is that he's being held because he's paying the price for the death of some Chippewa. Four of his warriors are sitting in the guardhouse with him."

Anton, after being turned away from the building holding the Indians, rode directly to Lawrence Taliaferro's quarters.

"What the hell happened?"

"It's not good, Annawon. Shakopee's being held along with four of his braves. looks like Snelling isn't fooling around. He's sentenced them to die, but not by hanging."

"Oh, no! What happened?"

"The day after you left, Hole in the Day came in under army protection to talk peace with the Dakota. We had a very good meeting and agreements were made with a little compromise from both sides."

"Doesn't sound like anything deserving of the death penalty so far."

"Well, the Chippewa offered a meal to celebrate the newly made treaty, and a handful of Shakopee's band attended. It was outside the fort, real sociable, and everyone seemed to be enjoying it. After Shakopee and his men said their farewells and left the wigwam, they turned their guns on it, killing and wounding several of those inside."

"What?" Anton was horror-stricken.

"Yep, that's right. Shot the place up pretty badly, then ran off into the woods when those inside returned fire."

"You sure that's what went down?"

"Unfortunately, yes. A few troopers saw it happen. The Chippewa brought their wounded to the fort for protection, where the injured were treated. Anton . . . the daughter of Hole in the Day died."

Anton was speechless.

"Snelling told Shakopee's band to turn in the ones responsible or suffer the consequences. A few days later, they showed up and turned over Shakopee and four braves. That was the number demanded by the Chippewa to even the score."

"You said they aren't going to be hanged."

"That's right. To let everyone know he's done fooling around, Snelling decided to let the Chippewa determine how they would die." Taliaferro paused. "They've been ordered to die by gauntlet."

A chill settled on him, and Anton shuddered. He had seen others die by this method and he had seen yet others escape with their lives. The chances were slim, but it was possible.

"If Josiah Snelling hadn't handled it the way he did, we'd likely have a tribal war on our hands. He had no choice. He had to let the Chippewa set the death terms since they're the ones hurt this time. Their chiefs have expressed some doubt about the army's ability to protect them. In fact, they question the strength of the white man."

"That's only talk, Major. Every single chief I've talked to respects the might of the U.S. Army. I've met Hole in the Day. He's an honorable man. His people would follow him into Hades if asked. He's smart. He knows the might of the army. He may not like them, but he knows their numbers are like the leaves of the trees. I know these two tribes have fought each other for years, and the Chippewa have done the same thing to the Sioux in the past. It just keeps changing sides. This time Shakopee's band did the killing. Next time the Chippewa are going to pull the same thing, just wait and see."

Taliaferro replied, "Damn it, Anton. Don't you see . . . that's why I was sent here! I have to keep peace between the nations, which will help keep peace between the Indians and the whites."

"They have a great respect for you and rely on your good sense to keep problems from escalating into outright wars. You can't change things that have been going on for decades. My advice is to keep doing what you have been doing, and leave it at that."

* * *

The Gauntlet
June 1827

ANTON'S HEART WAS HEAVY as he sat in the saddle, giving the mare her head. They were on their way to the fort, and his mind was elsewhere, confident in the knowledge that the mare would follow the trail she had taken many times. He rode alone by choice.

Today was the day his friend Shakopee would die. There was nothing that could be done. The sentence was irrevocable. The band was there to offer support and medical assistance should any of the braves run the gauntlet to the end, for then their lives would be spared. Hopes were low.

Reaching the clearing outside the fort, Anton saw a gathering of Chippewa near the graveyard west of the walls near the bluff. Separate from them was a line of young men, each focusing on the rifle he held, making sure all was in order, with extra powder, and extra balls and patches close at hand.

Then, from the fort, the prisoners were led, leg irons and chains restricting their movements.

Anton joined the other Sioux at the edge of the trees. This would be the destination of the warriors running the gauntlet. To make it to the trees meant life. It was a run of nearly a hundred yards, and failure was unthinkable.

As Anton looked on, the shackles were removed, and the men stood. At a word, one of them broke toward the distant Sioux. There was a discharge of firearms, and beneath the smoke, the man lay dead. A second dashed to the line only to be cut down before running thirty feet. A third, then a fourth suffered the same fate.

Finally, Shakopee, warrior and friend, made his dash. Rifle fire filled the air and dense powder smoke drifted across the open space. He ran on. There was a murmuring from the Sioux as their leader drew closer with every bound. Again, the rifles exploded, this time catching Shakopee and bringing him to the ground, dead.

Anton watched the horror unfold as men and women charged the bodies with their knives and tomahawks in hand. He could take no more. Reining his horse, he turned away and joined the others as they walked toward their encampment.

From the killing field he heard whoops and screams as bodies were slashed, scalps were taken, and the dead were horribly disfigured before being pushed over the cliff into the river below.

* * *

TWO DAYS LATER, ANTON was in the commandant's quarters. "Colonel, I think I'm done. Things are just too complicated, what with the Chippewa, the Sioux, the traders, the trappers, and the settlers all coming together. I'd be much obliged if we cut our agreement here and now. I've been working for you for more'n five years. Near as I can figure, I got a dozen horses owed me. If it's all the same to you, I'll just pick 'em out of the corral and be on my way."

It was done. The U.S. Army no longer employed Annawon "Anton" McAllister.

Chapter Nine

Anton's Marriage

IT WOULDN'T BE LONG until the snow would fall. Four months had passed since Shakopee's execution, and Anton had spent the entire time in the Indian village. The friendship between him and Colonel Snelling had grown cold, although not because of the death of the five Sioux. Anton understood the necessity for that. What he didn't understand was the colonel's all too often use of whiskey. Anton hated the drink because of what it did to men's minds.

Unknown to Anton, the conversation he'd had with the colonel about resigning his scout duties was to be his last. On October 2, 1827, Colonel Snelling, along with his family and all their possessions, climbed aboard a riverboat on the way to St. Louis, Missouri, where he was to report to Jefferson Barracks for reassignment. His time in the Northwest Frontier was over.

* * *

ANTON SAT CROSS-LEGGED as Rising Eagle took careful aim. His wide smile served as testament to his enjoyment of the game they played. At three years old, he was being schooled in the art of shooting the bow and arrow. Anton had cut a branch from a young elm near the river nearly a year ago, and had been seasoning the wood by hanging it from the center pole in their tipi. Figuring it to be dry and well-tempered, he whittled the branch to an oval shape along its length until it had an even bend when drawn. Cutting notches at each end, he tied on twisted sinew to serve as a string. Willow branches were used for arrows. With only a blunt shaft and no fletching, they were effective for fifteen or twenty feet.

The change in Rising Eagle would be gradual. In addition to helping him develop his own technique, the effort of repeatedly drawing the bow was strengthening muscles necessary for pulling the stronger bow he would use in warfare and on the hunt.

"Are you two going to play all day?"

Rising Eagle responded indignantly, "Mother, I am not playing! Anton tells me I must practice if I will be a great warrior."

"It's time for us to eat. You can practice more after we eat."

With a resigned sigh, Rising Eagle laid down his bow and started for the tipi.

Anton's stomach growled with hunger, anticipating Star Woman's special meal of fresh fish and wild rice boiled in a sauce made with raspberries, apples, and fresh spring water.

Although the meal had been prepared inside the tipi, they preferred to eat outside. The day had been warm for early October. With the sun low in the western sky, they could feel a chill in the air and smell the peculiar odor of a swamp in the process of preparing for winter. The weather was about to turn.

Rising Eagle spoke. "Tell us again about the land to the east." He had heard the story dozens of times, but he never tired of it.

Anton leaned back against the log upon which Star Woman sat. "There are great mountains, into which are nestled beautiful valleys," Anton loved to speak of the land of his mother's people. He relished his memories of her and their life together. "My mother trapped beaver, mink, otter, and muskrat. The mountain streams ran clear and pure, and you could feel the joy in the song of the lark as he clung to the tall grass of the meadow. The red-winged blackbirds praised the rising sun by singing their songs while perched on the swollen swamp cattail."

Now came the part Rising Eagle loved to hear.

"When I was four, I learned to set the snare. At five, I could read the weather by watching the sky and the behavior of the animals. When I turned six, mother began selling pelts, and I began to learn the art of barter."

"What was the first? The very first thing you bartered?"

"I remember it well. It was a badger pelt. It was my first pelt. I caught it, I skinned it, I seasoned it, I worked it soft."

"Tell me about the barter, Anton."

"It was about this time of year. The day was cool. Mother and I were at a French outpost, and she was trying to strike a bargain for steel traps. My pelt was taken that spring when the fur was heavy, thick and rich from the winter season. It draped over my shoulders and covered my whole back."

Rising Eagle was fully engaged.

Star Woman, aware of her son's affection for Anton, found herself drawn to the man more powerfully than ever before as she listened to his story yet another time.

"A young French boy, maybe fourteen, wanted that badger pelt. Mind you . . . I didn't want to trade it, but he wanted it badly. The more I held back, the more he offered. Turns out, when we left the post, he had my pelt, and I had everything except his long-handles." Anton tipped his head back and let out a guttural chuckle. "I got a pair of boots I wore for two years before I outgrew them, a French hat I tossed as soon as we left, britches that were too big, and a belt that carried a sheath and knife. The knife is what sealed the deal. I used that knife for a good ten years, before I lost it somewhere on the boat when I came up the river to Fort Snelling."

"Tell me again about my father."

"Do you know how late it is?" Star Woman interjected. "Don't get started on another story now. Best to wait for a new day to have time to do justice to the lesson."

* * *

IT WAS HER IDEA. SHE HAD ASKED HIM. It was the first night that he slept in her camp, and the warmth of her body against his was the best thing he had ever felt. They lay on their sides, his arm draped over her naked body, as he pressed against her back.

The very next day, Anton took eight horses to Star Woman's family, and he was officially her man.

Chapter Ten

Winter with Dokkins

THE PARTY OF FIFTEEN BRAVES approached the Chippewa encampment with extreme caution. Their leader was named Bends the Bow, a young Mdewakanton brave from the band of Gray Iron, known for his hotheadedness and questionable judgment. Gray Iron's band camped near the St. Peter River, two days hard ride west of Fort Snelling, and Bends the Bow was its most fearless warrior.

Nearly a year since Shakopee died running the gauntlet, some still just itched to get even. It wasn't that Bends the Bow knew Shakopee. He had never met the powerful chief. It was more the fact that he loved conflict and the bedlam rampant during the battle—that's what brought him to the edge of the Chippewa camp.

Caught unaware, the camp, which laid seven miles north of Fort Snelling, posted no guard, secure in the mistaken belief that the adjacency of their camp to the fort would keep them safe.

More execution than battle, the men moved through the camp killing everyone they encountered: men, women, and children. Bends the Bow counted seventy-three bodies—some eviscerated, all bound at the ankles, and draped head down over poles suspended between trees encircling the camp. The grisly scene was meant to strike fear and prove superiority of the Dakota over the Chippewa. It did the opposite.

The outraged Chippewa began a strategy of systematic attacks on individuals foolish enough to travel alone or in very small groups. When three braves from a small band of Chippewa attacked Anton's camp, they found more than they bargained for, losing their lives in the fight that followed. However, the experience convinced Anton he must move his new family to the west, away from the fort that seemed to bring bloodshed to those close to it.

* * *

IN AUGUST OF 1828, MAJOR JOSEPH PLYMPTON arrived to take command of Fort Snelling. On the day he arrived, Lawrence Taliaferro departed with a contingent of Chippewa chiefs, heading to Washington to be hosted by President John Quincy Adams. On that very same day, Anton McAllister prepared to move his family to a safer place.

"Yank that knot good and tight. We don't want any of our stuff falling out along the trail." Anton was walking the camp perimeter searching for anything they may have overlooked. Breaking camp was the job of women, although Anton, true to his mother's influence, joined in the endeavor. Rising Eagle was tying the rawhide strip to one side of the travois.

Star Woman was an excellent teacher and used the move as an opportunity to teach the young man accountability. He was responsible for the small camp items and blankets. Anton had constructed the travois and strapped it to the horse. Rising Eagle's job was to load and secure the items.

With no specific destination in mind, knowing only that he would take Star Woman and Rising Eagle away from the danger of Fort Snelling, Anton led his family northwest. After the lightning episode on the prairie, Anton had no intention of taking his family in that direction. Instead, he headed northwest, often making camp near the frequent lakes they came upon, catching fish for their meals, some eaten raw, some cooked over the evening fire, and some smoked for eating on the trail.

They had been making and breaking camp for nearly a month, all the while putting distance between themselves and the fort. Anton reckoned to settle in as soon as the right spot presented itself.

As was his habit while on the trail, he moved his head left and right in a casual manner, occasionally glancing to his back trail, eyes sweeping the area looking for anything that didn't belong.

He'd first noticed the unnatural movement nearly an hour earlier. He'd caught it out of the corner of his eye and knew it shouldn't have been there. Since that time, he'd been able to verify the presence of another person without giving the slightest indication he was aware. He nudged his horse and drew even with Star Woman.

"Somebody's been tracking us for the last few miles. Looks like a single man. At the first chance, I'm going to circle back and see who it is. You take the mare's reins and keep riding till you're well out of sight. This could take awhile, so set a camp someplace ahead, and stay there till I come in."

Within a quarter mile they crossed a depression, and Anton slid to the ground and cut to his right at a dead run. After fifty yards, he reached dense underbrush that hid his movement and allowed him to angle in the direction they had just traveled. His goal was to reach the bottleneck between the heavy woods they had traversed earlier. If he was right, he would have the opportunity to waylay whoever was following them and learn whether or not the man was a threat. Picking a substantial oak with branches extending over the trail below, he climbed and positioned himself over the path on which the man would be riding, and settled in.

* * *

THE MAN'S THOUGHTS WERE CENTERED on those he followed.

By damn, they're still heading toward the rock falls. Haven't seen nobody set a trap so maybe they're just passin' through.

He rode a wild mustang, broad of face and compact of body. Across the horn of his saddle lay a rifle, and his body was leaning forward and to the left, the better to see the tracks left by the three. The two parallel grooves left by the travois were not hard to follow.

Anton had been studying him for the past fifteen minutes when he first became visible. During that time, the rider never raised his head to survey his surroundings.

Anton couldn't help noticing that the man looked like he was made up of bits and pieces gleaned from a trash pile, which was close to the truth. The wide brimmed hat and black military boots were taken from a British corpse. The saber, broken in the conflict that took the Brit's life, was recovered a few yards from the body. The scabbard was nowhere to be found. The buckskins were those commonly worn by French trappers, and a Chippewa woman made the buffalo belt and sheath for the broken saber.

Riding slowly, head tilted forward, the rider approached the tree that concealed Anton.

Anton's muscles tensed as the rider drew within ten feet. At five feet, his left leg began to cramp and he knew if he didn't straighten it, his tendons would constrict, and the pain would be unbearable as the cramp set in. Unable to follow his original plan and wait until the rider passed to jump him from behind, Anton launched his body with the intent of dislodging him from the front.

The horse was the first to react. With something hurtling toward her, she shied to her left and nearly sent her rider to the ground. Anton's right hand reached out and locked on to the man's upper arm, pulling him completely out of the saddle and sending the rifle into the trees on the far side of the narrow trail.

They hit the ground with a thud that knocked the wind from the rider's lungs while Anton landed on both feet and propelled his body into a shoulder roll. Before the man could recover, Anton was on him, knife drawn, blade poised over his throat, a determined look on his face. As the rider began to recover, Anton sensed this man was no stranger.

"Dokkins . . . is that you?"

With wide eyes, the face looked upward. "McAllister! It's me, Dokkins. Put that damn knife away and help me up."

Anton sheathed his knife and stood upright. "Dokkins, how's it turn out that you been following us? Where's the rest of the party?"

"By damn, that's the second time you could've killed me."

"Sorry, Jeremy. I figured you to be someone after our stuff. Now tell me what brings you on our trail and where the others are?"

Dokkins righted himself and brushed the dirt and twigs from his buckskins. "You know . . . after you left, them boys started what I'd call a rebellion. Them ungrateful bastards started bitchin' about every meal I made 'em, so I left the party, hitched up with a Chippewa squaw, and started my own trap line."

"Why'd you start following us?"

"I figured by the direction you been heading you just might decide to set your line in some of my favorite streams." Dokkins was rubbing his arm where Anton had grabbed him.

"I got no intention of staying anyplace we aren't welcome, so you needn't worry about that." Anton was surveying the area, hoping to spot Dokkins' horse. "You doing the cooking for the squaw and you?"

"You kidding? I couldn't stand the shit I cooked. Now this here woman I got . . . now there's a cook. She can make damn near anything taste fit for a king." His head began to swivel. "You see anything of my horse? You scared the shit outta her. I'll bet she's still running." Dokkins turned and strode toward the underbrush, searching for sign of his rifle.

"Judging by the tracks, she's headed straight down the trail. With any luck she'll be waiting for you at our camp." Anton motioned with his arm to indicate the direction the horse ran. "C'mon. Way I figure it, we ought to have smoked fish waiting for our lunch. I'd be much obliged if you were to join us."

"Ah, I got 'er." Reaching down, Dokkins wrapped his hand around the temporarily lost rifle. "I'd love to join you." He stooped to retrieve his hat. "I didn't know you had a family, Anton. Seems to me you was single last time we was together."

"Let's just say I was uncommitted the last time we met." They began walking the trail in the direction of the camp Star Woman would have set by now. "If I recollect . . . you seemed to have had some pretty strong feelings toward Indian women . . . now you're settled in with one."

"You know, Anton, that time you damn near kilt me made me take another look at what I was thinking. I owe you a debt I can't never repay, 'cause I figure, in a roundabout way, you got me a good woman, and that makes all the damn difference in the whole damn world."

* * *

CARRIES STICK POKED AND PRODDED the fire to life as sparks rose with the hot air currents. Beyond the peninsula, across the large bay, she had spotted the two canoes, the first with Rising Eagle in the bow and Dokkins in the stern, moving with steady ease as it cut through the calm water. Star Woman and Anton followed them by some sixty yards. Since their first meeting, she had an immediate liking for the sociable Dakota woman and her son. Although he showed her great respect, Anton's physical presence and personal charisma frightened her. Nevertheless, she looked forward to their visits, and she had planned a special meal for this one. Although they first met only two weeks prior, Carries Stick decided she would use her influence with her husband to convince the newcomers to make camp with them through the upcoming winter.

Dokkins drove hard with the paddle, and the canoe slid smoothly onto the sandy shoreline.

"Woman . . . we're back."

Rising Eagle vaulted from the canoe, pulling at the gunwales to further its advance onto land.

"Got us a heap o' beaver needs skinning an' tanning. This was the best day of trapping we had yet." His eyes darted from side to side looking for the Indian woman.

WHACK! The blow, delivered to his left leg, stung like a burn.

"Don't you order me around, you soft-headed Frenchman." Carries Stick seemed to appear out of nowhere. She insisted on referring to him as "The Frenchman," because he had traveled in a canoe with Voyageurs out of Canada before he purchased her. In truth he was Canadian, the product of third-generation English and French.

"Damn, woman . . . that hurt like hell."

"You're lucky I only hit you once!" Her face showed a nervous concern as she bent to examine the welt she had given him. Her examination resulted in a change of attitude. "I didn't mean to hit you that hard . . . you set yourself on the canoe while I make a quick poultice to take out the swelling."

Dokkins placed his rump on the gunwale as Anton guided his canoe onto the shore.

"What's the problem? What'd you do to your leg?" Anton disembarked and walked toward his friend.

Before he could answer, Carries Stick appeared with a small bundle of moss into which she had placed a poultice of slippery elm. Her mother had taught her to keep water at a near boil, to which she could add berries, bark, herbs, or other natural cures for unannounced calamities. It took her little time to make a paste from the assortment of natural elements she kept in pouches.

"It appears I don't know my own strength. I only meant to get his attention."

"Ain't no problem, woman. I probably walked into it anyhow."

It only took a few minutes for her to wrap the leg with her leather sash, holding the poultice mixture in place.

Carries Stick stood from her kneeling position in front of Dokkins and turned to the approaching Star Woman. "I hope you like tail and loin, because I've been letting it simmer since morning. That big doe Jeremy got a couple of days ago gave us some pretty good loin steaks." They began walking toward the camp Carries Stick had selected.

Dokkins was following the two women, and he was dragging eight beavers tied together with a stout piece of buffalo hide. He interjected, "Of all the critters in the world, ain't nothing better'n deer loin . . . and beaver tail is a close second."

Carries Stick turned to share a look with her husband, and Star Woman saw that she cared deeply for the man she was with.

They had covered perhaps twenty yards from where the canoes were pulled ashore, and Star Woman saw no sign of a camp. It always amazed her the way the Chippewa woman was able to hide the substantial wigwam in the dense forest and heavy underbrush. She remembered the very first time she set foot in the small camp, and her sense of wonder at the near invisible nature of the good-sized dwelling. It literally appeared out of nowhere, and its construction was ingenious.

Saplings were cut, stripped of their branches, and the thick ends anchored into the ground. There were perhaps fifteen of them anchored to form a circle. Bowed inward, their tips were lashed together forming a large inverted bowl nearly ten feet in diameter. By weaving smaller branches among the structural elements, and using bark as shingles, they had built a secure dwelling that blended with the natural forest surrounding it.

* * *

THE FIVE OF THEM RELAXED around what was left of the cooking fire. Carries Stick had prepared a meal that rivaled any Anton had ever eaten. Her use of natural herbs and spices, liberally applied to the venison at just the right moment, brought the natural juices to the surface, making the flavor explode in his mouth.

"So things ain't good down on the St. Peter?"

Anton answered in a casual manner. "Well, it has nothing to do with the river, but you can bet things ain't good." He was reminded of the altercation at Star Woman's camp that precipitated his decision to leave for new ground. In retrospect, he began to realize that the three Chippewa braves he'd dispatched were not much more than teenagers.

"It'd be a big problem if the Chippewa and Dakota got into a full-blown war. The young braves seem to be causing the most disturbances. They're loaded with gall and itching for a fight. To top it off, the commander at the fort was transferred, and his replacement doesn't have the experience to know the best way to deal with the two nations, so I got a feeling that he may just add to the problem."

The women and Rising Eagle retreated to the lakeshore, leaving the two men to talk.

Dokkins gazed at the starlit sky through an opening in the trees. "I may be a long way from the action down on the river, but there's lots of rumors floating about. Carries Stick's got her a brother what knows where the action's at, and it ain't just down there. Seems there's a rub over a couple o' missionaries that's traveling the big river all the way to Itasca. They're pushing religion onto the Chippewa. Ain't making much headway, but they're raising a ruckus trying."

"These folks got names?"

"One calls himself Reverend Conrad. The other's Price, just Price. That's the two of 'em, Conrad an' Price, and they're gonna get theirselves killed if they ain't careful."

"This country's got lots of way to kill a man without 'em begging to find new ones." Anton had little time for anyone trying to push his way of life down another's throat. "Anyhow, how about you, me, and Rising Eagle do a little deer hunting tomorrow? He's been practicing. I got a feeling he just might be ready for the real lessons of a hunt."

"By jingles, I ain't been deer hunting for a damn long time myself. Don't be telling Carries Stick, but them loins we just ate was from a mistake deer, got herself tangled in a beaver dam. Skewered her leg for sure, and was stuck tight when I come across her. She was a fresh one so naturally I let on I kilt 'er by using my hunting skills."

"Why, you old coot, I was rightly impressed. I figured you outsmarted a whitetail for sure."

"You know, as much time as I spent with McCarin and Clacker, I ought to of learned a few things about hunting wild game. I wasn't always a cook you know. Lots of times I had to kill our dinner."

"Near as I can recollect, the boys complained a bit about eating lots of squirrel, beaver tail, and fresh fish every now and then. Don't think I can recall ever eating deer though."

"You were only with us a couple o' weeks. That ain't hardly time enough to sample the whole menu, Anton."

"Rightly said, Jeremy, rightly said. You got a spot in mind we can waylay a buck?"

"I do at that. That dam where I picked up the doe had some pretty heavy trails on the south end. I figure we can slip in before dawn and take 'im on his way to bedding down for the day."

* * *

THE NEW DAY BROKE CALM with a chill in the air and frost on the gunwales of the beached canoes. About an hour and a half before sunrise, the three men, for now Rising Eagle insisted on being counted as such, slid easily from the shore into the black water of the lake. Anton was in the bow, Rising Eagle in the center, and Dokkins in the stern where he could control the direction of the canoe.

Although he now considered himself a man, Rising Eagle could not hide the excitement held inside his five-year-old mind.

"How much farther?"

"Don't know for sure. Dokkins figured it to be a half-hour paddle."

"Do you think we'll get anything? I sure hope I get a shot."

"Hush up now. We don't want every critter in the woods to know we're coming."

They beached the canoe a hundred yards south of the beaver dam.

"You take the boy that direction," Dokkins jerked his thumb over his left shoulder. "There's a dandy spot right up there for him to get a shot. I seen some active scrapes and rubs on some sizable saplings last time I was here. I'll be heading that way," thumb jerk to his right. "Both ways look good to me."

Rising Eagle clutched his hunting bow around the grip, two arrows held tightly against the stave. With his other hand, he tucked the knife sheath into the waist strap of his deerskin leggings. The bow he now held was an upgrade of the one he'd practiced with during the summer. Although lighter in draw weight than what he would use as an adult, it was strong enough to take small game and birds of any size. Anton wanted the young warrior to experience the thrill of the hunt while holding no expectation for placing venison on the fire.

"You ready?" Anton surveyed the young brave, satisfied with what he saw.

"I'm ready."

Anton led them along a trail that twisted around a steep hillside and into a shallow ravine that exited to a large open meadow.

"What do you think, Rising Eagle? Where do you figure the best spot is to set an ambush?"

"Um, I think . . . um."

"Isn't easy to figure out, is it? Tell you what, this time I'm gonna help. Pay attention because the next time, you're on your own."

Rising Eagle nodded and the two of them retraced their steps to where the ravine began.

"We want to be above the animal—makes it harder for him to smell us. It also makes it harder for him to see any movement when you set for the shot."

They entered the wood line parallel to the cut and walked, every footfall bringing them higher, until Anton was satisfied with the position.

"Now take a lay of the land. We've got brush on both sides of us. This here boulder lets us get right out to the edge. You can darn near drop a rock on his head if he comes through here."

The eastern sky was just beginning to lighten as the two of them hunkered down for however long it might take. Thirty minutes later, Anton began to feel the morning chill and shivered. A glance toward Rising Eagle told him the five-year-old was feeling it too. Without a word, he removed his shirt and draped it over the young man's shoulders. Moments later, Rising Eagle's head spun around, eyes wide with excitement.

"There's one coming." The boy's voice was an excited whisper. "Look to the right. At first I thought it was a horse, but it's a deer I think."

Anton crawled even with Rising Eagle and peeked around the boulder. Sure enough, not the lone deer he expected, but three whitetails approached. Judging by their size Anton figured it was a doe and two early, nearly full-grown fawns.

Backing away, he gestured to Rising Eagle, indicating he should shoot when he thought the time was right.

The young Indian rose from his kneeling position to crouch behind the boulder.

Meanwhile Anton crawled to his left to the cover of bushes growing near the edge and worked his way under cover to a point that allowed him to view both the approaching deer and Rising Eagle as he waited for his opportunity to shoot.

Rising Eagle's mind flipped and turned, churning through all he had been taught in preparation for this moment.

Pick a spot. Aim small, miss small. Stay calm. Above all, stay calm.

Peeking around the boulder, expecting to see the deer nearly underneath his position, he was shocked to see them scarcely twenty feet from where he originally spotted them. They were nibbling leaves from bushes at the edge of the trail, apparently in no hurry.

Rising Eagle flattened his back against the boulder, and for the first time, realized his palms were sweating. Laying the bow and arrows at his feet, he wiped his palms on the shirt draped over his shoulders and felt a hot numbness in his stomach. He thought, *Is it getting hot?*

He felt the perspiration on his forehead as he shrugged Anton's shirt to the ground, bent and retrieved his bow. With arrow nocked, he peeked around the boulder.

Here they are! They're right here! I have to shoot.

A tremor started in his legs and traveled up his torso to his shoulders, then down his arms.

They were below him. He had to take the shot.

As he began his draw, his arms shook so violently the arrow clattered against the bow, and the doe raised her head. The moment their eyes met, he lost control, releasing the arrow. The three white-tails scattered as his shot clattered among the rocks on the opposite side of the ravine.

* * *

THE CANOE GLIDED ACROSS THE GLASSY WATER, tiny whirlpools separated by a barely perceptible wake, the only evidence of their passing. Rising Eagle was still recovering from the excitement. His disappointment was real, although secondary to the thrill of being within fifteen feet of three whitetails.

Anton spoke. "I'm proud of you, youngster. You're on your way to becoming a man."

"I couldn't believe they were so close. I was so nervous. I'm just now not shivering anymore. I think I forgot everything you taught me. I can't remember aiming at anything. She looked me right in the eye. I don't remember shooting. What a thrill. Wait till I tell Mother."

Dokkins, feeling the moment, expertly executed a maneuver learned while with Peter McCarin and Clacker. Dipping his paddle, a flick of his wrist, and Rising Eagle was doused with ice-cold water from an October Minnesota lake.

"Hey!" Spinning his head around, Rising Eagle looked angrily in Dokkins' direction. His demeanor softened when he saw the grin that was spread across the older man's face.

* * *

THEY WINTERED THERE, in the camp of Dokkins and Carries Stick. The two women enjoyed each other, and the men worked well together, setting and checking traps and sharing food provided by the three "men." Rising Eagle was tutored in the skills required of a good trapper, and he learned to skin beaver, otter, and the occasional mink.

The weather was mild for most of the winter with frigid spells during the second week of February. Other than that, there was little snow and unseasonal warm spells.

March arrived with mild weather. With it came unwelcome news from Carries Stick's brother. Anton had returned to camp after checking their trap line on the west end of the lake and was in the process of removing his snowshoes when he noticed the horse picketed alongside his mare.

"Ahoy, the wigwam." He had no intention of surprising those inside, and habit had him moving to his right, a fair distance from where he hailed.

The flap was pushed aside and Dokkins stuck his head through the opening. "C'mon in here. Carries Stick's holding court. Red Tail's here with news."

After greetings were exchanged and Rising Eagle was sent to the shelter built for Anton's family, Carries Stick's brother, Red Tail, explained why he was there. "Last time I was here I told Dokkins about a couple o' guys what was stirrin' trouble."

Dokkins interjected, "They be that Conrad and Price I was tellin' you about, Anton."

Red Tail continued, "They're dead now. The band's afraid of what might happen if them down at the fort on the two rivers find out."

"How'd they die?" Sure of the answer, Anton asked the question anyway.

"Hunts with Teeth, kilt 'em. They was playin' poker'n drinkin', and he caught 'em cheatin'. Kilt 'em both on the spot and left the bodies lying where they fell."

"Sounds fair to me." Dokkins was unimpressed. "You came all this way to tell us them two's dead? Seems like a terrible waste o' time."

"We went to their camp and found some papers with words writ on 'em. We was wonderin' if you could tell us what they says."

"Damned if I can help you, but I'll bet Anton here can read."

* * *

ANTON STRAIGHTENED. For the past three hours, he had been sitting at the rough desk he assumed had been the property of the Reverend Conrad, and he had learned a great deal about how the good reverend and Price were defrauding the Indians under the guise of religion.

Dokkins sat with his back against the inside wall of the rough cabin, enjoying the whiskey he'd found in a corner. He was fiddling with a hand-held telescope he'd found on a shelf in the cabin.

"This here's a dandy glass that's for sure. Brings things in nice an' close. Look here. It's got "Jim" carved on the outside leather." He got up and handed it to Anton.

Anton gave it a quick look, then handed it back. "Yep, she's a good one all right."

"Get Red Tail in here, Dokkins. You might see if you can round up Hunts with Teeth too while you're at it." Anton spared no words. Dokkins had been drinking whiskey for the last three hours and seemed unaffected by it. Nonetheless, that he was drinking at all was an irritant to Anton.

The two Chippewa must have been close by, for Dokkins returned immediately with them following him.

Anton went to the heart of the matter. "First off, let the wolves finish those two. Nobody at the fort's going to miss either one. I'd advise you to take their clothes and burn 'em, then set the bodies in the woods someplace away from camp."

Nods all around.

"These papers tell what they were up to, and it wasn't anything good. Seems these boys were getting the Indians drunk while playing poker, then getting them to make their sign on these documents." Anton waved a stack of papers he held in his fist. "These papers sign over land to prove ownership. It doesn't mean a thing now. Depending on what might happen it could've made them rich in the future. Agent Taliaferro told me this was a danger around the fort. He never figured it would happen way up here."

Hunts with Teeth's eyes sought those of Red Tail. "Them two was drinkin' two to one of mine. They was fallin' down drunk, worse'n me. I seen 'em share a look, and I saw their eyes. They weren't drunk like they looked. That's when I kilt 'em."

"By damn! I thought there was something strange about that whiskey I was drinkin'." Dokkins moved toward the stash of whiskey in the far corner. There were a dozen bottles, each corked with a sprig of maple. Off to the side were another three bottles corked in a similar manner. On each sprig a notch was cut. Grabbing one of the twelve, he yanked the cork and took a swig.

"Jehosephat, that's some strong stuff. That ain't what I was drinkin' before. Them bastards was diluting their bottles with water."

"That explains a lot." Anton's anger rose to the surface. He turned to face Hunts with Teeth.

"You did the territory a big favor by killing those two. They were stealing your land just as sure as if they held a gun to your head. When you burn their clothes, slip these papers on the pile too." He smashed the bottles with the barrel of his rifle, spreading glass shards and whiskey over half the small room, and stalked out of the cabin.

* * *

On March 4, 1829, Andrew Jackson was sworn in as the seventh president of the United States. That morning found Anton McAllister moving his family from the shared camp of Jeremy Dokkins and Carries Stick. The discovery of the method used by Conrad and Price to steal land from the Indians made an impression that Anton couldn't shake. He began to realize that without the concept of land ownership, both the Chippewa and Dakota could be cheated out of thousands of acres. How widespread could the problem be if it was happening this far north?

"You sure you wanna head on down to Lac qui Parle? I heard there's lots of trappers what come into the area. Could be you stick your nose into a heap o' trouble."

Anton considered awhile before answering. "Jeremy, I owe you and Carries Stick a debt for sharing your camp with us. I figure to move on to where I can get word to Taliaferro about this land swindle thing. Besides, Red Iron's village is down there on the St. Peter. I figure to settle in, give Rising Eagle a chance to make friends with kids his age."

"Well, you know you're always welcome here."

"Thanks, partner. You've got a good one in Carries Stick. Seems like her family's a good one too. You take care now, and if you ever need my help, send word and I'll be here."

They said their final good-byes and Anton's small family headed south to the source of the St. Peter River, then on to the camp of Red Iron.

It took them four days of easy travel, arriving midday at Fort Washington on Lake Traverse. Not wanting to enter Red Iron's camp after dark, they stayed the night at the trading post where Anton reacquainted himself with Joseph Renville, who he encountered in the post commissary.

"Joseph, my friend. How wonderful to see you again."

"Sir? I recall the face, but unfortunately, the name escapes me."

"I met you back in '25 while accompanying scribes for Josiah Snelling to study your methods."

Renville studied the face of the man before him. "Of course. Forgive me. Anton McAllister, I believe? That seems like a lifetime ago. What brings you to this area again?"

"I'm moving my family from up north, and hoping to find someone who can deliver a message to Agent Taliaferro for me."

"Well, believe it or not, I'm heading down to Fort Snelling in three days. I'd be happy to deliver your message to the agent." Anton's reference to moving his family from "up north" piqued Renville's curiosity. "You say you're moving from up north. If I'm not mistaken, you were chief scout for the fort the last time we met."

Anton told him of the troubles around the fort that resulted in his leaving the area, and he told him about spending the winter with Dokkins and Carries Stick. Finally, he explained the swindle scheme that had been uncovered.

"So, now we're on our way to Red Iron's camp. I count him as a friend, and we'd like to settle in with his band."

Renville set a puzzled look on his brow. "You know, he's quite a ways down river from here, in fact, it's only about a day's ride from his camp to the fort."

"Oh, I thought he was just east of here, least wise that's where he was last time I saw him."

"I don't recollect him ever being this far west. Only time he was in this area was when he was on a quest for stone to make a ceremonial pipe, and that was back in '25."

"Oh, right. That was it. He stepped up and gave me a hand with Snelling's scribes after lightning nearly blew us up." Anton soured at the thought. "He even gave us a couple of horses to replace the two that got fried. We sat and talked for a good long spell, and he told me about the pending marriage of his daughter."

"It went without a hitch. From what I hear, they're doing fine. Red Iron's an honorable man. You'd do well to tie in with his band."

The two talked until well after sundown before parting ways with a handshake and a friendly good-bye. The next morning, Anton left for his reunion with his friend Red Iron. From there, he would go on to the fort and deliver news of the land swindle to Taliaferro personally.

* * *

LAWRENCE TALIAFERRO LISTENED with building anger as Anton described the method used by Conrad and Price to fleece the natives.

"By damn, Annawon. if there's a way to circumvent the law, there are those who will find it. I'll get a dispatch off to Washington, with the information."

Chapter Eleven

Treaty of 1837

THINGS ON THE FRONTIER SEEMED to be changing at lightning speed. Chetanwakanmani, the third in the Little Crow dynasty and the man loved by Lawrence Taliaferro, died of whiskey poisoning at Prairie Du Chien. In 1834, Wakinyantanka, known to the whites as Big Thunder, became the fourth chief to be known as Little Crow, leader of the Mdewakanton band of the Seven Fire People.

Lawrence rode west, his mind totally occupied by thoughts of the last forty-eight hours. He couldn't help dwelling on what he'd seen as his Indian friends made their marks on the treaty just signed. The Treaty of Saint Peter essentially ceded all land east of the Mississippi and called for the removal of all Native Americans to west of the river. Although primarily affecting Chippewa land, he saw it as a flashpoint for the Dakota because, although only a relatively small number of Dakota were required to relocate, it established firmly and forever the idea of boundaries.

He entered the camp of Red Iron in the early evening and was directed to Anton's tipi. Anton and his family had lived with Red Iron's band for the past eight years. During that time, they had grown together as a family while Rising Eagle grew into a fine young man. At thirteen years, he was nearly ready to take on the mantle of a warrior.

After a few words of greeting, Lawrence told Anton about the treaty signed two days earlier at the agency near Fort Snelling.

"We knew it had to happen. Now that it has, I feel we're going to see some very large changes in the next few years." The two men were on the east edge of Red Iron's main camp, Anton's tipi at their backs.

Anton shook his head slowly. "Yes, I'm afraid you're right. This territory is going to bust wide open. I figure this is just the opening gambit in a game that the red man always loses."

"It's inevitable. This treaty dealt mostly with Chippewa land. At least with Washington calling the shots, we can rest assured that the tribes are paid compensation for the land they give up. I don't know if the bands understand the finality of the agreement, but it's better than what you saw up in the North Country with that Conrad fellow."

"Yeah, likely so. What do you suppose is the next step? I see lots of white men coming up the river, and many are bringing their families. They don't mix well with the fur traders and trappers already in the area. I'm afraid all hell's gonna bust loose."

"All hell's already busted loose, Anton." The agent stood and, snatching a stick from the ground, began to pace. "This treaty turned over the Wisconsin territory to the United States. That part's fine and good, because stipulations for setting up Indian reservation land were written into them, but the American Fur Company is already stepping in and muddying the waters."

His eyes were on fire as he snapped the stick in two, throwing the pieces to the ground.

"A trader, name of Warren, broke into the meeting with some phony papers that claimed he was owed money for purchases on credit that nobody remembered."

Anton's countenance changed immediately, sensing the similarity to the illegal scheme perpetrated by Conrad and Price.

"He claimed he was owed twenty thousand and demanded payment. I should have just shot the bastard. When it was over, he got his money. Damn shame."

Anton stood. "Why'd he get paid? Can't you stop something you know isn't right?"

"Anton . . . a commission was appointed to oversee the treaty. I'm just there to represent the law and say what I figure is right or wrong. That doesn't mean they have to listen to me. They ended up paying that thief his twenty thousand dollars. Moreover, a guy named

Dousman claimed five thousand and got it written in, and there were others doing the same."

"Can't anyone else see the fraud?"

"Well, Anton, I gotta tell you that Hole in the Day knows what's going on. In fact, most sensible-minded Indians and intelligent onlookers can see it. Damn shame."

Anton barked, "I'm going to rethink my confidence in the U.S. Government if they appoint a commission that won't listen to the man they chose to keep the peace."

"Anton, it doesn't matter if . . . " Lawrence was distracted by an angry discourse taking place some distance from where they talked.

He moved to the side of the tipi with Anton at his heels to find the source of the racket. Just outside the encampment, in a clearing where large boulders bordered the river, two young braves were engaged in a serious argument. Both the young men were about the same size, although one looked about two years younger. They each grasped opposite ends of a bow held between them. Lawrence recognized neither. He watched from the shadowed area behind the tipi.

"Now. Give me my bow."

"Your bow? This bow belongs to me. It's been mine since my father made it for me."

"I found it by those boulders. It's mine and I want it back."

"Look, Braided Tail, I just laid it there two minutes ago while I fetched the arrow I shot at that clump." The younger boy pointed to his left, indicating a tuft of grass that was darker than its surroundings.

"Ain't no never mind. I laid claim to it when I saw it layin' there. Now give it to me." Braided Tail made a sweep with his left leg, connecting with the younger boy behind the knees and knocking him to the ground. The bow clattered among the rocks a short distance from them. Before the younger boy had a chance to recover, Braided Tail pounced on him and pinned his arms to the ground with his knees.

By this time, Anton had made his way to the agent's side and immediately recognized Rising Eagle as the boy on his back.

"Now I'm gonna take that bow and be on my way. Don't you do a thing to try to stop me or I'm gonna give you a good beating."

As the older boy rose and turned to leave, Rising Eagle jumped to his feet and charged, taking him to the ground in a heap.

"You're doing nothing of the kind, and if you don't admit the bow's mine, I'm gonna teach you a good lesson. I'm not afraid of you. Open your mouth and admit it's mine."

Lawrence turned to Anton. "Isn't that Rising Eagle?"

"Seems like."

The older boy seemed to be thinking it over while being held down. "Yeah, okay, so it's your bow. I saw it layin' there and didn't see anyone around, so I figured I might as well take it."

The younger boy rose to his feet and Braided Tail followed. "Say, what's your name anyhow?"

"Name's Rising Eagle. My father is Annawon and my mother is Star Woman. This here's our camp. That's our tipi right over there."

"Well, good to meet you Rising Eagle. They should have named you Big Eagle. My name's Braided Tail."

"I know. I've seen you with some of the other boys."

They continued to talk while the two men slipped back behind the tipi unnoticed.

"You got a pretty good boy there, Anton."

"Yes, he's a good one all right. He isn't mine from natural birth. His father was one of the bravest men I've ever known."

"Yeah, I know the story of Tomawka and his killing of the three-toed wolf. I'd say the boy has his father's mettle."

"Seems that way, doesn't it?"

As they turned and walked toward the center of Anton's small encampment, Lawrence said, "I was saying . . . it doesn't matter what any one man knows to be the truth unless he's able to convince others. I'm learning there are too many others with closed eyes and uncompromising minds. They only see the red man as a problem to be dealt with."

"Well, they're gonna find that the Dakota don't like to be told what's good and what's bad. These treaties are going to drive a wedge that splits us right down the middle."

Lawrence continued, "My job's to keep peace out here the best way I know how. I've got a commander at the fort who doesn't know which way is up, I've got two nations just chafing to get at each other, and I've got the federal government doing their best to open the whole damn area for settlement. Now President Van Buren wants me in Washington with influential chiefs from the Dakota Nation to deal with the fighting here between the Sioux, and between the Fox and the Sacs on the south side."

"By damn, you got a thankless job. All's I can do is wish you the best of luck."

* * *

Washington
August 18, 1837

UNDER ORDERS, LAWRENCE GATHERED twenty-one chiefs from the Dakota Nation and escorted them to Washington with the belief that they were to negotiate a Dakota treaty with the Sacs and Fox. Unknown until their initial meeting was the fact that talks would center on the purchase of Dakota land by the U.S. Government.

Chief Standing Cloud voiced his negative view of the deception. "We never dreamed of selling our lands until your agent . . . invited us to come and visit our Great Father." He was standing ramrod straight. "Now you wish for us to sell our land that belongs to all people. This is not right."

He was ignored.

On September 29, 1837, all parties signed the document agreeing to the sale of approximately five million acres, resulting in the relocation of hundreds of Dakota people. Although the Dakota chiefs were unhappy with the meeting, they resolved to accept the reality of its outcome. However, the Treaty of 1837 would not be ratified by Congress until June 15, 1838. During that nine-month period, attitudes would develop that would lead to a calamitous end.

* * *

Lake Calhoun and Lake Harriet Mission, Northwest Frontier
1839

THREE BRAVES KNELT ALONGSIDE the trail leading to the mission. They were from separate Chippewa bands, and each had suffered the loss of a family member to the Dakota during the last decade.

Yellow Head, no relation to the chief of the same name, spoke to the others in a hushed tone.

"We are agreed then. We will kill the first Dakota passing this place."

"Eha, I would strike him with my war club as he turns to my hail." Flat Stone was the largest of the three braves and somewhat of a bully among his band. "I would sever his head if it was up to me, but I will concede that honor, to your plan."

Hunts with Knife spoke, "We pledge ourselves to each other. We will each strike a blow in our own way. The scum will die three times. The war club must be the last death, for his crushed skull will be his final grave."

"Aazhida." Yellow Head agreed.

"Aazhida." Flat Stone echoed.

"Eha. Yes, revenge. My grandfathers speak." Hunts with Knife grabbed a fist of loamy soil from the ground beneath the ferns where they crouched, spit to moisten it, and rubbed it on his cheeks. The Dakota would not see him until he had already died his first death.

* * *

NE-KA, KNOWN AS BADGER to the whites, left his father's tipi with the book given to him by Reverend Jedediah Stevens. Stevens called it the Bible, and Ne-ka was being educated in Christianity at the Lake Calhoun and Lake Harriet Mission, less than an hour's ride northwest of Fort Snelling.

Young, just twenty-three years, Ne-ka was an excellent student and a valued member of Cloud Man's village. Considered wise by his elders, he was the proud father of a three-month-old son. Held in high esteem, he was marked for greatness by the village chief and encouraged to study the white man's ways so he could teach them to the band.

His father bid him safe passage, "Learn well, my son. I fear much depends on our understanding of the whites."

"Yes, father."

As he walked, Ne-ka thought of his wife and infant son, and his mind turned inward. *I wonder if Pond will be at the mission today. He is a great man and will some day write the words of my people. I feel I am doing much good in helping him translate our language into writing.*

Ne-ka was approaching the mission on the trail he always followed after traversing the Little River.

Of the two Pond brothers, Gideon was more to his liking. They sat for hours talking about the cities to the east and the amazing things therein. Lamps lighted the streets, and the stores offered everything a man could wish for. Ne-ka vowed that someday he would take his family there to see the wonders for himself. Perhaps his son could be an owner of such a store.

"Dakota!"

The word startled him from his reverie. Not sure he heard correctly, Ne-ka slowly turned toward the source.

Yellow Head, surprised at the ease with which the lone enemy would die, slashed his knife blade right to left, opening Ne-ka's belly from side to side, exposing the Dakota's entrails. Yellow Head was ecstatic. This was the first death.

Ne-ka, caught off guard with no chance to unsheathe his knife, stared wide-eyed, not comprehending what had happened. He looked down as bile rose into his mouth and he saw his own intestines slide from their cavity. Then Kills with Knife delivered the second death.

He approached from the front, body leaning forward in a taunting manner, meeting the vacant stare of the dying Dakota, making sure his earth-blackened face was the last vision the man would see. Slowly and deliberately, he reached around the dying man and plunged his blade into his lower spine.

With a convulsive jerk Ne-ka collapsed to the ground, unable to force his arms or legs to function. He lay there for what seemed a very long time, when he noticed a third man approaching. The man held a war club, and for the first time Ne-ka realized he would die. As he opened his mouth to begin his death song, his life ended in the third death as his skull was bludgeoned time and again.

* * *

RISING RIVER, WIFE OF NE-KA, drew the blade over her arm as her plaintive wails were heard throughout the village. It was one thing to lose a husband while on a raid, another to lose one as he walked in peace. She was inconsolable. Only the presence of her young son kept her from joining Ne-ka in death.

Word spread like wildfire, drawing many warriors to the village of Cloud Man. Their leaders held a counsel.

"Ne-ka had much promise. His death must be avenged." Cloud Man set the course. "It is decided. We shall form war parties from each village and take our revenge."

War parties were formed, each with responsibility for a given area. They moved in swift retaliation, first north to the Rum River, then east to the St. Croix, entering conflicts with all they encountered. With no way to identify the killers, retribution was taken upon any Chippewa encountered. It was swift and without mercy. Ninety-five scalps were taken before the war parties returned to their camps. It was one of the most destructive revenge campaigns ever executed by the Dakota Nation.

Chapter Twelve

Rising Eagle's Vision

THE SUN WAS HIGH IN THE SKY, and Anton had just listened to his friend Lawrence Taliaferro lay out his views on the future of the Northwest Frontier and the frustration of having to stand by as an observer while things decayed around him.

"Used to be that I could have some effect on the Indian nations and the way business was done with them. Now, with most of the beaver gone and muskrat skins bringing less than a nickel, it seems the American Fur Company has given up trading in pelts. Instead, they're concentrating on building a house of lies claiming money owed them by the red man. Every time a treaty is made, they claim to be owed thousands."

"What about this business of the latest Dakota skirmish with the Chippewa? I hear there were plenty of scalps taken for the loss of only one brave." Anton knew the particulars, but was asked by Red Iron to learn what the agent had been told.

"That's another thing that sticks in my craw." The whole mess sickened Lawrence. "I heard three braves, some say from Hole in the Day's band and others say from a Pillager band, murdered a favored son of Chief Cloud Man's village. Only they didn't just kill him, they desecrated his body in a grisly manner. By the time I got word, the Dakota were already on the move to exact their revenge. The mutilated man had strong medicine. The people demanded payback."

The two men sat in silence for many minutes, each immersed in his own thoughts, gazing into the dappled tapestry of dancing light as the breeze rustled the cottonwood leaves and the river gurgled. Their moods were dark. Recognizing a certain danger in pursuing that line of thought, Anton spoke of lighter things.

"Rising Eagle was fifteen in July. Soon he will go on his vision quest."

Lawrence responded, "Little Crow has spoken of such a quest. I know little of its meaning or its importance."

"Its importance is central to the soul of the Dakota people. Its meaning is spiritual and directed to the individual. If I were twenty years younger, I would relish the quest myself. It reveals much about a man's character, and at times it discloses future events."

"C'mon, Annawon! Surely you can't believe in knowing the future."

"Lawrence," for the first time Anton addressed the agent by his given name, "you expressed ignorance in the ways of the vision quest. I am only telling you what the people believe."

Feeling the sting of Anton's rebuff, Lawrence aid, "Please forgive me. It was not my intention to insult the ways of the people. It's just that such a thing is foreign to me . . . I'm sorry."

Again, they sat without speaking, each looking inward. Finally, Anton said, "Rising Eagle's blood father once told me of a dream he had. We discussed the possible meanings, wondering if it foretold future events, and he was sure it did. It was nonsensical on the surface, however, he believed it to portend what was to come."

"Is this something you can tell me or is it some kind of secret to be kept from other men?"

"No secret . . . near as I can remember he was floating above the action as a flock of crows ripped flesh from a man's bones. Ended up with the man jumping rock to rock across a river, and finally with a skull floating in the air. Who knows what that could mean? One thing he knew for sure was that it wasn't literal."

Lawrence was stunned. "What the hell could that possibly foretell about future events? Sounds like a simple nightmare to me."

"Yeah, but he was sure it had some meaning." Anton's mind returned to the memory of his own nightmare after nearly drowning in the Red River. "By dang, I never put the two together. After Mc-Carin pulled me from the Red, I had a dream that I didn't remember until just now."

"We all have dreams. I've learned that the only thing they tell us is what we fear, what we long for, or what we've already experienced at another time."

"That's exactly the point. I have no idea where this thing came from. It had nothing to do with anything I've ever thought about."

"Anton, if I thought every nightmare I'd ever had foretold the future, I'd either be stuck in a well or drowned while sitting in a tree."

"No, this is different. I can't explain it, but I get the feeling it was trying to warn me about something coming." Almost involuntarily, Anton pulled the dream from the recesses of his mind. *The unnamed Indian was gesturing wildly as his face elongated, thinly stretching from forehead to nose, lower jaw distorting terribly, first one direction, then another. He was mid-air, screaming words without voice . . . as his head exploded. The skull floated upward, twisting, turning, finally morphing into swirls of vapor, dissolving into the surrounding blackness, itself all encompassing, until only a fearsome darkness remained.*

A shudder coursed through Anton's body. "Whatever it was, I hope I never have another."

Lawrence responded almost before Anton finished talking.

"I've resigned my post."

"What?"

"I've sent my resignation to Washington, Anton. I'll be leaving before the snow flies."

"Good Lord, man. You're the only piece of sanity these people have. You can't leave now."

"I've had it. These last ten years since Snelling left have been getting worse. Henry Schoolcraft is about to get a promotion to Superintendent of Indian Affairs for this area. I'm out."

"Who's in? Surely, they won't leave your post unfilled."

"From what I hear they're going to move Amos Bruce out here to take over. I don't know much about him. If he's an honest man, he'll do a passable job. It took me twenty years to gain the trust of the two nations. I guess you can't expect a man to come in and make a difference on the spot."

"Lord, help us."

* * *

THERE WAS NO SINGLE REASON for Taliaferro's leaving and he spent many sleepless nights before making his decision. The frontier was becoming civilized, and he had been a primary participant in governing its growth. Now, serving under his sixth U.S. President, his authority was being diminished, and he found it unpalatable to have no say in treaty negotiations. His friendships were deep and he couldn't bear to watch those he had grown to love destroyed.

Major Lawrence Taliaferro, Indian Agent of the Northwest Territories, boarded a steamboat on October 7, 1839, on his way to Washington after twenty-two years on the frontier. His time in the Northwest Territories was finished. The first, and for many, the only agent the Indians had ever known was gone.

* * *

The Mississippi River
July 31, 1840

THE BLUFF WAS JUST SOUTH of Red Wing's village on the Mississippi. There could be no better place than this, for it was imbued with the spirit of a warrior chief.

Red Wing, one of the most fierce war chiefs of the Mdewakanton, was a legend to Rising Eagle. There were two stories about how he got his name. One said he carried a talisman of a swan's wing that had been dyed red. The other, and the one Rising Eagle preferred, said the name was given to him because of his speed while covering vast distances to attack his enemies, and the fact that he always carried a red blanket. He died at age seventy-nine when Rising Eagle was five.

The village was on the west side of where the Mississippi widened to form Lake Pepin. A sheer rock face over 300 feet high stretched for nearly a half mile along the river. Although close in proximity to Red Wing's village, it could have been a thousand miles from nowhere. Rising Eagle was at the very top of the highest point.

It took him nearly twelve hours to set the poles required for the vision quest. The center pole was especially difficult. At fifteen feet, it weighed as much as the other four together, and he carried it nearly twice as far as the others. Knowing there would be no trees at the summit, he picked carefully from the downed trees on the back slope during his ascent. In fact, the center pole was his second selection. Marking its location, he continued climbing, choosing the four corner poles and carrying them as a bundle all the way to his chosen spot. Dumping them, he retraced his steps to secure the largest and most important to his quest, the center pole, which represented Wakan Tanka, the Great Mystery, and the center of all things.

With boulders, large rocks, and random pieces of broken wood used as wedges, Rising Eagle raised the corner poles in the four directions. They represented the four elements: fire, air, earth, and water. To each of them he tied a cloth of a specific color—to the north, he tied a white cloth; to the east, yellow; to the south, red; to the west, black.

He had chosen the four pole placements equidistance from a schism in the granite that served as the platform for his quest. The break was of sufficient width to allow placement of the center pole within it, where, through the use of stone wedges it was held in place.

The outer poles represented a circle inside which the seeker would walk and symbolized wholeness and helped the seeker remember Wakan Tanka, who, like the circle, has no beginning and no end.

Rising Eagle would have no water or food for the duration of his quest, and sleep would be sporadic, taken only when exhaustion or the spirits dictated.

As instructed by the elder in Red Iron's camp, he navigated the circle very slowly, very deliberately, shuffling only a few inches each hour while facing the center pole, looking inward, searching his soul, all the while summoning the Great Mystery to appear.

On his third day into the vision quest, having gone without sleep, food, and water for eighty-six hours, he lapsed into a transcendental state.

Perhaps it is time to rest my head near the center pole. Wakan Tanka will find me there. He lay down, his head near the pole.

After a time, from beneath the total blackness of his closed eyelids, he sensed a great light, and his ears detected a barely audible buzz. *What is that sound? It is familiar yet foreign, as if something . . . no, several paddles are beating the air.*

* * *

STRUGGLING TO OPEN HIS EYES, Rising Eagle rose to one elbow. The sun was high in the sky with light so intense he was forced to slam his eyes shut to avoid blindness. Lying there, eyes closed, he sensed shadows passing over him and a breeze against his face. Afraid to look, for fear of blindness, he nonetheless forced his eyes to open a mere crack. The intense light was a corona encircling all things, and he felt himself being lifted into the air. The breeze he'd felt on his face now enveloped his entire body, and he opened his eyes wide.

He was mounted on a dragonfly high in the air, and below him, he saw seven crows dipping and swooping between the branches of a great oak tree.

Specks appeared on the backs of the crows. The specks revealed themselves to be evil tricksters who began pulling feathers from the crows until all seven fell to the earth. They shrank in size until each became a swarm of grasshoppers that rose as one to join Rising Eagle high above. As the swarm approached, it split into small groups that surrounded him. To his right he counted thirteen, to his left another thirteen, and flying behind him a final group of thirteen.

As if by magic, each of the flying grasshoppers took the shape of a whitened skull, visible for a short time before vanishing into nothingness. As he watched, one skull reappeared and continued flying alongside him. At once, it became a dragonfly like the one he was mounted on and it was caught up in a wind vortex that took him high above the world. Magically, Rising Eagle found himself mounted on this dragonfly, and they were inside a vortex he recognized as a great tornado. They were lifted so far above the land he could see rivers and lakes below. Suddenly, they fell toward the earth.

Then there was only blackness.

* * *

AN ACHE IN RISING EAGLE'S LEFT SIDE awakened him. He lay as he remembered, head at the center pole. As he stretched the stiffness from
his body, he saw that he was surrounded by darkness.

*How much time has passed? Wasn't the sun high when I lay down?
What's happened to me? Was my vision true or was it simply a dream?*

Rising Eagle moved into position in the circle. "Great Spirit! Cre-
ator of all that is good! Reveal my spirit guide that I may understand all
I have seen. I will remain within the circle until my guide appears."

With that pronouncement, he began a chant, not with words,
and with a cadence and utterances from someplace deep inside. He
neither understood their meaning nor sought understanding. The only
thing that mattered was the song.

He was unsure of how long he sang to the circle, and not caring,
he knew only that it was a very long time. Dawn was breaking when
he finally stopped his chant. His head began to spin, and he reached
for the center pole for support. Finding it difficult to maintain his balance, with arms firmly encircling the pole, he slid down to his knees.

Only then did he see the old man.

"You seek understanding of your vision?"

Rising Eagle was incredulous yet unafraid. "Are you my spirit
guide?"

"I am your essence. I am all that is good. I am here to interpret
your vision."

As Rising Eagle looked upon the man who seemed to have appeared from nowhere, he saw that he was very old with very gray hair.
He was wrapped in a buffalo robe, with a single eagle feather hung from
the braid that extended over his left shoulder. His face carried deep wrin-
kles from many years in the sun, and beneath wide cheekbones, his
mouth was shriveled and toothless. On either side of a nose that looked
to have been broken many times and below his deeply creased forehead,
was the most amazing feature of this old man's countenance.

His eyes were the color of turquoise and seemed to fill the center of his face with blue lightning that penetrated to the very soul of

Rising Eagle. So clear and deep were the pools of blue that Rising Eagle feared being pulled into them.

"Tell me what you saw, and I will tell you the meaning."

"I was high in the air with the wind blowing through my hair. I was astride a giant dragonfly, as though upon a horse." Rising Eagle paused, waiting for the old man to interpret the meaning.

"Go on. What else did you see?"

Disappointment filled the young man, disappointment that he was given no explanation to latch onto. He looked into the old man's eyes wanting to ask the meaning, afraid to pose the question.

"Go on, what else did you see?" The old man repeated.

"I looked below me, into the forest where seven crows dipped and swooped among the branches of a great oak. Their powerful wings carried them with ease."

Again, Rising Eagle paused.

This time he received an answer.

The old man gazed as if in a trance, as though looking into the future. "The seven crows represent the Seven Fires of the Dakota Nation. They are proud. They are powerful. They go swiftly wherever they wish, and they control all that is around them."

His eyes focused on Rising Eagle. "These are very good signs, they speak well for the future. If there is more, tell me now."

Rising Eagle responded, "On the crows I saw specks of white that revealed themselves as tricksters. They pulled the feathers, one by one, from the crows." Again, he paused, waiting for the old man to comment.

"Go on. What else did you see?"

"I saw the crows lose their fathers and fall to the earth where they shrank in size until each became a swarm of grasshoppers that flew to meet me. As they drew near, they became three distinct groups, and they joined me in flight. On my right was a group of thirteen, on my left, another group of thirteen, and behind me was a third group of the same number."

"Let me tell you the meaning of what you describe." The old man interrupted Rising Eagle, stopping the account of his vision.

"The white specks you witnessed on the backs of the crows were the white men that move to weaken the people." The old man stopped as if to gather his thoughts before continuing. "I fear for Oyate, the people. Your vision was one of sadness for the Dakota Nation. Continue speaking your vision."

Rising Eagle barely heard the command to continue, his mind having fixed upon his vision being one of sadness for the Dakota Nation.

"Please go on. What else did you see?"

Deeply troubled, he continued, nonetheless. "I looked again at each of the grasshoppers and saw they had taken the shape of a whitened skull. No sooner did I see the skulls then they vanished into a smoking nothingness. As I watched, one skull reappeared before taking the shape of a dragonfly identical to the one I was mounted on. As we flew, it was caught up in a tornado that sucked him high above everything. Suddenly I joined him as we fell toward the earth."

They sat in silence. Rising Eagle was sweating profusely, and the old man seemed to be lost in thought.

Finally, the old man spoke. "I don't understand the meaning of your vision, but I will tell you what I see in it." He paused for a long moment before continuing, "The three swarms of thirteen equal the number thirty-nine. Its meaning escapes me. All vanish, yet one returns. This one has a special meaning to you. Your lives are tied together somehow."

The old man's eyes held much sadness as they locked on Rising Eagle's.

"You must take the name Four Wings, to honor the dragonfly that took you into the air. You must always be aware of the wind that surrounds you. It can bring both harm and good. Much will happen during the time of great sorrow that your vision portends. Follow your heart. It will guide you true."

Rising Eagle looked out over the river toward the horizon. When he turned to speak to the old man, he was gone.

The young Dakota was left with no sign that what he had seen and heard actually happened. Was the old man just a dream, a figment, an apparition with no substance? That was when a dragonfly landed on his forearm, and Rising Eagle became a believer.

He returned to his people and the ceremony that finalized Four Wings as his name. As normal, his vision was his own and no questions were asked regarding the quest. The respect he garnered was an extension of the respect for the vision and his spiritual enlightenment. It was the prerogative of the seeker to share his vision. It was seldom done.

* * *

THEIR SECOND NIGHT OUT and Anton and Four Wings had already killed a nice deer. The family would eat well, and Anton's promise to Star Woman of fresh venison would be realized.

Anton stoked the fire as Four Wings spread grease on the skillet. They both looked forward to returning to Red Iron's village, a mere day's ride east. After rubbing tallow onto the skillet, Four Wings cut the heart into thin slices to be fried alongside slices of fresh liver. Both had been washed thoroughly in the nearby stream.

The two men, now equal in the eyes of the people, settled back in comfortable silence as their meal sizzled in the skillet.

Four Wings said, "Father, can I ask you a question?" Although he knew Anton was not his real father, he also knew Anton had raised him and taught him as a true father would teach his son.

"Certainly. You know you can ask me anything."

"When you met my real father, Tomawka, what was your first impression?"

"Your father was a man I respected from the moment I first met him. The way he carried himself, the way he spoke, the way he accepted the things he could have no power over; he was magnificent. Your father, although I knew him for only a short time, was likely the greatest man I have ever met."

"Do you think he ever had a vision?"

"I can't say exactly. I don't know I fully understand the vision quest, although I do know if I were twenty years younger I'd be taking mine. On the night I met your father, he told me of a dream he'd had just before we met."

"Do you suppose you could remember parts of his dream? I've been troubled since my quest, and I don't know what I can do to gain peace of mind."

"Was your vision that upsetting? I've noticed a change in you, a maturity that seemed to come from nowhere. You went away a boy and returned a man. Is there anything I can do to help?"

"No, not really. I was just wondering if my father had a vision."

"I think I can remember some of what he told me. It was quite a while ago, you know. The only reason it's relatively fresh in my mind is that I had a recent recollection of an experience I had when you were only a toddler. It reminded me of your father's dream."

Anton gathered his thoughts.

"As I recall, Tomawka's dream started with a flock of crows that were intent on killing somebody. Tomawka was like a spirit and was watching from above. Somehow, a grasshopper figured into it," he paused, gazing into the fire, struggling to remember the details. "The man was an Indian, and he ran to the cliff edge and jumped."

It was beginning to crystallize. Details were coming into focus.

"He saw the Indian become a grasshopper trying to ford a river. With every jump, the other side got farther away. With every jump, boulders appeared just as the grasshopper was about to land in the water. I recall four boulders, and when it jumped from the last it rose high above the water and turned into a skull before disappearing altogether."

Four Wings sat in stunned silence while the fire popped and crackled, sending sparks into the sky. There was no wind. The air was dead still. The sounds of the night permeated his senses: crickets, frogs from the nearby stream, and somewhere a coyote howled. The fresh, earthy smell from the rotting tree trunk he used as a backrest blended with the odor of the sizzling dinner and filled his nostrils. Everything was alive. His fingernails traced the contours of his arm and it was as though every hair follicle served as an impediment to the light touch.

"You all right?" Anton broke the stillness.

His question came through as if in a fog, from far away. Four Wings returned to the present.

Anton continued, "We talked about the dream, but nothing made sense. In the end we moved on to other things." He repeated, "Are you all right?"

"Yes. Sorry. I was just amazed at the similarity between Tomawka's dream and my vision. Father . . . the vision itself was interpreted by an old man who appeared from nowhere. He was very old and wrinkled and toothless, but his eyes were those of a young man. They were intense, almost like they were lit from behind, and they were the color of turquoise. His long gray hair lay over his shoulder in a single braid with a single eagle feather tied into it."

Four Wings began explaining his vision and the old man's interpretation. They ate what they had prepared and continued to talk until the night was half gone. Anton was told every detail of the vision, never interrupting, allowing the story to unfold at the teller's pace. When he had finished, Four Wings leaned back on his elbows waiting for Anton's reaction.

"Well . . . that's quite a story. The old man was part of the vision itself. If his translation is true, it just deepens the mystery of the vision. Oh, it's pretty clear the Dakota Nation is in for a lot of trouble from the whites. It doesn't take a visionary to see that coming. It's amazing that Tomawka saw nearly the same thing fifteen, twenty years ago."

"You know, this gives me a feeling of closeness to him I've not felt before."

"And that's good, son. He was a powerful man and would have loved you very much." Anton spoke from the heart. "He would have taught you many things."

The two of them bedded down for the night, each with separate thoughts—one with thoughts of the past and things lost without ever being held, and the other with thoughts of the future and the meaning of the vision he had just learned

Chapter Thirteen

Star Woman and the Missionary

RAINSTORM, A CHIPPEWA from the St. Croix band, crawled to the spot where several of his men lay hidden. "Hold this position until you hear my war cry. They have no idea that we're anywhere in the area. Remember, wait for my signal." Then he was gone as silently as he had arrived.

The main group of attackers hid in the deep ravine near the mouth of a creek east of the Mississippi. Directly in front of them was Kaposia, the camp of Little Crow. This was a retaliatory raid, and it was intended to strike a deadly blow to the hated Dakota.

With no feats of bravery to celebrate, yet newly delivered whiskey to polish off, half of the braves in Kaposia were reveling and celebrating nothing in particular.

This will be like child's play, thought Rainstorm. His people would honor him when he brought home many Sioux scalps. Since the murder of Ne-ka near the mission at Lake Calhoun, raids were followed by counter raids, followed by counter raids, in a never-ending escalation of fighting.

This day a strong message will be sent. While Rainstorm was anxious to begin the attack, he was no fool. All they had to do was wait until a number of the drunken dogs lay on the ground in sleep. Then they would attack, and maybe . . . take the entire village.

As the sun passed midday and shadows began to lengthen, some of the Chippewa braves, hidden a short way distant, just in front of Pig's Eye Lake, began gambling with river stones dug from the ground. A friendly game ensued, centering mostly on things of relatively little value—a piece of jewelry bartered from the trading post, beads, and other trade goods. As the day progressed, the stakes got higher. One of the braves, Spotted Fawn, had been particularly unlucky, losing his moccasins. To make matters worse, the man who won them became full of braggadocio, casting verbal darts with careless fervor.

Spotted Fawn fumed. His honor was being assaulted and he could do little about it. To strike out at the perpetrator would bring derision from the others and only make matters worse.

Then he heard the women's voices from the direction of the river. Grabbing his rifle, he alerted the others and crawled to the edge where the tall grass gave way to open shoreline. Unable to see anyone, and with the sound of voices coming closer, he slowly raised his head to get a better look. At that particular moment, one woman pitched a river stone into the clump to the left of where he was hiding. Her sharp eyes caught the movement as Spotted Fawn dipped his head.

With a shout of warning, she broke into a dead run toward the camp, followed by the others she was with close on her heels, all screaming out to alert the warriors inside the camp.

Spotted Fawn, already angry at his gambling losses, raised his rifle and fired. At the sound of the discharge, his mates behind him began to fire at the retreating women, killing a few while others continued toward safety.

Rainstorm, perhaps fifty yards distant with the largest group of warriors in the war party, had no choice other than to give the signal to begin the attack. Although not particularly skilled with rifles, the amount of lead raining into the camp tore holes in everything in its path including a few men, women, and children.

The firing rallied the camp against the attack, and in spite of being filled with whiskey, or maybe because of that fact, a running battle commenced that lasted a few hours. Although they lost more men during the skirmish than the Chippewa, Little Crow's warriors chased the attackers from the area in defeat. The results would have been much different if Spotted Fawn had not gambled away his moccasins and the attack had gone according to Rainstorm's plan.

* * *

STAR WOMAN HIKED THE PACK a little higher on her hip while working her way across the stream. Filled with prime pelts, it weighed nearly fifty pounds, and she intended to trade for camp supplies to help them through the winter. Each year it seemed to take more and more to trade for winter rations, and she expected this year to be no different.

Red Iron had moved his camp to a heavily wooded area and marked with uneven ground where rain and melting snow had eroded the surface, leaving jagged scars on steep hillsides. She'd found the ideal spot for their tipi, with access to a small cave where they could keep flour and salted meat through the winter. She had already set aside a quantity of apples as far from the opening as possible, hoping they would stay fresh during the coldest months.

She had no inkling of the battle ensuing to the northeast of her position at Little Crow's camp. Red Iron, a friend of the whites, knew the area close to Fort Snelling was a dangerous place, especially after the murder near the Lake Calhoun and Lake Harriet Mission, so he made it a point to stay well west of the fort.

Star Woman was on her way to the Traverse des Sioux Mission site and the newly constructed trading post nearby. Although the mission was planned for completion the following year, she knew the post was open for business, and she intended to be one of the first to trade there.

She approached from the north, angling toward the back of the large cabin that was the post. She knew nothing of the men who operated there, and she was not going to announce her arrival until she entered. She had seen the goings-on in other trading posts and had no inclination to be an easy mark for ne'er-do-wells hanging around this one.

At the rear corner of the building, she set the furs in front of her, adjusted the knife position on her waist, hoisted the bundle, and walked around to the open doorway.

There were four windows: two in the front wall either side of the door and one on each end of the structure. Beneath each of the windows were shooting slots cut through the logs. The back of the building had three such slots evenly spaced along the width of the wall. In spite of the windows and open doorway, the interior was in deep shadow, and Star Woman took a few minutes to acclimate and let her eyes adjust from the afternoon sun.

"Hello, madam. Did you per chance bring pelts to barter?"

She looked for the source of the voice, and with eyes now adjusting to the shadowed interior, saw the man behind the voice at a long table set off to the left.

"I have prime winter pelts. Fox, wolf, beaver, mink, weasel . . ." Her eyes now penetrated the darkness. Two others sat with the man who had spoken.

"What exactly, do you wish to trade for? I have very warm wool blankets, fresh over from England."

"I am in need of flour, blankets, rifle ammunition, powder, and patches. If you have warm coats, I will take three."

"I think you may be getting ahead of yourself, madam. Let's take a look at those pelts of yours. Then we'll barter." The affability present at their first exchange had now vanished.

She dropped the bundle in front of her, noticing that the other two men had not changed position. Rather than dumping the contents on the floor, she slid the bundle toward the table, and dipping her hand, began stacking whatever skin she happened to grab, one by one, on the table. She had counted eighty-seven skins while filling the bundle. After depositing twenty beautifully tanned hides in front of the trader, Star Woman stood erect waiting for a response. She had seen Anton do this for fifteen years, so what came next was expected.

"You call these prime skins? My dear madam, these are some of the mangiest examples of fur I have ever seen."

She had learned that the most critical time for the barter was at hand. She also noticed that one of the other two men in the room had advanced in a bit too casual a manner toward her position.

"If you have no interest, I will kindly take my pelts and be on my way." Star woman reached for the skins.

"*Tuer la femme stupide maintenant.*" The man behind the table assumed the woman had no knowledge of French, and, therefore, did not attempt to hide his command to the other. "Kill the stupid woman now!"

"Si votre freind prend un pas de plus vous allez mourir."

He reacted to her words as though he'd been struck a blow. She had said, "If your friend takes one more step, you will die." When she moved to his side with lightning speed, knife in hand, the blood drained from his face.

"No, no! Jon, back away!" The trader was truly afraid for his life.

"Monsieur, take one more step and he dies." Her knife blade lay on the trader's throat.

The man stopped in his tracks.

Then, from the other side of the room, the third man reminded them of his presence.

"You boys seem to have run into a bit more than you bargained for here." Addressing the second man, "I think it's best if you just step out that door and consider this a good day for a walk, mister." The second man took his leave like a dog with his tail between his legs, making for the closest trees.

Star Woman released her grip and lowered her knife, took two steps, and turned to face the man she had just reprieved.

"Shall we begin anew? I wish to trade these fine pelts for the supplies I mentioned. You know as well as I, that these are not only prime, but of a superior quality seldom brought before you." She reached down without looking, grabbed the first skin she touched, and flipped it in his direction.

The trader snatched it from the air and it settled on his wrist and forearm, draping easily, its softness and flexibility obvious.

"Yes, we will begin the barter."

The haggling was minimal, Star Woman in definite control of the transaction. The unidentified man, still near the far wall, approached for a better view of the barter and was amazed at the proficiency and skill of the woman in dealing with the reprobate trader. Before the transaction was completed, she had added a gallon container of dry, fine-ground English tea to her take.

When all was said and done, she came away with more than a single person could carry.

"May I introduce myself?" The unknown man spoke.

She looked at him with suspicious eyes.

"My name is Thomas Williamson, Doctor Thomas Williamson. I run the mission at Lac qui Parle. May I help you with your burden?"

"I don't have far to go, I can manage."

"It is clear that there is more than you can manage, and being close means I will not have far to go out of my way. Please, allow me to help you."

"Suit yourself." She would watch this one closely.

By the time they reached her camp, she began to feel the sincerity of this man. "Would you allow me to prepare a cup of this fine tea for you? It is purported to be the best England has to offer."

"Nothing would please me more."

Star Woman brought water to a boil and poured it into cups. She poured ground tea onto rifle patches, gathered and twisted them, then dipped them in the water to infuse the liquid with flavor.

"This is indeed a very nice tea. Thank you."

She nodded. "What brings you to this post?"

"I've been ministering to the Dakota at the Lac qui Parle Mission since thirty-five and now I'm to direct a mission effort at Kaposia. I'm on my way there to assess the situation."

"I fear you may be walking into more than you bargained for. There is much conflict between tribes, and the closer to Fort Snelling, the greater the danger seems to be with the whiskey peddlers, whites, Dakota, and Chippewa all living in the same space."

"The territory's opening up. As you know, the mission here at Traverse des Sioux will soon be in operation. A man, Stephen Riggs, who is with me at Lac qui Parle, will soon be here to direct this mission effort. He, like I, feels a true connection to the Dakota people. If they cannot adapt to the ways of the white man, it will be very bad for them."

"What good can you possibly do? Our way of life cannot coexist with your people's. Where can we go? What can we do?"

"You must learn to farm. I'm told the beaver are gone and soon there'll be no game left to hunt. The buffalo are plentiful now to the west. When the railroad comes, they too will be gone."

"Before the fort where the two rivers meet was built, wild game was plentiful. With the army comes trouble. There is now much whiskey and too many whites, each seemingly intent on robbing us of our very existence. No, Doctor Williamson, few of my people can read and even fewer can write their name. They are unlearned in your ways."

They sat in silence for some time before the doctor said, "You understood that they intended to kill you at the trading post. When the trader called you a foolish woman and instructed his crony to dispatch you, you understood his tongue."

"*Oui, je parle la langue française*, but I believe he referred to me as 'stupid woman.'"

"Yes, so he did." Williamson chuckled at her reply.

"I am happy that he believed me when I told him he would die if his friend came any closer. I would not have enjoyed killing him."

Doctor Williamson looked around the camp. "You traded for three warm coats, where are the other two people?"

"My husband is Anton McAllister, and my son is Four Wings. They will be back soon. My name is Star Woman"

"Your French is very good. Do you speak any other languages?"

"Thank you. Yes, I speak the Santee Sioux dialect. My tribe is Mdewakanton Dakota. I also speak Chippewa and have a passable understanding of Sac, Fox, and Winnebago. Of course, you know I speak English."

"Excuse me, Star Woman. Do you read and write those languages as well?"

"French and English, yes, of course. The others . . . only the words that can be defined. For many Dakota words there is no written definition. They represent a feeling or rely upon a situation for their meaning."

"Please allow me to make a proposal to you. Mr. Riggs, who will serve the Dakota in your mission here at Traverse des Sioux, is an excellent speaker of Dakota. We are attempting to translate the Holy Bible into your language. Helping in this endeavor, besides Riggs and myself, is a man named Gideon Pond, and another, Joseph Renville. Renville is half Dakota. He claims to be related to Little

Crow through his mother's blood. Anyway, his father was a Canadian trapper, and his mother was a Dakota for sure."

"How does that work . . . with the four of you?"

"Well, typically I read a verse from a French Bible, Renville speaks it in your language, Gideon and Riggs write it down, then we all agree on the truest translation of the original verse. It's all very cumbersome, very slow, however, it gets the job done."

"How do you think I can help with the process? Seems to me the last thing you need is another person slowing things down."

"The way it is now, our confidence, or lack of confidence, requires that we all be involved in the process to avoid errors. With your linguistic skills we may be able to spread the burden through simultaneous translation of multiple verses."

She listened, and as he spoke a flame began to kindle inside her with the knowledge of the benefits this project could bring to her people.

* * *

Lac qui Parle
November 1842

ANTON AND STAR WOMAN had been making their way to the Lac qui Parle Mission where she was to meet Doctor Williamson and the others involved with the translation. They were nearing the Chippewa River crossing, the most dangerous part of their journey. Just a week earlier, four Wahpeton braves had been cut down, murdered, their bodies mutilated and left on the frozen ground as food for predators. Their deaths were the third instance of senseless killing near the crossing, and Anton was taking no chances.

Finding an open area backed by a granite outcropping, he reckoned it would be a safe place for Star Woman to wait while he surveyed what lie ahead.

"Take the rifle. This is a good place to defend. If anyone comes in view, shoot over his head. I suspect there are at least four men doing the killing, most likely from ambush. Otherwise the Wahpeton that died would have been able to defend themselves."

After supplying her with percussion caps, powder, patches, and shot, Anton mounted up and headed for the crossing a mile and a half ahead. "If I hear a shot, I'll come on the run, so just hunker down, and I'll be here shortly."

Star Woman replied, "I'll be fine. You just mind yourself."

A subtle shift of his weight in the saddle, a gentle nudge to the mare's sides with his heels, and she responded with a shake of her head, and they were on their way.

He rode slowly, paying attention to everything around him. The smallest patch of prairie grass drew his scrutiny and his head was on a swivel. The farther he rode, the more uncomfortable he became, and the more convinced he was that somewhere ahead people were waiting to kill anyone traveling this way.

Guiding the mare down a gentle slope approaching the river, the feeling of being watched became overwhelming, and every one of his senses became heightened, none more so than his hearing. As he drew close to the river's edge, the muted echo of water splashing over and around exposed rocks became secondary to the myriad sounds of the bordering woods. Even during the cold of a November day, it was filled with sounds of life. From somewhere behind came the raucous call of a disgruntled jay, and from his right, the call of the chickadee and flutter of wings of a larger bird, perhaps a crow fighting to become airborne.

This place among the rocks was the only spot to ford the expanding river without swimming across deeper and wider stretches of open water extending at least three miles in either direction. The east approach to the river was a heavily wooded gradual decline. On the west side, after an embankment of four feet or so, was a stand of swamp willows and a single cottonwood tree of huge dimension, beyond which the prairie came into full view.

* * *

THREE BRAVES PEERED through the dry fall grasses in front of the holes they'd dug into the earth. They were spread a total of forty yards from first to last, the last being no more than five feet from the water's edge. Knowing that human nature would force anyone approaching the crossing to be focused on the river just steps ahead, those lying in wait would gain the total surprise necessary for their murderous intent. They watched the single rider approach from the east.

* * *

ANTON, NOW FULLY ALERT, had already, unknowingly, ridden past the first brave and was drawing even with the second Chippewa hiding to his right twenty-five yards from the trail.

As in times past, his mare was the first to detect danger. By some miracle of nature, she knew that death was close by. Anton saw her ears lay back and felt a tremor in her withers as she sidestepped to avoid the danger she sensed on her right.

* * *

THE CHIPPEWA BRAVE was from Hole in the Day's band, as were his two mates. They were outcasts, held in contempt by the others because of their lack of moral character. Acting as one perverted mind, they preyed upon red or white. It made no difference to them. They didn't kill for possessions or personal gain. They killed for the thrill of killing, and this traveler would be their next victim.

As the rider passed the first position, the Indian hidden there crawled from his hole toward the trail to act as a blocker in case the man wheeled and tried to run back in the direction he had come.

The second brave's position was the killing location, and the third was a backup in case number two failed.

When the rider drew even with the second brave, the Indian raised his rifle, and with his finger caressing the trigger, cocked the hammer with his thumb in preparation for the shot.

* * *

THE WARNING FROM HIS MARE and the distinct click made by the hammer being cocked set Anton into action. He reached forward, right hand on the saddle pommel while violently twisting his body to the left, flattening himself to the mare's neck. With his movement, she jumped ahead into the shallow water.

The shot tore through the air, passing inches above Anton as he charged to the cover of the willows on the other side. Entering the trees, he vaulted to the ground while the mare was still at a dead run.

Among the scrubby trees were patches of swamp grass separated by dry stretches of open dirt. Spring rains and the swollen river had created a marshy area, gone dry under the hot summer sun. Now, the autumn cattails, swollen to the point of bursting, spread their seeds like snowflakes as man and horse crashed through them.

Anton sprinted to his left, keeping low to hide his position, wishing he had not left his rifle with Star Woman. Careful to avoid thickets of bulrushes and the telltale cattails, he moved about twenty yards from where he'd dismounted, and slowly parted the reeds to view the other side. All three Indians had come together. They were pointing their guns at the spot he'd just come from. As though on signal, they fired into the tall grass, covering a wide area, apparently hoping to hit their quarry through blind luck.

He realized his predicament as the three reloaded. With only a knife, he stood no chance. His only hope was to put distance between him and the three killers and gradually work his way back to Star Woman and the rifle. The open river now lying between them posed a problem. The dry swamp in which he hid was small, easily covered by the three killers in a few minutes, and if he bolted to the open ground beyond or tried to swim the river, he would become a defenseless target.

His eyes searched for something he may have missed, anything to give him hope. Nothing.

Looking back toward the three, he saw the brave on the left go down. He had hardly hit the ground when the second collapsed without a sound. The third Chippewa turned to look behind him and death in the form of an arrow caught him in the throat, ripping through his jugular. His wound sprayed blood like a fountain, and he was dead before he hit the ground. The man taking the shots had crawled into position to hide in one of the holes vacated when the three gathered at the river's edge to plan the final kill.

While Anton looked on in incredulous disbelief, a squat figure stepped from the seclusion of one of the holes dug by the murderers and lifted his right arm in greeting.

* * *

THE STOUT INDIAN was a lead man from a Wahpeton band named Tatemina, known to the whites as Round Wind. He was sent by Joseph Renville to provide protection at the crossing. Renville feared problems in light of the recent killings, and though he knew Anton would accompany Star Woman, he reasoned that a second protector would do no harm.

While Anton was quite tall and blessed with a chiseled, angular body and handsome looks, Tatemina was a full ten inches shorter, squat and powerful, with a simple, round face that belied the intelligence that lay behind his dark, piercing eyes. Those eyes demanded attention and were the source of his elevated station within his band.

In spite of the fact that Anton was nearly eight years younger than Tatemina, a strong friendship developed between the two. They visited often, for it had become habit to attend translation meetings, not as participants, but as warriors traveling in concert with the participants. It was a dangerous time, strewn with peril from rogue Indians and whites alike. They came to view themselves as bodyguards, protecting and ensuring safe passage.

Tatemina was a brother to Big Thunder—Little Crow IV—and shared mutual friends with Anton. He was known for his considerable battle skills. During a raid on a Chippewa camp, it was said he moved among the enemy without notice, stealthy as a cat, counting thirteen coups by laying his war club on the shoulder of thirteen warriors without injury to them or himself. His skill with bow and arrow was legendary. He'd once shot seven arrows through a ten-inch ring in under a minute, from a distance of sixty feet.

Tatemina had seen forty-nine summers, while Anton was in his forty-first year. They sat for hours telling stories. Anton was fascinated with stories of buffalo on the plains of the Northwest Territory and the Minnesota River bottoms and the methods used to hunt them. He listened in rapt attention as Tatemina spoke of Canadian French traders on the Red River, and of his personal war with the Chippewa.

They were both good listeners, which drew them close, and Tatemina became lost in the stories Anton related about the White Mountains, Ohio, and the journey that had brought him to Fort Snelling.

* * *

Anton's tipi, Red Iron's encampment
March 1846

ANTON AND TATEMINA HAD BEEN FRIENDS for three years when Joseph Renville died. His death was followed by another great loss: Chief Big Thunder was killed by the accidental discharge of his own gun. The fourth in the Little Crow lineage to accept leadership of the band, his position passed on to his son, Taoyateduta, who became the fifth chief named Little Crow.

Taoyateduta's ascension caused contention within the band and resulted in a conflict in which two of his half brothers were killed and the young chief was wounded. The bullet passed through both arms resulting in a deformity that would mark him for the rest of his life.

"What can you tell me about Taoyateduta?" Anton asked. "It seems there was a little trouble as a result of his appointment as chief." Like all others, Anton had heard of the rivalry within the band.

"Big Thunder would have preferred either of two sons born of his second wife to succeed him. Both died in 1841 during a raid on the Chippewa. He had four sons with the same woman, and the two remaining tried to kill Taoyateduta. That's how his arms got injured, during that fight."

"What's your opinion of his ability to lead?"

Tatemina thought for a short time before answering.

"Taoyateduta, like his father, desires peace. He believes his people will benefit by farming. We will see what the future brings."

* * *

Kaposia
August 1848

CHIEF WABASHA AND ANTON rode their horses at a walk side by side and very close together so they could speak without raising their voices. The two had known each other since Anton's days as scout for Colonel Snelling, and there was a mutual respect between them.

Wabasha's village lay nearly a day's ride south of Fort Snelling on the shores of the Mississippi. They were meeting at Kaposia—where the rivers joined and Little Crow made his camp. Following the greetings and exchange of small talk common among friends, the Indian chief came to the point.

"I would ask a favor of a trusted friend."

"Of course. What can I do for you?"

Wabasha had an intrinsic understanding of political issues and made it a point to actively seek information that could be used for the betterment of his band. He had heard things that alarmed him, and he wanted Anton's help in gathering information around the rumors.

"I have heard of a meeting to be held in the town of Stillwater. It will be of great importance and could change the dynamic of the whole frontier. I heard it will organize the settlers into a single body."

Anton replied, "I have not heard of this. What's the favor?"

"A meeting of this sort would not welcome the red man in its midst. You have the appearance of a white man. I would like you to attend their meeting and learn what they intend to do."

* * *

On August 26, 1848, Anton strolled into John McKusick's store in Stillwater, found a nail keg against the rear wall and settled in to follow the proceedings that centered on creating a territorial government.

It was referred to as the Stillwater Convention, and it resulted in the selection of a man named Henry Sibley to represent them in Congress with the goal of establishing the Minnesota Territory. At the conclusion of the meeting, Anton ambled out the door in much the same manner as he'd arrived, and disappeared into the crowd gathered in the street.

* * *

Anton was in the camp of Wabasha reporting what he had learned.

"Perhaps the White Father in Washington will not grant the request. Perhaps this country will remain as it has been for hundreds of years." Wabasha was hopeful.

"There's no way to turn back time. I think this is going to add to the problem, not only with the Chippewa, but with white settlers that are bound to follow. As your ancestors and I both came west from the eastern mountains, so will the white men come."

In March of 1849, the Territory of Minnesota was created, bringing settlers in a seemingly endless stream. The St. Peter River was beginning to be referred to as the Minnesota River as the new arrivals began to settle into the area. Unaware, and often uncaring, they trespassed on Indian land while the traders in the area continued to bilk the Indian of anything they deemed of value. Speculators laid claim to choice pieces of property with little or no regard to the Native American.

Graft was widespread, touching even government officials appointed to oversee the fair treatment of the Indians. Amos Bruce, the replacement agent for Lawrence Taliaferro, was sued with the claim that he overstated the amount he sought for reimbursement for expenditures by ten thousand dollars.

Suspected of behavior unfitting a public servant, Henry Sibley himself, was accused by some of profiteering.

Game became scarce, and by the end of the decade the light of the Seven Fires was beginning to dim.

Chapter Fourteen

Treaties of 1851 and 1858
Let Them Eat Grass

MAJOR CHIEFS AND LEAD MEN from the Sisseton and Wahpeton bands stood with dignity, and the air was filled with a solemnity as thick as that surrounding a burial. They were dressed in the beautifully beaded buckskins and moccasins reserved for important ceremonies like the one they now attended.

Chief Big Gun, representing the Wahpeton, and the Orphan, head chief of the Sisseton, stood in front of their contingents, both wearing full headdresses, stunning and impressive to behold. They were accompanied by delegations consisting of the principal men of each band. There were women present as well, and a cadre of warriors from the various bands in high paint and feathers milled about and looked on from a distance as goods intended as presents from the White Father, were heaped in a pile.

Through this treaty, the Sisseton and Wahpeton ceded their lands in southern and western Minnesota Territory, along with some lands in Iowa and Dakota Territory for a promised payment of $1.665 million in cash and annuities.

As Stephen Riggs read the contents of the treaty in the Dakota language, all present knew deep within that their lives would be changed forever. One of the Wahpeton chiefs, Sleepy Eye, who made his camp a short way upstream from Traverse des Sioux and would soon move his band further upriver, spoke to the commission.

"I seek provisions within this treaty that will guarantee help for my people before the ground becomes white. My people will be very hungry when that time comes." He began to deliver a long speech, complaining that the amount paid for their land was insufficient, and began listing other grievances. He was silenced by the commission, as terms of the treaty had already been agreed to.

There were others who spoke, and then signatures were affixed to the document. In many cases, the Indians were able to sign their own names, a result of the schooling given by the missionaries. After signing the treaty documents, they moved to a makeshift table made from an upright barrel where they signed a second document presented by Joseph R. Brown and Martin McLeod, which authorized payment of claims by traders from the Indians' annuities. Those placing their mark on the paper had no idea what they were signing.

It seemed there was no end to the treachery of the traders or of the agents of the U.S. Government present at the proceedings.

Thirteen days later, on August 5, 1851, at Mendota, near Fort Snelling, the Mdewakanton and Wahpekute bands added their signatures to the treaty documents. Chief Wabasha, as head of the Santee delegation, was dressed in his ceremonial attire, looking splendid and larger than life. To his right sat his number two chief, Little Crow, and the chiefs and headmen of all the bands including Anton's good friend, Tatemina. Shakopee, son of the Shakopee who was killed running the gauntlet, was there as well. All signed the treaty, all doing so with remorse.

The treaty ceded all land in the Minnesota Territory with the exception of the newly established stretches along both sides of the Minnesota River running a distance of 150 miles, each strip averaging ten miles in width.

In addition to annuity payments, provision was also stipulated that specified amounts of money to be provided for the erection of mills and blacksmith shops, opening farms, fencing and breaking land, and other "beneficial objects as may be deemed most conducive to the prosperity and happiness of said Indians . . ."

With these treaties, Dakota people sold most of their land to the U.S. in exchange for $3.75 million, at an estimated price of twelve cents per acre. When the treaties were signed, the traders claimed to be owed almost half a million dollars for goods given to the Indians on account.

As recognized by Lawrence Taliaferro with the signing of the Treaty of St. Peter in 1827, it was clear to anyone wishing to look with open eyes: the fur trade had transformed itself into land speculation and outright thievery through entries for fictitious credit given by the traders.

What easier way to make money than to steal funds the Indians would receive for their lands after signing the treaties? Land speculators, including Henry Sibley as agent for Pierre Chouteau, began buying land adjacent to the reservation established by the treaty.

Before the end of the year, seven thousand Dakota Sioux were moved from their native land to the Minnesota River strips, opening huge parcels to settlement at the purchase price of one dollar twenty-five cents per acre.

The 1851 Treaty of Traverse des Sioux was the catalyst that set in motion the Indian wars that would wrack the Dakota Nation and culminate with the massacre at Wounded Knee, South Dakota.

* * *

Dokkins' Camp
February 27, 1855

WITH A STRONG, ALMOST PRIMAL longing to retrace his journey along the Red River of the North and make a sweep to visit the camp in which they wintered, Anton had asked the others to accompany him. Now in his fiftieth year, and seeing what was happening to the territory, there was a sense of urgency inside him. He was able to convey that urgency to Tatemina, who readily agreed to travel with him.

To Four Wings, five months short of his thirtieth birthday, it represented an exciting adventure to see where Anton had almost drowned during the blizzard of 1826, where he'd met Dokkins, and finally to visit the camp where he himself had spent the winter of 1828/1829 and to see the two people he had learned to love.

The three horsemen made no attempt to conceal their approach. Anton remembered that Dokkins could be a loose cannon, and he didn't want anyone to get shot.

"Ahoy, the camp!"

"Ahoy, yerself!"

The voice seemed to come from within arm's reach on his left.

Anton spun in the saddle, startled, nonetheless recognizing the voice as that of his friend Dokkins.

"That you, Anton? I figured it was you first glimpse I had."

"You old horse thief. When'd you get so savvy?"

"When'd you get so stupid? Last I knew you was supposed to be half Indian."

The three men dismounted, and Anton introduced his two companions.

"This here's my good friend Tatemina . . . and I think you know this young man," pointing to Four Wings, "you knew him as Rising Eagle. Since his vision, his name is Four Wings."

"By damn! Four Wings, eh? How long's it been anyway? Last time I seen you, you was up to here," holding his hand mid-torso, "and you clattered arrows among the rocks. You remember that?"

"Sure do." Four Wings was grinning ear to ear. The two embraced and clapped each other's backs.

There was general conversation as they walked toward the wigwam where they picketed the horses and greeted Carries Stick.

After sharing a meal, they settled in around the fire.

"By damn! It's good to see you again, Anton! Me an' Carries Stick talks about you all the time."

"Jeremy, you know that's hardly the truth," she shifted her eyes to fix on Anton's face, "but we do think of you often. Tell me the news of Star Woman. Is she well? What has she been doing with herself?"

"Set yourself back, woman. We're gonna talk men things."

She snapped her head in his direction, took a grip on the ever-present elm switch lying by her side, and Dokkins reconsidered.

"Well . . . I guess we can get that out of the way first. It's just that there's lots o' stuff to catch up."

Anton addressed Carries Stick. "Star Woman has been running our camp with the efficiency of a military exercise. We've been spending our time with Chief Red Iron's band . . . by the way," he shifted his eyes toward Dokkins, "Taliaferro agreed with the handling of the Conrad and Price situation."

Dokkins nodded in approval. "Them boys'll like hearing that piece of news. They ain't never been comfortable since then."

"Well, you can tell them to rest easy. Taliaferro left the agency in '39, and the new guy's got his hands full trying to manage the present, let alone the past."

Anton looked in Carries Stick's direction, "Seems like Star Woman is into something she really likes. She's been helping the missionaries down at Lac qui Parle do translation work of the Bible. They're making good progress too." He grabbed a stick and prodded the fire. "She's still the best I ever seen at skinning and tanning a quality pelt."

Tatemina sat in respectful silence, enjoying the exchanges going on around him. While Anton was conversing with Dokkins, Four Wings was deep in conversation with Carries Stick. She was starving for information concerning Star Woman, who, since their winter together, she considered her best friend.

Dokkins said, "You know this is Winnebago land. Awhile ago a few of the chiefs left for Washington to talk about a treaty."

"No, I knew nothing of this. I do not know the Indian agent. I spend my time in the villages or various places where translation meetings occur." Turning toward Tatemina, Anton asked, "Have you heard of this treaty?"

"Like you, I have heard nothing. I'd be willing to bet there isn't a Dakota chief who has heard of it either." Tatemina appreciated the fact that his friend had worked him into the conversation.

Turning his head toward Dokkins, Anton asked, "Are you aware of the treaty at Traverse Des Sioux?"

"Yeah, news of that one reached us. Seems like it ain't gonna be long before there ain't no land to set a trap line on what ain't owned by the government."

Tatemina offered, "It's been nearly five years since Traverse Des Sioux. The Dakota, at least those who haven't moved west to the Missouri, are planting crops and blending into the white man's ways.

All the camps have moved west on the Minnesota, and every lodge is finally collecting pay as promised in the treaty of '51. It's the crops that keep everything on an even keel."

They had never talked of how the treaties affected the Indian, and Anton had never heard Tatemina weigh in on the subject. "It seems like more and more whites are moving in, and it seems like they're set on buying land adjacent to our stretch along the river."

Tatemina answered, "That's a fact. We already know most of the game's gone, so as long as the weather doesn't stunt the crops, we'll have food for our bellies. Those that reject farming spend their allotment on whiskey. I see that as a big problem."

Dokkins, always anxious to enter a conversation, blurted, "By damn, Anton, do you remember that day I was drinkin' that watered down crap from the good Reverend Conrad?"

"Sure do, sure do. I reckon whiskey's always going to be a problem as long as there's those that refuse to give up the old ways."

* * *

March 1857
Spirit Lake, Iowa

DURING THE SIGNING of the 1851 treaty, a Wahpekute band under the leadership of Wamdisapa, known as Black Eagle to the whites, had broken from the main tribe and was not a part of the treaty. Consisting of outcasts and murderers from Yankton, Sisseton, and Wahpekute bands, they were considered a bad lot and shunned by other Dakota. Outlaws and renegades, they roamed southwestern Minnesota Territory and Iowa.

By 1857, the band had been reduced to ten or fifteen lodges under the leadership of Inkpaduta. They had settled in the area near the Missouri River, west of Minnesota Territory, ranging east into Iowa and the southwest corner of the territory.

Early that year, Inkpaduta, and eleven of his warriors were on a sweep that brought them up the Little Sioux River in Iowa to Spirit Lake.

At that time, few whites had settled in the area. Although Spirit Lake was on ceded land, it was far enough separated from white settlements to place it in the heart of Indian Territory. Nonetheless, a settlement consisting of a few buildings was erected at Spirit Lake, and the same occurred around a trader's house a little further south.

Roaring Cloud, a son of Inkpaduta, crouched low behind a fallen tree just off the game trail. To his left knelt Fire Cloud. They were twin brothers who had left the main group of renegades hoping to return with food for the others. Although brothers, they could not have been more different in character.

Neither was particularly gifted in athletics. Both were feared. Roaring Cloud was lustful, cruel, and a senseless killer with no re-morse. His brother, although of vile character, was effeminate in ges-ture, relying on his wiles to survive in the company of killers. The two now surveyed the cabin ahead and the half dozen chickens that pecked to one side.

Roaring Cloud said, "There is our evening meal, brother. We have watched for over an hour with no sign of anyone. Let us take our dinner."

Exiting their hiding place, the two walked in a casual manner, crossing the fifty or so yards to the edge of the building. There, Roaring Cloud handed his rifle to his brother and dashed to grab the neck of the closest bird. Among flapping wings, flying feathers, and the ruckus caused when one grabs a chicken by the neck, the Indian drew his knife, severed the head, flipped the kicking carcass aside, and raced to grab another.

Seemingly from nowhere, a dog with bared fangs leaped toward the Indian, locking canine teeth on his forearm, causing them both to crash into the side of the cabin. Within seconds, the animal lay dead, stabbed through the heart.

Roaring Cloud climbed to his knees and turned to look in his brother's direction. The boot caught him square in the jaw propelling him into the cabin wall. From a distance, Fire Cloud watched in fear as the white man beat his brother into unconsciousness, then de-manded their weapons, which were quickly given up.

Injured, embarrassed, and containing a rage that could not be hidden, they limped into the party's temporary camp, where Inkpaduta and ten more of his warriors waited. Before the brothers could complete their story, several men on horseback, no doubt responding to pleas by the dog's owner, surrounded the camp and the entire Indian party was disarmed.

The following day the weapons were returned under the condition that they leave the area immediately. As much as it ground upon his pride, with the odds heavily against him, Inkpaduta took his band of twelve and headed north.

About the sixth or seventh of March, they came upon the settlement at Spirit Lake and so great was their rage that they massacred everyone there, killing all the men and some of the women, and taking four women prisoners.

Moving further north and encountering more whites at the Springfield settlement, they killed everyone, leaving bloody bodies in their wake. The total number killed was forty-two.

Little Crow was outraged and led an expedition to eradicate the outlaw band, and was successful in putting an end to their murderous ways by tracking down and killing most of them, and rescuing several hostages.

Although not linked to the Dakota uprising, this was a harbinger of things to come.

On May 11, 1858, Minnesota became the thirty-second state admitted to the Union.

* * *

June 1858
Washington

LAWRENCE TALIAFERRO SLID onto the chair at the kitchen table in his quarters on the corner of E Street. As had become his morning custom, he poured a cup of hot water for his tea. He'd had a fitful night, and it had been well after midnight when he last looked at the bedside clock. When he finally fell asleep, he dreamed of when he was a child. He knew she loved him, but in his dream his mother shunned him, ordering him to run a gauntlet. Men lined the path with whips and books that morphed into ax handles, and each man looked like Sergeant Pitt. He awakened in a sweat, knowing it was a dream yet unnerved by its content and unable to stop reflecting on it and what it might mean.

Of all his remembrances, the worst was the day that Timmy Overton died. That was the day he'd first realized evil existed in the world. It showed him the power that words possessed when used for evil, and the necessity for protecting the innocent from the duplicitous intent of others. It did in fact, form the cornerstone of his career in the Northwest Frontier while serving as agent to the Dakota Nation, who were childlike in their trust in the words spoken by the white man. He had done his best to protect them, and there was no doubt to the satisfaction he felt while remembering friendships made. That experience had been the most fulfilling in his life.

He was interrupted from his reverie by a tapping on his front door. Rising with some difficulty, for he was now in his sixty-fourth year and bothered by rheumatism, he walked somewhat unsteadily to the front room and opened the door.

Facing him was a man of medium build who he vaguely recognized. Behind him, Lawrence could see the top hat and black jacket of another individual.

"Major Taliaferro, I am Joseph Campbell, the oldest son of Scott Campbell, who was your interpreter for eighteen years."

Lawrence extended his hand.

"Yes, yes . . . I see your father in your face, so good to meet you. How is your father?"

"He is in fine form, and sends his regards. There are three gentlemen that wish to speak with you, sir."

He stepped to one side and the three men came into view. Lawrence found himself face to face with three Mdewakanton Sioux.

Campbell, motioning with his right arm, said, "I give you Taoyateduta, the son of Little Crow—Wakinyantanka—Big Thunder, who along with his father you counted as friend when you were Indian agent. Taoyateduta is the fifth to take the Little Crow name."

Lawrence addressed the Indian. "By George, you were only a lad the last time I saw you. I felt terrible at the news of your father's passing. I'm so sorry."

The Indian leader grasped the hand offered by the older man. "Thank you."

Turning to the next man, Campbell offered, "This is Shakopee, the third to take that name."

Lawrence again extended his right hand. "I knew your grandfather well, and your father also. I'm sorry to say I don't recollect knowing you. It was a long time ago, and I'm afraid my memory isn't what it once was."

The remaining Indian stepped to the front.

"I am Chief Wabasha. My father was also Wabasha, known as Red Leaf. He spoke of you many times. I remember sitting in my father's tipi while the two of you talked of important things."

"It's so good to see you again. Come in, come in. Join me in sharing tea." The four men entered the foyer. It was all Lawrence could do to keep from embracing them. These were men with a connection to his past and their presence was unexpected.

They sat for well over an hour, during which time they explained that President Buchanan had invited them as a social gesture to meet with him and introduce them to James Denver, the newly appointed commissioner of Indian Affairs. They were also there to sign another treaty.

Toward the conclusion of their visit, Little Crow, who was an elegant speaker and needed no translator, paid tribute to Lawrence Taliaferro. "You took my grandfather with you to this great city in 1824. You took my father also to this city in 1837. He did good for our people. He made a good treaty, because you stood by him."

Lawrence inquired as to the welfare of his friend Anton McAllister and was brought up to date on his status, as well as that of the various missions in place along the length of the Minnesota River. After telling stories and recounting many shared experiences, it was time for them to leave. They exited with the promise that they would visit the next time they were in Washington.

They would never meet again.

* * *

On June 18, 1858, a treaty was entered into whereby the north side of the Minnesota River, the same land that the government granted them in the treaty of 1851, was ceded to the U.S. Government, removing all bands to the ten-mile wide stretch on the south side of the river. The chiefs and headmen from the Mdewakanton and Wahpekute bands signed the treaty. It was the biggest mistake of their lives.

Almost immediately, steps were taken by the government to move seventeen hundred Dakota families off the ceded land to the south stretch. When Little Crow's band learned the extent of the treaty, he lost the respect of his warriors and others within the tribe. Furious with the thought that the white men had duped him, they responded by appointing another, Traveling Hail, to replace him as their spokesman.

Annuity payments under prior treaties were made in gold, with distribution handled by crooked traders claiming false debts and siphoning large amounts before distributing funds to the Indians. Nevertheless, annuity payments were being made, corn was being grown, and relative calm prevailed. The treaty of 1858 severely restricted the Dakota to a thin strip of land devoid of game.

Everything seemed to work against the Indian over the next three years. Bad weather adversely affected the crops and annuity payments became sporadic. When the Civil War erupted, the government considered offering the Indians script, or a means of payment other than the customary gold. The Indians complained, and the government relented, promising payments by the standard method.

The summer of 1862 was particularly trying. Annuities were hit or miss, finally ceasing to come at all, and they had a poor crop due to spring weather patterns. They were starving. The Sisseton and Wahpeton were extended credit by the traders on their reservation to the west, while those on the Mdewakanton and Wahpekute reservations were stingy and unwilling to offer supplies without payment up front.

As the summer wore on, the tribes became more and more desperate. The agent in place, Thomas Galbraith, the most recent in a succession of men more interested in their own welfare than that of the Indians, called a meeting where they discussed giving food on credit from their packed warehouses. It was his decision to hold the food until the annuity payment arrived, since in the past both food and money were distributed at the same time.

A warehouse was broken into and food was taken. The warehouse raid was halted by troops and a meeting was called between the Indians and the traders. There was much discussion around past credit issues and questions surrounding the late annuity payments.

Eventually the discussion turned to the Indian spokesman who made a passionate plea, "My people are starving, and you have warehouses full of food. The payments are late, and my people go hungry. You have taken our land, your cattle eat reservation grass, you cut our trees for your buildings, and you shoot our game. We ask only for food."

Thomas Myrick, storekeeper and spokesman for the merchants replied, "If they are hungry, let them eat grass."

There would be no credit and no food until the payment arrived.

Chapter Fifteen

The Uprising Begins

Brown Wing crawled toward the pothole where he'd seen them land. The four of them were hunting game, and couldn't resist the possibility of taking a few wood ducks back to camp. The plan was for Brown Wing to crawl to the edge of the swamp grass, and take one on the water. He had done it before while hunting alone, now with three others, he figured they should be able to take two, maybe three out of the flock.

When Brown Wing fired, the others were free to shoot. With any luck, they'd be close enough to pick another off the water. If they were unable to get off a shot before they flew, they would try to take one in the air, a difficult shot with a rifle.

Opposite Brown Wing was his best friend, Runs Against Something When Crawling. The two had been friends for as long as either could remember. In addition to being the same age, they had like interests and even had similar physical characteristics.

Approaching from the left was Killing Ghost, eighteen and the youngest of the four. To their right was Breaking Up, the oldest and most assertive.

Brown Wing placed his hands with careful precision as he crawled through the heavy marsh grass that grew all the way to the open water. He carried his rifle in his left hand. Another ten feet and he could set for the shot. The heavy grass surrounding the pothole reached well above his back while he crawled, and to get the best chance of killing a duck on the water he would need to rise to his knees, take aim through any available opening, and kill one before they could react.

The mosquitoes had been relentless since he began his approach, and he could ignore them no longer. He swatted at several that had landed on his forehead and ears, and with that movement, bedlam ensued.

Not more than a foot in front of him, a whitetail doe had bedded down for the day. She had no idea he was there, and his abrupt movement startled her into immediate action. She scrambled to her feet, crashed through the grass that mostly covered her body, and bolted past the startled Indian. Brown Wing recoiled to his left as she charged, and before he'd untangled his rifle from the heavy cover, she was gone.

While this was taking place, the ducks took to the air, following the path the doe had taken nearly smacking Brown Wing in the head as they skimmed along, inches above the grass, heading for parts unknown.

He stood, dejected and defeated, for he knew what to expect from the others. They could be merciless in their degradation after what must have looked like a total failure on his part.

He was dead on in his expectations.

They assembled, asked what happened, and after hearing his explanation, began mocking him with much fervor. Even after they resumed their trek toward the main camp, there were occasional references to his lack of hunting prowess.

They were nearing the town of Acton when they skirted a farm owned by Robinson Jones. Jones had built his farmstead to accommodate a small general store and post office.

"I'm in no mood to talk to any white men today." Breaking Up was in a foul mood. "Let's just take the fence line around the edge."

All agreed.

They were well past the buildings when a chicken bolted from the base of a fence post. Breaking Up, the closest to the fence, bent to discover a hen's nest with three eggs.

"Look here brothers, the Great Spirit has given us our dinner."

All gathered at the nest to look upon their good fortune.

Killing Ghost was the first to speak. "We can't eat those eggs. That's stealing from a white man. If we got caught there'd be hell to pay."

Breaking Up reached down and grabbed the nest, hurtling the eggs to the ground.

"Even though you are almost starving, you're afraid of the white man? You coward."

"I'm not afraid of the white man."

"You're a coward, and I will tell everyone you are a coward."

"I am no coward. I will prove to you that I'm not afraid. I'll go in there and shoot a white man. Are you brave enough to go with me?"

Breaking Up, in the mood for a fight, decided he would take the challenge and kill one himself.

The four men approached the Jones's public house, entered, and rummaged about. Jones could see they had little intention of purchasing anything so with two children safely in the back room he left for the Baker place about a mile down the road where his wife was visiting. The four Indians followed at a discrete distance.

Jones entered the yard with outward calm, although his insides were aflutter as he addressed Mr. Baker.

"Howard, I got four Dakota behind me, and I got a bad feeling about what they got on their minds."

"Just settle on down, Jones." Howard Baker looked toward the road. "I see them . . . and they don't look like much. We got Webster in his wagon just yonder. I'll wander over and get him out here."

By the time the Indians arrived, Baker and Webster were joining Jones in front of Baker's house.

Pleasantries were exchanged, and the Indians asked for water, which was given.

Not too much later, the conversation turned to the subject of marksmanship. Breaking Up spoke as a friend, though his heart was full of hate.

"I've heard much about the accuracy of the white man while aiming his rifle. I propose a contest of skill."

The whites agreed because it seemed guileless, and the Indians, because it fit their agenda.

Webster walked thirty paces distant, placed a sawn board firmly in the crotch of a tree, and returned to his place on the firing line.

"We will shoot first and our shots will be marked, then you will shoot to beat our effort." Breaking Up spoke with authority.

All agreed, and the Indians toed the line. Each aimed and carefully shot in succession, each shot accompanied with a "well done" or a groan of support.

Baker caught Jones's eye and gave him a wink, as if to say, "See, nothing to fear here."

After all had shot, Webster, who'd opted out of the competition, walked to the target, marked the holes, and returned to the line.

"One miss."

The first white to fire was Jones, with a clear hit. He turned to his companions with a wide grin.

Webster turned and walked toward the Baker house where Mrs. Baker stood on the stoop. This left only Howard Baker to try his hand.

Taking careful aim, he squeezed the trigger. His shot was an obvious hit as the piece of wood flew from its perch. Laying his rifle on the ground, he moved to reposition the target in the crotch of the tree.

Unrealized by the whites, while they were shooting in the contest, the Indians were reloading.

They raised their rifles as one, each with a separate target, and released a rain of lead on the unsuspecting men, killing all three of them and Mrs. Baker where they stood.

Realization of what they had done hit home. Now there would be real trouble. They had killed three men and a woman. They wasted no time in heading for their main camp, some forty miles distant, where they would tell their chief, Red Middle Voice, about their deed. On their way past the Jones place, fifteen-year-old Clara Wilson, adopted daughter of the Jones's, stepped into the doorway, and was shot dead.

On their way back to their village, they enticed another white man outside under the guise of friendship, and killed him with a single shot.

* * *

August 17, 1862
The camp of Red Middle Voice
8:00 p.m.

CHARGING INTO THE CAMP, riding double on two horses stolen from a settler, the warriors came screaming, "Prepare for battle. Prepare for a war with the whites, which we have now begun."

Chief Red Middle Voice, a man with an inherent desire to stand up to the whites, firmly believed they could be defeated. He met with the four young men to learn of their deed. Stirred by their acts, he made them go over their story multiple times before he reached a decision.

"We must take this to Shakopee. He will know what to do."

When they approached Shakopee's camp, word had already reached there and the five were greeted with shouts and whoops from Indians itching to go to war with the whites.

Chief Red Middle Voice was convinced the timing was right to make war against them and drive them out.

"They have fewer soldiers than we have warriors. My people have seen with their own eyes fewer soldiers than before. They have been sent to fight their war against the south. Now is the time to take our land back and drive every white man from our country."

Shakopee did his best to counter the argument. "It is true that they are fighting a war with themselves, but there are many more soldiers than what we see."

Red Middle Voice answered, "With the strength of all the tribes we will be unstoppable. We need a leader, a war chief who can rally all the people to join us in the fight."

The two men were speaking in a public setting. All around them young men itched to go to war. Shakopee had no other choice.

"We will go to Little Crow's house. He is a great war chief. We will ask him what he thinks on the matter. It is my feeling we should turn the four over to the authorities and be done with it."

Little Crow lived in a house built for him by the government and situated a short way downriver from Shakopee's village. Shakopee and Red Middle Voice led a group of warriors in that direction. Other braves joined them along the way. When they arrived, Little Crow was rousted from his bed.

Like a pack of snarling wolves, they surrounded his house. From among them came war cries, pleas, and threats.

"A war has begun with the whites! Lead us in battle." The voice came from somewhere to Little Crow's left.

From another, "Unite the nation. We will take our land back." From yet another, "We will kill every white and send them back where they came from."

Little Crow raised his arm for silence. "You have seen fit to replace me with another. Let him lead you into battle. I have been to Washington and seen the might of the whites. We cannot beat them. Our friend Mahsabusca, the agent Taliaferro who we all knew and trusted, has told me this."

From the crowd a voice spoke, "Traveling Hail is not a great war chief. You can unite the nation."

There were whoops and cheers, and Little Crow, like any other man might, began to think it possible to restore himself through leadership in battle. As the fever of war increased, so did his desire to lead his people. Finally, he succumbed.

"I will be before you at every battle, but I have many white friends. I will not kill my white friends."

Cut Nose was selected as his war chief and the stone aimed at the white nation was in the air.

* * *

Lower Sioux Agency at Redwood
August 18, 1862   .

DAWN BROKE WITH OVERCAST SKIES and sporadic showers along the river. Abigail Samuels awoke early. Her husband, Felix, had a great snore going, making it impossible for her to get back to sleep, so she crawled out of bed and half staggered to the stove. Striking a match, she lit the kindling prepared the night before and put on the kettle of water over the heat.

It was a morning like many others since they had come here from Ohio, the humidity was what she hated, even though the stagnant, moist air worked wonders for her skin.

Thinking she heard something outside, she stepped through the doorway and cocked her ear toward the west in the direction of the Redwood agency. She heard the sound again. It was unnatural, yet not unlike what she heard when she put green pine logs in the stove—a popping sound. There was something else . . . a strange wail . . . then realization hit.

Spinning on her heels, she turned and raced into the cabin, "Felix, wake up! There's shooting at the agency. I swear I heard Indians yelling. There's something going on across the river. Something's wrong at the agency.

"What the hell?"

"Get up, we've got to move . . . now."

Felix, finally with his wits functioning, knew exactly what she was talking about. All the settlers along the river were aware of the degradation in the relationship with the Dakota. It was happening. They were revolting.

"We have to get to Fort Ridgely. No time to hitch the wagon. You'll have to ride Victor without a saddle. We've got to go now!"

The two of them ran to the barn, where Felix grabbed the halters from their pegs, slipped them on the horses, and boosted his wife onto Victor's back. They rode at a gallop toward the fort.

Back at the Lower Sioux Agency, the Indians under the leadership of Little Crow were in the process of burning the government warehouse, setting fire to the private stores and homes, and breaking into barns and stealing horses. During the first few minutes they had killed twenty white settlers and traders. Among them was the storekeeper Thomas Myrick, the same Myrick who had made the proclamation "Let them eat grass!" Of no surprise to anyone who'd attended the meeting when those words were spoken was the discovery that his mouth had been stuffed with bloody grass.

* * *

FOUR WINGS AND STAR WOMAN were quiet leaving the agency, careful not to awaken those still asleep. The two were on their way back from St. Paul, where they'd picked up gill nets for Red Iron's band. Star Woman was partial to travel, especially when in the company of her son, so she'd jumped at the opportunity to make the trip. With many of her friends clearing land and planting corn, she relished the independence and freedom of the trail.

They were on their way back, and had reached the lower agency the day before as the sun was setting. They'd spent the night and were getting an early start with the morning light. They wanted to make the Upper Agency at Yellow Medicine before nightfall.

They were about five minutes west of the agency when Four Wings grabbed the bridle of Star Woman's horse and hurried the two of them down an incline and behind a stand of young cedars.

In a low voice he explained, "Someone's coming."

"A Chippewa war party, or perhaps it is Inkpaduta?"

"It could be. Whoever it is, we'll let them pass."

The first horseman reached their position within moments. As the party filed past their hiding place, there was no talk between them. The riders were Sioux and they were painted for war. Four Wings and Star Woman shared a look of horror as warrior after warrior rode passed them in deafening silence.

They had not bothered to count the warriors, guessing there were well over a hundred. They were mostly young men, each showing tension in their bodies and their faces, common before battle. Some carried rifles, some lances, and others bows and arrows. Many had tomahawks and knives tucked into sashes at their waists.

Four Wings and Star Woman held their position for a little while after the warriors passed, and Four Wings turned to his mother. "This is a major raid. I know of no Chippewa in the area."

"Whatever is happening is a big deal. I wonder . . ." She stopped mid-sentence as they heard gunshots coming from the direction of the Lower Agency.

Urging their horses up the incline, they rode at a canter toward the source of the shots, pulling up before coming into view of the agency buildings. In the distance, they could see smoke rising and fires burning and people running.

They watched in horror as tomahawks rose and fell. Neither dared to move, nor could they entirely grasp the meaning of what they were witnessing. Finally, Star Woman broke away from the mindless slaughter, wrenching her gaze from the image unfolding before them.

"Four Wings . . . Four Wings!" He shook himself free from the scene. "We must ride to the Yellow Medicine Agency and tell them what we have seen. A war has been started."

* * *

AS NEWS GOT OUT THAT THE LOWER AGENCY was being attacked, soldiers were dispatched from Fort Ridgely under the command of Captain Marsh to thwart the attackers. As Marsh approached the Redwood Ferry, Indians crossed from the other side, upriver, to attempt a flanking maneuver while a single brave held the soldiers' attention at the ferry crossing.

From the west side of the river that man yelled, "All is well now, things are settled at the agency. Come across. The chiefs wish to have a peaceful conference with you."

Captain Marsh held his men to the east side of the river.

"Come, we will conference at the agency."

What Marsh may have lacked in experience was made up for with cautious bravery. "I will come. My men will follow on my signal."

During this exchange, the Indians who had forded upriver had circled and were now closing on the rear of the column. The Indians on both sides of the river opened fire. The soldiers, unable to retreat, fought back in unorganized confusion. Many died, but a few were able to make it back to Fort Ridgely.

When the killing ended, there were forty-four whites dead and ten civilians held captive. To those captive families held at the agency, Little Crow spoke. "I did not wish to go to war, but my young men forced me to. We have begun and must do the best we can. I spare the lives of some of you for the sake of our good old Father,

Mahsabusca. His words are this day in my ears. Had he been here, this war would not have begun."

* * *

Twenty-five miles south of Fort Ridgely

TATEMINA DUG HIS HEELS into the sides of his mount, urging him to increase his speed. He bent his body forward against the stallion's neck, feeling the power beneath him. The seven that followed were intent upon killing him. Were it not for his magnificent horse, he would already be dead.

He was on his way home from Mankato, where he had been visiting family. As was his normal way while visiting a white settlement, he dressed as a "cut hair," to avoid unnecessary trouble with the city's residents. Cut-hair was used by the more militant Indians and was meant to be derogatory toward those who dressed like the white man and adopted the white man's ways. Tatemina first heard of the Lower Sioux Agency attack while passing a settler's cabin and being challenged by those within. They soon recognized him as a friend of Doctor Williamson, so they spoke freely of the attack.

The men he now ran from had confronted him moments earlier as he rode from the dry marsh to higher ground. Closing from both sides and blocking his path in front and rear, they demanded he dismount. None were familiar, and Tatemina figured they were Yankton from farther west, drawn by the recent events. News of the trouble at the Lower Agency spread quickly, and just as quickly drew troublemakers intent on personal gain or personal glory.

The leader of the seven rode onto the trail, blocking the way. He sat his horse in a casual manner, rifle horizontal in front of him, relaxed and confident.

Tatemina reined in.

The man in his path spoke as one used to having his way. "Get off that animal and you may live another day . . . You are a cut-hair. I should just shoot you and ride on."

The reaction was immediate and likely saved Tatemina's life. Supremely overconfident, the Yankton expected him to dismount immediately. Instead, he yanked the reins and simultaneously urged his horse forward, causing him to rear. Then strong legs propelled them into the horse blocking the road. The stallion, much larger than the ponies ridden by the seven, drove through the roadblock, sending the horse and rider to the ground. Tatemina rode through the chaos, reaching the trees before the others could react.

The downed Indian quickly recovered and swung onto his horse to give chase, followed by his companions.

It was really no contest. They weren't carrying carbines so they couldn't shoot while riding, and Tatemina's stallion easily outpaced the slower ponies. They trailed for nearly a mile before giving up the chase.

Tatemina slowed to a walk, eyes always moving to search for others who may lay hidden.

This is worse than I thought. His mind raced as the tension in his body began to subside. *Those Yankton must have ridden all day and all night to get this far so soon, likely changed ponies too. I must be cautious.*

When he'd set out from Mankato he'd intended to ride west a ways until he figured he'd covered enough distance, then cut north to Fort Ridgely. Now, however, in light of the attack on the Lower Agency and his run-in with the seven, he thought it best to continue on the same course, bypassing the villages until reaching the Yellow Medicine River. He'd follow that north to John Other Day's camp. Other Day was a Wahpeton Sioux chieftain and friend of Tatemina, who had taken early to the white man's ways, and was their true friend.

* * *

St. Paul, Minnesota
August 19, 1862

ALEXANDER RAMSEY, THE SECOND GOVERNOR of Minnesota, sat behind his desk. Across from him was Henry Sibley, the first governor, who now carried the rank of colonel in the U.S. Army. He had no combat experience and little knowledge of the Indians, his only experience being that of a trader in the St. Peter River Valley.

"Colonel Sibley, it's imperative that you lead American volunteer forces against these savages. They've murdered those at the Lower Agency and attacked troops from Fort Ridgely. I suspect this is a local uprising, a relatively insignificant event, although one that must be dealt with."

"Governor, we know the cause of this. It's the annuity payments. They haven't been made. The settlers horn in on reservation land, and it's a hundred different things that total up to this mess."

"So, what's your point?"

Sibley replied, "I guess there is no point. It's just a huge problem with no solution I can see."

"Well, I've got a solution! Drive all the savages out of the state and keep them out. That's the solution! I want you to chase those killers into the ground, and I want it done yesterday!"

With that directive, Colonel Henry Sibley began his campaign to eradicate the Dakota Indian problem in Minnesota.

* * *

LATE IN THE AFTERNOON on the nineteenth, Tatemina charged into Other Day's camp, unaware of the attack on Fort Ridgely. He had been on the trail since leaving Mankato, sometimes racing across open ground, sometimes walking his horse to avoid bands of marauding troublemakers. On two occasions he'd encountered unarmed settler families and advised them on the best route to safety.

"Where is Other Day?" he asked the first person he saw.

"He's been gone from camp since yesterday. He heard about the trouble at the Lower Agency. I think he's gone to the Yellow Medicine agency to help the whites."

"Do you know the man named Anton, from the camp of Red Iron?"

"Yes, I know him. I also know his family, Four Wings and Star Woman."

"Do you know where they are?"

"I do not know. Four Wings and the woman rode west just this morning. They were going to the Hazelwood Mission."

Tatemina, who had not dismounted, wheeled his horse and rode west.

He had pushed the stallion hard during his ride, seeing no other way. Once he located the others, he would give the animal time to rest. Until then there was little choice but to go on.

He now entered an area interspersed with heavy woods, deep ravines cut away by centuries of runoff, and rocky outcroppings that seemed to grow out of the surrounding land. This was Wahpeton land, and he was at home here. If he were to ride twenty miles beyond, he would again encounter rolling hills and prairie.

Tatemina rode to the mission and dismounted. As he approached the door, it swung open and Stephen Riggs stepped out.

"Tatemina, I didn't expect to see you for a couple of days what with you being down in Mankato. From the looks of your horse you've been riding him pretty hard."

"Yeah, we've been on the move going on two days now. How are things up here? I know it's a mess down at the Redwood Agency. I'm told Little Crow attacked and murdered everyone there."

"That's only partly true. A few riders tell us the Crow spared some lives."

"Have you seen my friend Anton and his family?"

"They should be close to the Upper Agency by now. They were here, all three of them. With the trouble down south they figured they should go support the folks at the Upper. I understand Other Day's heading that way too. Star Woman rode toward the post by Lac qui Parle."

"Good to know. Have you got a place inside I could rest? I'm all done in. It's been a long ride."

"I'll take care of your horse. You go right in and pick a spot to lie down."

"I'm grateful." Tatemina nearly stumbled through the door, found a corner, and was sound asleep before Riggs came back.

It was mid-morning on the twentieth and he awoke with a start. Riggs was deep in conversation with an Indian Tatemina did not know, but they were speaking in Dakota. He caught only the occasional word, unable to follow the distant conversation. Abruptly their talk ended and Riggs turned in his direction.

"Little Crow has attacked Fort Ridgely with hundreds of braves. Bands are roaming the river valley, killing every white they see. Bear Tooth just told me they're moving west. To top it off, the Chippewa are muddying the waters by taking scalps from both sides."

"You said Anton's family went to the Upper Agency. Has Little Crow reached that far upriver?"

"I'm told they've been fighting at Fort Ridgely since sunup."

"I must go there. I have both white and red friends there." Tatemina moved toward the door.

"There's more. While you slept, I heard from one of Other Day's men. The Sisseton and Wahpeton will join in the fighting. Most will not kill. All will plunder and take what they can." He paused to collect his thoughts, and then continued, "John Other Day spoke against joining. He has gone to the agency to take his friends to safety."

Chapter Sixteen

Tatemina to the Rescue

TROOPER GERALD KINCAID STRETCHED the sleep from his body and swung his legs over the edge of his cot. What a day yesterday had been. He, along with about seventy others, had mustered into the army thinking they would be heading south to fight the Confederates. Instead, they were sent to Fort Ridgely for the purpose of quelling the recent trouble with the Indians. Grabbing his straight razor and towel, he headed for the pump house.

Looking at the sky, he could see the day would be clear and warm. They had worked well into the night settling in and learning the fort rules and the layout. Their arrival had apparently been unexpected by the regulars and it proved a difficult task to get everyone situated.

As he lathered his face, he felt the nervousness of a greenhorn. Upon arrival at the fort, he heard about the attack on the Lower Agency and the fate of Captain Marsh and his men. Adding to his general discomfort was the influx of settlers entering the fort and the stories they told. Throughout the night, he heard the sound of gunfire in the distance, nothing alarming, just the occasional *bang*. This was, after all, the frontier, and they had been sent to put down the Indian revolt. Had the shooting been the only factor, he would have thought little of it. However, the arrival of families during the night and the stories they told proved to be very unsettling.

The razor slid smoothly over his skin as he drew it from his lower neck toward his chin. With deft strokes, he cut away the two-day growth of whiskers, all the while turning things over in his mind.

Kincaid was a romantic at heart, never giving a thought to the dangers of army life, only the idea of heroism under fire. When the call went out for men to fill a Minnesota volunteer battalion, he was first in line. At twenty-three years of age, he'd signed up to fight Lincoln's war. He now began to doubt that decision.

With a clean-shaven face, he wiped the remaining lather from his chin, swished his razor in the bucket of water, snapped it shut, and stepped through the door. Before his foot hit the ground, the bullet caught him in the forehead, and he died instantly.

The next few minutes were total chaos as the regulars mounted a defense while lead rained in from the east, and green troops cowered, waiting for someone to tell them what to do.

In spite of the disorganization within the ranks of the troopers, they were able to hold their own against the attackers. By nightfall the fighting tapered off, stopping completely when darkness set in. They had lost four men, but were becoming more organized as a fighting unit.

The next day the sunny weather yielded to wave after wave of heavy rain, with only sporadic attacks by the Indians, more as a harassment tactic than a full-out battle.

On the twenty-second, the four hundred Dakota had increased to twice that number, and the fort was in serious jeopardy. Were it not for their heavy artillery pieces, they would undoubtedly have been overrun and defeated. With clearing weather, the battle intensity increased, and it was clear the Sioux had used the prior day to good advantage by adding warriors and dispersing them to attack from all sides.

A vicious attack from the north commenced with the Indians burning several buildings and using others for cover. Those being used as cover were set aflame by the garrison to prevent them from being of benefit to the Indians. Unable to break the defense of the fort, Little Crow's men laid siege and prepared themselves for a drawn-out battle.

Settlers from the entire river valley had abandoned their homesteads to bring their families to the safety of a larger city. New Ulm and Mankato were destinations for wagons full of frightened whites. Many were attacked and many died at the hands of small bands of renegade Indians. Cabins were aflame everywhere, and it seemed the whole Minnesota River Valley was burning. There were stretches where bodies lined the road, scattered where they fell, with no dis-

cernment between man, woman, or child. If they were white, they
died.

* * *

August 22, 1862

AS LITTLE CROW PLACED FORT RIDGELY under siege, Tatemina was
about halfway to the Lower Sioux Agency when he heard the shots
from the direction of Astor Bennett's place. He jabbed his heels into
the fresh mount, a mare Riggs had given him, and she surged forward,
headed for the house apparently under attack.

Bennett had brought his family to the Northwest Frontier from
Illinois, where he had farmed out his parcel to the point that it would
no longer produce a decent crop. After the frontier was opened for
settlers, he moved his family west. Accustomed to the flatlands from
whence he came, he chose a parcel devoid of trees, with wood close
enough to provide for his needs.

Bennett, through some providential miracle, had placed his log
house in a perfect spot. The wellspring had been discovered by a fortuitous accident. While driving a stake to tie his horse, water bubbled
to the surface around the pole he had driven. Fortune had smiled. The
discovery of the spring dictated where he would place his house and
outbuildings.

It wasn't long before his homestead was a favored gathering
place for Indians and whites alike.

It was now under attack.

Dismounting on the backside of a knoll, Tatemina tied his
horse inside a thicket of cedars, took his rifle, powder horn, and bag
of shot, and dashed to the corner of the building opposite the shooting.

"Astor, it's Tatemina—Round Wind. I've come to help. Do
not shoot me if I enter."

There was no reply from within.

"Sarah . . . Astor! Hear me. It is Round Wind. Let me in."

"Yes . . . yes, I'll open the window. Slip through there." It was Sarah who answered. The window was above his head, heavily shuttered to protect against harsh weather and attack.

He heard a board slide and the shutter swung upward. He poked his rifle through the opening and followed it with his body.

"Round Wind! We're sure glad to see you!" Astor was in the process of reloading, while his son of thirteen years, David, worked on reloading a second rifle.

Tatemina said, "Do you have any idea who might be out there? You know most of the Sisseton in this area. Did you get a chance to see if any of these looked familiar?"

Sarah answered in place of her husband, "Sisseton? These are Chippewa. We heard about the trouble downriver. These are Indians from north of here . . . just trying to get what they can."

A volley smacked into the building, one round penetrating an open area in the chinking and lodging harmlessly in the rear wall.

Tatemina said, "You got any idea how many there are?"

"Near as I can figure, can't be more'n four or five. Trouble is, we can't get at them from here. Our only hope is to go outside and meet them where we can move around."

"I wouldn't advise that. Best case is your son here grows up without a father. Worst case is everyone dies. Here's what I'm thinking," Tatemina spoke in a positive manner, "all we need to do is fire an occasional shot just to let them know we're still here. We've got water and I know you've got lots of food stored up, so we can hole up here for a week if we have to. By that time, they'll either rush us, or leave. That is, unless you got someplace else to be in the next week or so."

So they settled in, uncomfortable, yet willing to outlast the opponent.

It went that way, the occasional shot coming from the cabin, followed by a volley from those outside, for the next three days. On the fourth day, the Chippewa made a move to break the stalemate.

Under cover fire, two braves crawled toward either side of the house with the intention of lighting the roof and setting the cabin aflame. The sharp eyes of young David Bennett spotted them while they were still some distance out.

"Pop, there's two of 'em crawlin'. One left, t'other right."

"Good eyes, boy."

Astor, while keeping his barrel fully inside the house, aimed through the narrow shooting slit and squeezed off a shot, finishing one of them.

"I can't see t'other. I think he's behind the house already."

"I'll find him." Tatemina leaned his rifle against the wall, and pulled his knife sheath around to the front of his body. "If he gets to the roof, we're all done."

With agility belying his sixty-five years, Tatemina was through the window opening and crouched near the rear wall.

Tatemina thought, *Where would I go if I wanted to gain the roof?* He knew he didn't have much time. Having visited this place many times before, the spring water being of exceptional quality, he recalled the lay of the land around the house, considering the single most advantageous place from which roof access could be gained. Remembering what he had seen, he moved swiftly to his left, the side opposite from where the attackers were firing.

There, on the corner of the dwelling, was the skinning tower. Not really more than a low roof with a beam running six feet out from the house wall was used to string up large game for butchering. Underneath was a table about thirty by twenty inches for cleaning rabbits, prairie chickens, and all manner of small game. On the table, facing the back corner stood the Chippewa.

As Tatemina came around the corner, the brave, about to climb to the roof, turned in his direction, and their eyes met.

Instinct, the same instinct that saved his life when the Yankton intercepted him, took hold, and Tatemina moved. With cat-like quickness, he attacked, drawing his knife as he closed the distance between them. One clean swipe and the Achilles tendons were severed on both legs and the warrior collapsed, striking his face on the table and driving the drying whitetail antler through his eye socket into his brain, killing him instantly.

Reaching the fallen Chippewa, Tatemina grabbed the hair on the dead man's head, pulled his tomahawk from his waist, and with one stroke severed the head from the body.

With supreme confidence, he stepped around the side of the building holding the severed head aloft, and screamed, "Aiee! Chippewa scum. Your friends are dead. Think about death. Are you ready to die today? Are your ancestors ready to receive you?"

There was silence.

"I ask you, are you ready to leave this life?" Tatemina said again.

The birds were silent and there was no rustle of leaves in the trees. Everything was eerily still.

"I have taken the head of your pathetic warrior with my bare hands. I am the ghost of battles past. You will not see me until it is too late. Now I come for you."

The effect of his words was chilling to those in the cabin. It was devastating to the Chippewa braves. The last glimpse of the three remaining warriors was their scramble to escape the area.

* * *

August 23, 1862

AT THE TIME TATEMINA was riding to rescue the Bennett family, Anton was moving due east from the Upper Agency with the idea of warning settlers on farms and small communities that had sprung up some distance north of the river. His plan was to ride a well-worn wagon trail, which would, if he followed it far enough, bring him to the river just north of St. Peter.

The wagon road he was on followed a narrow ridgeline bordering a dry swamp to the north and a heavily treed swale to the south. The day was clear. The sun's position indicated it to be mid-morning.

They were moving parallel to him on the backside of the dry swamp where the trail they followed came within yards of the heavy swamp grass. It took him a while to count the wagons as they labored along with only sporadic moments of visibility while they passed intermittent breaks in the tall, heavy grass. He counted three wagons, each overflowing with men, women, and children. Totally unaware of his presence, he could clearly hear their loud conversation float over the distance between them.

Anton was familiar with the wagon trail he followed, and he knew it intersected with the other, less than a quarter mile ahead. Urging the mare forward, he intended to wait for the settlers at the junction. The trick would be to do it without getting shot.

He picked a spot to the left of the trail behind a large cottonwood that had fallen long ago. The branches were naked, and large pieces of bark had fallen off the thick trunk. Heavy vegetation had grown through the fallen tree's skeleton, offering a thick blanket of cover for anyone behind it. Anton stationed himself in a position that offered unimpeded passage onto the trail after the wagons passed.

He heard them approaching.

"How long do you think it'll take us to reach St. Peter?" A woman's voice asked.

"It could be another day or two. We can't go too fast in these wagons." A man answered.

There was constant chatter as each wagon passed. After the third had passed his location, he walked the mare onto the rutted trail behind them. It appeared that they had no concern for watching their back trail since he followed for a good eighty yards before making his presence known.

"Hello, the wagon."

Heads spun in his direction and one man scrambled to locate his gun.

"I am a friend. Do not shoot me. See, my hands are empty, I bear no ill will." The first two wagons trundled forward unaware of the rider that had joined the procession.

Anton urged his horse forward until he came alongside. "I am riding from the Upper Agency to warn settlers of the Indian danger."

The man had found his weapon, yet Anton saw he held it pointed upward in a non-threatening manner. Turning forward, he yelled to the wagon in front, "Rufus, hold up there."

Rufus turned and looked to the third wagon.

"Hold up, Rufus. We got us another that wants to join the party."

Rufus turned to the front wagon, cupped his hand and brought it alongside his mouth, "Jim Edward . . . hold it up."

The front wagon continued forward. The chatter from those riding was incessant, making it impossible to hear anything over the racket they were making.

"Jim Edward . . . hold up! We got a rider here."

With no response from the front wagon, the man named Rufus drew a pistol, pointed it in the air, and pulled the trigger.

With the sound of the shot, all talking ceased in the front wagon as heads spun, and Jim Edward slapped reins on the team's haunches without looking back. The horses dug in and were running at a gallop before Jim Edward turned to see where the shot came from. What he saw were two wagonloads of people waving and apparently yelling for him to stop. He pulled up and waited for the other wagons to catch up.

"What the heck were you shooting at, Rufus? Scared the crap outta me!"

Rufus answered, "With all the yapping going on behind you, it's no wonder you couldn't hear me yell. I figured that'd get your attention."

"Got my attention all right. With a wagonload of folks counting on me, I wasn't taking any chances."

"Sorry. I guess that wasn't the smartest thing to do." Rufus motioned toward Anton. "This fellow wants to ride along with us. I figure it can't do no harm, in fact he could come in handy if we need to defend ourselves."

Jim Edward, the apparent leader of the group, looked Anton up and down. "What's your name, mister?"

"Anton McAllister."

Jim Edward looked skeptical. "Are you that Anton chap that used to hunt for the fort?"

"One and the same."

"Well, by gosh, you're sure enough welcome to ride with us. We'd consider it a privilege to have you in our company. I figure there isn't a better person alive to have as a guide, just to make sure we don't get turned onto the wrong trail . . . are you going all the way to St. Peter?"

"I figured to cover a lot of ground on the way. Yeah, St. Peter's where I'm headed." Anton broke his focus on the man in the wagon to scan the area around them. "Are you familiar with any others that may have homesteads between here and St. Peter?"

"We come down from just north of Acton. That is, them that's in my wagon. Acton's where the whole shebang started. At least that's what we heard. Don't know much about this area. As far as we know, all the other families have cleared out. We're the last."

Anton had tallied the number of adult men in the group. There were ten between the three wagons. He counted eight women and seven young children.

"What's your plan for defending your party?"

"We figured to make it to St. Peter, and fall in with the citizens if we get attacked."

Anton began to understand why he had so little trouble joining the party. "I mean . . . what's your plan in case you run into a band of renegades on the way?"

The man named Jim Edward stared at Anton, and his face drained of color.

"Well . . . now . . . to be honest, we never gave that much thought. We just figured we'd get to the city and find safety there. I can see now, we never planned for protecting ourselves along the way, and that was a big mistake."

Anton hid his anger. Divine intervention had kept the group safe so far. Without some kind of action plan, they would be helpless if they ran into a band of Indians with murder on their minds.

"The whole river valley is awash with blood from settlers trying to make it to the safety of a fort, agency, or large city. This isn't an afternoon picnic." He knew they needed his help if they were to survive. Twenty-six souls now relied upon him to bring them to safety.

"I suggest we drive the wagons about three miles up to a wash I know. I think it best if we pull into it and set about making a plan. There's good cover there, and it'd be a good place to spend the night. In the morning, we can set out. The way I figure it, we're just about due north of New Ulm right now. If we tend to our business we should be able to make St. Peter tomorrow."

The people in all three wagons were silent as they rumbled along the rutted track. For the first time, everyone realized the danger they were facing. There was no more chatter, no more laughing. Anton had struck a nerve.

* * *

ANTON SAT AMONG THE MEN gathered off to one side of the small encampment. He wouldn't let them build a cooking fire, and he set guards at the three points of access to the small clearing. He configured the three wagons to form a triangle, with the open area in the middle serving as their camp. The horses were unhooked and picketed in the areas between the wagons.

"You say this is your third day on the trail? I can't understand how you could've come the distance you've come without running into a single war party. You have to be the luckiest people in the territory."

The men shared looks.

"Are all three wagons from north of Acton?"

Jim Edward answered, "No, just mine. I hooked up with Rufus about noon of the first day. Wasn't until this morning we hooked up with Clarence over there." He pointed to the driver of the third wagon.

The men gave Anton a brief rundown of their individual situations.

Jim Edward was the oldest of the group. He had six grown sons and four near-adult daughters in his wagon. Together the family carried nine rifles. None of the family members had ever shot at a man.

The next largest group was in wagon three. Clarence Mooner had moved from Green Bay with his wife, mother-in-law, and three children, none over the age of twelve, and all girls. They didn't offer an explanation for where the father-in-law was, and Anton didn't ask.

Rufus was the most competent of the three. His age was somewhere between the other two, Anton guessed about forty, and he had served in the U.S. Army under Colonel Leavenworth. When his enlistment was up, he went back to Ohio, picked up his wife and family of four, all boys, and moved them to Minnesota Territory where he set up his farm on the most fertile soil he had ever seen. After three months, his wife's brother came to help him farm the homestead.

"The entire river valley is scattered with corpses of settlers caught unawares." Anton needed them to realize how serious things were.

The men nodded, and Jim Edward said, "Now that you've scared us good and proper, how do we proceed without getting our throats cut?"

"The way it sits right now . . . we're in a dangerous place. I don't know where the bulk of Little Crow's band is, but they're feeling pretty powerful. If we were to be attacked in force, there's not much we can do except hightail it out of here. The only chance we have is to spot them first, and decide to run or fight. Either way, we need to see them before they see us."

"That seems like a pretty tall order if you ask me," Clarence observed.

"It is. It's also vital to our survival." Anton's years on the frontier and the many close calls he'd had honed his decision-making skills. His experience with Kanti the day they'd watched the battle unfold between the Americans and the British had taught him the advantages of splitting a force to flank the enemy. The lesson learned had been used to one extent or another in many battles he had fought since coming to the frontier.

"This is how I see it. I want to see only armed men in the wagons. We have enough rifles to make a respectable showing."

Jim Edward interrupted him, "Are you suggesting the women and children follow on foot? These women and youngsters can't walk more than a mile before tiring."

"I said *see* armed men only. I propose the women and children lie on the wagon bed, invisible to anyone viewing from a distance. I figure armed men should dissuade any small bands we come across."

"What happens if we run into a larger group, say twenty or thirty?"

"We should be able to handle twenty or thirty. I count ten adult men capable of firing a rifle, plus eight grown women."

Anton turned to Jim Edward. "You've got four grown daughters. Do you suppose they could tuck their hair up under their hats, put on some shirts and trousers, and pass as men?"

Jim Edward understood immediately and gave a satisfied chuckle. "They're mostly tomboys anyhow. They're going to love this."

"Can all the women handle a team?"

All three husbands nodded in unison.

Anton continued, "I think it's best if we split them between wagons to give the impression of a lot of firepower. Dress them all up to look like men. Two wagons are going to be driven by women, the third will be driven by you, Jim Edward." Anton nodded in the older man's direction.

"We put three in the front wagon, a woman driving, three in the trailing wagon, including the driver, and Jim Edward driving the middle wagon with the children plus one woman dressed as a man."

"How many weapons do we have?"

Jim Edward spoke first, "My wagon's got nine rifles and two of my boys have pistols."

Anton looked toward Clarence.

"I've just got the one rifle, and the wife has a pistol for personal protection."

"That's thirteen firearms, how about you, Rufus, how many in your party?"

"I got just one . . . just one legal that is. The army kinda gave me another one when I left. They just don't know it. Then, of course," he jerked his thumb toward his brother-in-law, "Carvell here has a rifle too."

Jim Edward and Clarence exchanged looks.

"Okay! Between all of you, there are sixteen weapons, and thirteen of them are rifles. Rufus, I figure since you've been in the army you can shoot straight?"

"Straight as anything."

Anton questioned each man as to their shooting skills and was pleasantly surprised to learn they each considered themselves to be good shots. Jim Edward went as far as to say his whole family were expert marksmen. "I made them practice every day."

"We're going to single hitch all three wagons, which will free up three horses. That's three riders besides me to scout ahead for trouble. We take it slow and easy. You other men are going to walk with the wagons just in case the scouts miss something. At the first sound of trouble I want you to head to cover and shoot while you move from one place to the next."

The men exuded a confidence that had been lacking just a short time ago.

"You men know which of the women are the best shots. They're going to be firing from the wagons, and with any luck you'll catch the attackers in a cross fire."

* * *

WITH DAWN CAME THE RAIN, a slow, steady drizzle that dampened the sound of the wagons rolling through the mud. The four men on horseback rode about a half-mile ahead of the wagons, ranging left and right, looking for anything unusual. Anton took the lead, and was ahead of the others. Upon clearing a rise, he saw smoke coming from the edge of a lake. He looked around him for sign of the other three scouts. He saw no trace, which was no surprise since they were ranging behind, and up to a quarter mile each side of the wagon road.

Suspecting the smoke to be from a cabin lit up by a war party, he urged the mare forward at a gallop, drawing up well out of rifle range to survey the situation. He had ridden on the north side of the wagon road so he could remain in the cover provided by the swampy ground that ran all the way to the lake just west of the cabin. He could smell the pungent odor of burning pine, but the smoke had dissipated substantially since he first saw it.

Tying the mare on the edge of a thicket, he grabbed his rifle from its scabbard, removed his tomahawk from a saddlebag, stuffed the handle through the belt at his waist, and carefully approached the source of the smoke. He heard no shooting. In fact, the drizzle and wetness of the foliage dampened all sound, which leant an eerie presence to the moment.

The building came into full view as he stepped free of the swamp.

Anton could hardly believe his eyes. Instead of a small settler's cabin of the type common on the frontier, he saw a building large enough to hold two or three normal-sized cabins. It appeared to be well built with heavy shutters with shooting ports cut into each.

The smoke he saw from a distance had come from the south side of the dwelling where a man and woman were throwing brush on a large pile of hot coals. The leaved branches sat a moment on the smoking remnants before bursting into flame, sending sparks into the air. The area around the building had been cleared of trees and brush.

"Hello . . . hello . . . I am a friend!" Anton raised his arms, holding his rifle above his head as he approached the couple.

The man dropped the ax he was holding and picked up a shotgun from the ground. Stepping in front of the woman, he leveled the barrel at Anton.

"State your purpose, mister."

"I mean no harm. I'm scouting for a party heading for St. Peter. They're two or three miles back."

"You riding alone?" The muzzle remained pointed at Anton.

"There are three others scouting for three wagons full of settlers came down from the north. They figured St. Peter would offer protection . . . you mind if I put my arms down? This rifle's getting heavy."

The man approached as he spoke.

"I guess it's all right, but I'd rest a lot easier if you were to lay that thing on the ground."

"No problem." Anton slowly lowered the rifle and carefully laid it at his feet.

"What's your name?"

"Anton McAllister. I've been riding from the Upper Agency at Yellow Medicine to warn settlers and help those in need as best I can."

"You said there's three wagons. How many in the wagons?"

"We got . . ." Anton paused and counted on his fingers. "I figure there's twenty-five living souls all totaled."

The man had finally lowered the shotgun. "It's still a far piece from here to St. Peter, and there's killing going on dang near all the way to St. Paul."

The woman stepped alongside the man. Anton figured her to be his wife. She turned to face the man with the shotgun.

"Alfred, I'll bet we can accommodate them strangers. It'd give them Indians pause before attacking that many in a single building like ours."

The man named Alfred answered, "Yeah, it would, at that. Mister . . . go ahead and pick up your gun if it'll make you feel more at ease."

Anton gratefully retrieved his rifle.

"You've got the biggest place I've ever seen that isn't in Mankato or St. Peter. Seems like it's more than the two of you need."

"Excuse me, Mr. McAllister, this here's my wife, Greta. My name's Alfred Maas, and what we got here is the beginning of a town, at least that's what we'd like to think. What you see is the beginning of a place we're going to call Maasville, right on the shore of this here water they call Titloe Lake. This roadhouse is the start."

The woman named Greta became alarmed and pointed toward the wagon road that passed a few hundred yards to the south, where three riders were approaching.

Anton turned his attention to where she pointed.

"Not to worry. Those are the three riding with me ahead of the main party."

* * *

THE WAGONS WERE STRUNG OUT in a line from the building to the lake, and the horses were tethered to a picket line running parallel to the wagons. Inside, the unlikely gathering discussed the strategy for defending the building. As they planned their defense, Anton began to think more and more that they had come together through providence.

The presence of Rufus and his background in the army, although impulsive and quick to act, gave Anton confidence in the group's chances. Jim Edward brought rifles and the equivalent of ten fighting men. His daughters were competent beyond many men Anton had met. An added bonus was their skill at shooting. Clarence and his brother-in-law were young enough to take orders, pliable and strong, willing to give their lives to save the four daughters. Finally, Alfred Maas was a born leader, with a sharp mind and with clear intentions for his life.

All in all, they were a substantial group to be reckoned with by anyone who was looking for trouble.

Anton spent the night in the most comfortable setting he had seen since the whole thing started, and with a clear mind, slept like a baby. The next morning he rose at dawn, saddled the mare, said his good-byes, and was on his way back upriver, looking for others that may need his help.

* * *

August 26, 1862

TATEMINA RODE HARD TOWARD the Upper Agency, anxious to reunite with his friends, Anton and Four Wings. Being stuck in the Bennett place for the past four days had been driving him crazy. Not knowing if the Mdewakanton had attacked that far upriver was the worst.

He reached the agency just after noon on the twenty-sixth, only to learn that the two he sought had gone to warn the settlers scattered across the area from St. Peter to Lake Traverse. He was told that Anton had headed downriver, while Four Wings went upriver, both intending to range some distance from the river itself.

Doctor Williamson and John Other Day seemed to have things in control at the agency after moving many whites to secluded places where they would be safe from marauders.

Tatemina had only to decide which way to go, and like a great majority of his decisions, it was made immediately. He mounted and headed upriver. Surely, Anton would be harder to kill than the son. Yes, it was the son he would seek out and protect.

On the twenty-seventh, Colonel Sibley was finally on the move. Troopers sent ahead from the main force arrived at Fort Ridgely and the siege was broken.

* * *

Points west
August 29, 1862

FOUR WINGS TRAVELED WITH A HEAVY HEART. It was five days since he and Anton rode in separate directions to warn settlers of the coming storm. Working a zigzag pattern in an attempt to warn as many white settlements and cabins as possible, he worked his way west, encountering bodies along the way. Most cabins he came across were already burned, families butchered and left to lie where they died. He had encountered seven or eight wagons at different places, all were filled with women and children, and all heading downriver directly into the maelstrom. Were it not for his advice to go another direction, there would have been a significantly higher number of deaths. With each wagon, he inquired about settlements and locations of white men's houses, and if they had knowledge of the problems with the Sioux. Their answers determined the direction he would travel.

At the rate he was going, he figured it would take two more days to reach the mission at Lac qui Parle. Although deserted in 1854, there were still buildings intact, and he knew that many whites had been taken there.

* * *

TATEMINA WAS CLOSING IN ON HIS FRIEND. Encountering some of the same wagons and talking to those people, he got a rough idea of Four Wings's general plan to cover as much ground as possible. Rather than taking the circuitous route chosen by his young friend, he would ride a more or less straight line, which he had been doing for the past few hours.

He was now on a stretch of open prairie he knew continued for the next twenty miles or so before yielding to the outcroppings and wooded terrain of the Chippewa River. The day was bright and the heat from the blazing sun had the effect of lulling him into a drowsy introspection with thoughts about his past, and the circumstance that now controlled his future.

Tatemina's reverie was broken when he realized how far he had come. In the distance were knolls and depressions marking the edge of the Chippewa River. It was time to pay attention and concentrate on the task at hand.

As he approached the changing landscape, he realized he was much farther north than intended. What lay ahead was not the Chippewa, but a smaller river that flowed into the larger Chippewa, itself working its way into the Minnesota. He had allowed himself to drift northward during his reflections, to the extent that he was in unfamiliar surroundings. Knowing the river he sought lay to his left, he reined his horse in that direction, electing to stay on open ground where he would see anyone approaching from a long distance. Urging more speed from the mare, he brought her to a canter.

After riding for about a half-hour, he could hear the pop of gunfire in the distance. Heels to her side, the mare increased to an easy gallop while Tatemina made mental notes of topographical changes and landmarks unique to the area. There was no telling what he may ride into, and he wanted to know as much about the lay of the land as possible.

He was entering rolling country, typical of that bordering most rivers, and he was getting close to the shooting, which had increased in intensity. Topping a knoll, he reined in and backed toward where he had come, disappearing from view of those below.

Dismounting, he tied the reins to a bush and crawled to where he could see what was happening. Below was an isolated log cabin built close to a stand of mixed hardwoods. It was large by frontier standards and looked to be well suited to withstand the harsh winters of Minnesota. The back wall stood an easy ten feet tall with a roof that sloped evenly toward the front of the building, extending a good five feet past the front wall. The result was a covered porch with floorboards that appeared to be even with those of the interior. Centered on one sidewall, a stone chimney climbed past roof level. A window on each side flanked a centered door and there were windows in each of the other walls, and shooting ports cut to allow shot coverage to any part of the woods.

Among the trees, by the telltale powder smoke accompanying each discharge, he could discern several places where muskets were being fired. They seemed to be fairly evenly spaced along the tree line.

I wonder how many people are in the cabin. Looks like a dozen or more in the woods. Tatemina watched for quite some time, studying the positions of each man in the woods, the closest about fifty yards from the cabin. He began to think there were no more than seven or eight.

Unsure of whether the shooters were Sioux or renegade Chippewa, he decided it didn't really matter. He was committed to saving those inside the cabin. Things being what they were, he figured stealth was the only way to do what needed doing. He left his rifle with the mare Riggs had provided.

Moving with speed and staying behind the rise, he worked his way to a depression heavy with wild grasses that would provide cover all the way to the woods. Inside of a minute, he was twenty yards in and studying the lay of the land. With sporadic shots being fired from the tree line, he tried to get a better feel for how many attackers there were, and where they were located.

The edge of the open field behind the cabin became thick with underbrush and heavy bushes where it met the trees. Tatemina now realized why the shooters were spread out over a wide area. Staying behind the larger trees for protection, they had to find an open line of fire to the cabin, and open sight lines were infrequent due to the heavy bushes. Hunkering down and moving in a near crawl, he approached a shooter whose attention was fixed on the cabin. Coming from behind, and covering the final ten feet in a dead run, it was easy to dispatch the warrior without a sound.

Turning the Indian on his back, he was stunned by what he saw. The attacker was neither Sioux nor Chippewa; instead, he found himself looking at the body of a Winnebago brave.

He took no time to analyze the meaning of this before moving off to dispatch the next closest, which he did without incident. In like manner, he was able to kill seven of those firing at the cabin without alerting the others. Creeping deeper into the woods, he sat upon a log to ponder his next move and realized the shooting had stopped. He knew there was at least one more warrior to deal with, and with only a rough idea of his position, he slid to the ground to wait for him to make his location known.

He squatted, facing away from the field, leaning his back against a large oak tree. In his right hand, he held his tomahawk, in his left, the knife. He had no idea how long it had been since entering the woods. His mouth was dry as cotton, and his thighs burned from extended periods of creeping through the trees and scattered bushes in a low crouch. His breathing was deep, filling his lungs and expanding his chest, and he had a deep appreciation for the many hours he had spent running during his lifetime.

His heart rate had returned to normal and he was considering his next move when he heard the dry branch snap. Aware of the presence of another, he remained motionless as his senses climbed to a new level of alertness. Straining to hear any unnatural sound, he discerned the occasional footfall of one moving with great stealth. Keeping the oak tree between them, he slowly stood.

At the same moment that Tatemina stepped from behind the tree, the Winnebago brave turned in his direction. As their eyes made contact, each responded by charging forward to meet the challenge of the other. The Winnebago thrust his rifle butt, intending to catch

Tatemina in the head. A quick movement by the Dakota resulted in a jarring blow to his right shoulder. Spinning to lessen the impact, he swung with his tomahawk at the passing body, but feeling no contact, knew he'd missed the mark.

The Winnebago threw his rifle to the side and unsheathed his knife. The knife was his weapon of choice in close combat and this Dakota would feel the steel of his blade. Tatemina dropped the tomahawk, moving his knife to his right hand.

Again, they charged each other, coming together in a deadly embrace, each with a firm hold on the other's knife wrist. The Winnebago struck out with his leg, attempting to knock Tatemina off balance, with no success.

To counter the leg kick, Tatemina moved in the direction of his opponent's momentum, effectively using the Winnebago's weight to gain the advantage. Surprised by the move, the Indian's grip lessened and Tatemina was able to jerk his knife hand free, slashing upward as the two of them tumbled to the ground.

Then it was over. This was the last of those firing from the trees and with that realization, Tatemina felt something he had never felt before. His hands began to shake uncontrollably. Lowering himself to the ground, he sat next to the slowly spreading red blanket of the Winnebago's blood saturating the earth.

He wasn't sure how long he sat there waiting for the shaking to stop. Eventually, he arose and walked to the edge of the trees. In front of him, where the bushes were the heaviest, lay the body of another warrior. Approaching with caution, he made a cursory inspection of the body and concluded this one had died from multiple knife wounds. Without a full understanding, he crawled to the front edge of the heavy bushes.

"Hello the cabin." He yelled in a loud voice, getting no reply.

"Hello the cabin. I am a friend. These Indians are dead."

"Who are you, white or red?" The voice was that of a man and seemed to project from a shooting slot in the cabin wall.

"I am a friend. I am Dakota, but I am your friend. My name is Round Wind. If you have been to the Upper Agency, you may know me. I am a friend of Doctor Williamson and Reverend Riggs."

There was only silence and Tatemina was about to hail the cabin again, when a man appeared at the corner of the building.

"Come ahead. Let me see you."

Doing as he was told, he arose and walked through the bushes until fully exposed on the open ground.

"Come ahead. Please come ahead. There is someone here who knows you."

"I will gather my horse and be there straightaway."

"You might want to come directly. Your friend is badly hurt. I will send my daughter for your horse." Turning toward the front of the cabin, he spoke to someone inside, "Helen, would you please get the man's horse. He will point the way."

His teenage daughter appeared and Tatemina pointed to where the horse was tied. "I laid a rifle by the bush. Kindly bring that back as well."

Walking through the front door, he found the inside to be surprisingly bright. The sun was low in the western sky, striking the front of the cabin and streaming through the open door and adjacent windows.

In the corner, near the fireplace hearth, he saw a body.

"There . . . that man said he knows you." The settler pointed to the prostrate figure.

Tatemina was looking at the back of someone obviously in a bad way. Crossing the floor, he knelt and gently took the man by the shoulder and rolled him so he could see his face. His heart stopped and he could not draw a breath. The man was Four Wings, and he was unconscious.

Chapter Seventeen

Fort Ridgely

August 31, 1862

SINCE HIS ARRIVAL, COLONEL SIBLEY'S men had been doing cleanup and repair of the buildings. Some among his men thought him to be a poor leader, slow to react and timid in the dispatch of his duties once he reached a decision. Rather than pursue the Indians, Sibley drilled the militia and had his men participate in various training exercises.

Having seen the dead on his trek from the Upper Agency to Fort Ridgely, he organized a burial party of about two hundred fifty men with infantry, horsemen, and wagons to locate and bury the dead at the Lower Sioux Agency, Redwood Ferry, and the vicinity.

"The last thing we need is an epidemic of cholera. Major, I want you to bury every body you come across in this whole area." Sibley was addressing Major Joseph R. Brown. "Keep your eyes peeled for hostiles, and destroy any that you encounter."

* * *

BROWN LED HIS PARTY TOWARD the Redwood Ferry, where Captain Marsh had been ambushed on the eighteenth. Along the way, they came across and buried sixteen bodies. Upon reaching the ferry, Major Brown took a detachment of cavalry to the south side of the river, while Captain Hiram P. Grant and his infantry stayed on the north side. They began searching for bodies in their assigned areas, meeting up at a place called Birch Coulee a few hours later. Between the two detachments, they had buried a total of fifty-four bodies.

"See any sign of Indians on your side?" Major Brown asked. If the answer was yes, they would find a more defensible position for their camp.

Grant answered without hesitation, "No sign anybody's been there since they hit the fort. I'll bet there isn't an Indian within fifty miles. Funny how they turn tail when somebody can put up a fight."

"You men there!" Brown got the attention of half a dozen of his greenest militiamen. "Get over there," he pointed to the line of wagons, "and get some tents. Check with the quartermaster and start setting up camp. This is where we'll spend the night."

They formed a large U with the wagons, and picketed the horses at the open end.

Assigning four guards per station, he situated them around the circumference of the camp and considered the party secure.

* * *

LITTLE CROW WAS LEADING about a hundred warriors upriver from New Ulm, while one of his war chiefs, Gray Bird, was coming downriver with three times as many fighters.

Running Fox, advance scout for Gray Bird's unit, rode to report movement of white soldiers to his chief.

"Many soldiers came up the north side of the river. They are burying the dead, so there are wagons and maybe one or two hundred men. I watched them on the other side of the river. They will camp at Birch Coulee tonight."

"Did anyone see you?"

"I was invisible. They did not see me."

Gray Bird, knowing that Little Crow was coming in their direction, instructed the scout to ride and inform him of the soldier's camp. "Tell the Crow I will meet him before he reaches the white man's camp at Birch Coulee."

The two men met well after sundown and laid their plan for the following day. By dawn at Birch Coulee, over four hundred Sioux flanked the soldiers on three sides.

* * *

"HEY, THERE . . . JAKE, you better be awake over there! We're due for replacement any time now."

"Yeah, I'm awake, you worthless horse apple. Whatta ya think, I've been sleepin'?"

The two troopers had been on watch since three in the morning and Jake had a reputation for having trouble keeping his eyes open. Truth told, he was scared to death, and sleep was the last thing on his mind. They were both part of the Minnesota volunteers, and right about now they wished they were at home.

"I know what you mean, man. I'm as jumpy as a long-tailed cat in a room full of rocking chairs. This just ain't natural." Tom Peterson looked in the direction of trooper Jake Hathaway, whose attention was focused on something thirty yards distant.

"What's that? Who's there? Tom, take a look here." Nerves were worn to a frazzle, and Jake's were no exception. Thinking he saw an Indian, he raised his rifle and fired.

The shot served as a clarion to action for Little Crow's men to open fire from all sides. After the first moments of withering gunfire, ninety horses lay dead. The troopers fought back, however, the ill-placed camp was set in a hard to defend location. Without horses they were unable to do much except lie on the ground using the bodies for cover, and return fire. Fear of the big artillery cannons kept the Indians from overrunning the camp, so once again, a siege was underway.

At Fort Ridgely, sixteen miles downriver, they heard the gunfire. Colonel Sibley ordered a detachment to rescue the troopers.

"Colonel McPhail, you take two hundred men and relieve Brown and his men. If it looks like that ain't enough men, send word back and I'll lead a party out myself."

McPhail left the fort with two hundred forty-nine men, expecting the worst. Even before reaching Birch Coulee, he thought the Indians had him surrounded, so he sent word back, and Sibley formed a detachment that included an artillery brigade and moved toward the coulee.

Upon reaching the battle, the artillery opened up and forced the Indians to retreat from their positions. After nearly thirty hours, the siege was broken. The cost was high. Ninety horses and thirteen soldiers were dead, forty-seven men were severely wounded, and many others suffered lesser wounds.

It was the worst defeat suffered by the U.S. Army during the Dakota War of 1862.

* * *

Settler's cabin, Chippewa River
September 9, 1862

WHILE FOUR WINGS LAY NEAR THE HEARTH, his fever raged. Every few hours his wound was checked and clean dressings were applied. Tatemina went to the river just past the trees and filled two buckets with fresh water, poured them in the holding tank in the corner, and made another trip before they all settled in for the night. The family didn't want to lose the goats, so they shared the cabin.

It was a fitful night for Tatemina, with goats nudging his body awake and constant worry about Four Wings, he was awake more than he was asleep. He found himself wondering where Anton was at that moment, and then he pushed the thought to the back of his mind.

He welcomed the dawn as one would a lover. Mrs. Hayes was up and had coffee on the stove. Tatemina enjoyed having someone to talk to even if they did have to talk in hushed tones.

The frontier family owed much to Tatemina, for they had been almost out of ammunition and coming to terms with their deaths when he'd hailed from the wood line. They were equally indebted to the man who lay dying in their cabin. In fact, had it not been for Four Wings, they would all have been dead long before Tatemina came to the rescue.

While Tatemina prepared and applied a poultice for the wound in Four Wings side, he learned about the family he had saved.

He believed they had very few visitors because they seemed compelled to talk non-stop. Charles and Anna Hayes, along with daughter

Helen, had been living there for the past four years, so were well settled in. They had planted a small plot on the south side of the cabin where they grew vegetables, and not much more. They did have a couple of goats they used for milk. Charles had intended to bring home a goat buck to build a herd to use for fresh meat while selling the occasional animal. That was before the trouble with the Indians.

Charles was speaking to Tatemina, "We heard there was trouble all along the river valley. We were asked to go with others to Fort Ridgely, but we decided to ride it out here."

"Well, at least you're still alive. There's plenty that didn't make it to the fort."

"Don't know what happened. We've enjoyed the company of Sioux since we've been here. Generous, good people. Always our friends."

"Have you ever been touched by the Chippewa?"

"A few . . . we know the band of Hole in the Day, and they're good Indians too. We got the same treatment from them as we did from the Sioux."

Tatemina looked puzzled. "Those braves I killed in the trees yonder were Winnebago. You got any idea what they were doing this far north?"

Charles's eyes sparked. "There's been rumors that a band of renegade Winnebago were in the area for the past six or seven months. Nobody's been hurt. Some livestock's come up missing, and our dairy cow was killed about two months ago. Some have been saying it's Winnebago that's to blame."

"How'd Four Wings get cut up so bad?"

Anna answered. "I've never seen such a thing. They were right on us, no more'n twenty yards out, when this young man galloped into the fray whooping and hollering something fierce. He was swinging his tomahawk like it was a saber. Must a made them others think the bloody devil himself was riding in. They all turned and ran for the woods."

Anna Hayes spoke in a shaky voice filled with emotion. "This young man slid off his horse and stood alone out there in the open while the first to reach the woods began firing at him." Her voice broke and she paused befpre continuing. "I've never seen such bravery. He turned toward the cabin, and then he was struck by a bullet and went down. The last of the savages, not yet into the woods, ran at him to finish him off and they had a terrible struggle."

Charles broke in, "I fired into the woods to keep the others at bay while the fight commenced out there in the open. Next I knew, it ended and the other ran to the woods while your friend staggered to the cabin and we let him in."

"That explains the dead Indian I found in the heavy bushes just this side of the tree line. He must have died from injuries he got during his tangle with Four Wings. How long were you under attack before I came along?"

"It started at sunrise. Helen was dumping the slop bucket and saw them outlined on the hill east of the house. That gave us a good head start to get ready. They came at us fast, but we've got three rifles and all of us were shooting. Didn't hit a darn thing, but neither did they. Drove them into the trees, yonder." He jerked his thumb toward the woods.

"How long before Four Wings came along?"

"We must have been shooting darn near steady for almost a half hour. That's when they decided they was going to take us, and that's the time when your friend rode in making enough noise to wake the dead." Charles paused, shook his head as if in disbelief, then continued, "If he hadn't come along we'd all have been dead within an hour. All that shooting used up most of our powder and almost all of our shot."

"They kept pestering us with careful shots. None got through. I'd say we had been here a good ten, eleven hours since your friend got hurt and you came along."

"That explains why he's got such a fever. Nobody would last long with the beating he took. The bullet must have ripped open his side and the fight tore it even more. There's nothing we can do except wait for what will be." Tatemina spoke with resigned helplessness.

Four Wings slipped in and out of consciousness for the next three days while they waited for the fever to break. There was nothing that could be done, other than what had already been done.

On the fourth day, everyone's hearts beat a little faster when a group of Indians approached the cabin.

"Everyone stay inside, and make sure nobody sticks the barrel of a rifle out any opening. They look like Sisseton, so I'll go out and talk. If they shoot me, open fire and take every one of them you can."

As the Sisseton charged up to the cabin, Tatemina stepped through the door closing it behind him. No one made a threatening move, as if they were honoring some native protocol.

From inside the cabin, they watched with a guarded eye. There were fourteen Sisseton braves. Tatemina talked, gesturing with his arms while the lead man in the party sat his pony in a relaxed manner. They talked for a surprisingly short time before they reined to the side and rode off. Tatemina came back inside.

"What was all that about?" Charles was respectful yet forceful.

"That . . . was about dodging a bullet. Luckily, I knew the lead man in that party. They figured to take everything of value, burn your place to the ground, and set you loose. Seems that particular group was against killing the whites. He said they had a big argument before coming out, over killing or not killing." Tatemina strode to the stove and poured his cup full, turned to the others, and lifted his cup in a salute before sipping the hot coffee.

"Let's hope for two things: Four Wings' recovery and no more war parties."

* * *

IT TOOK THIRTY-SEVEN HOURS for the fever to break, and another week or so before the young Dakota could sit up. During that time, four war parties stopped at the cabin. Tatemina's presence and that of the very ill Four Wings inside the dwelling was sufficient to convince them to go elsewhere for their mischief.

Four Wings's horse had run for parts unknown during the fight with the Winnebago, so they were a horse shy when it came time to leave the cabin. On September 19, with a travois tied to Tatemina's borrowed mare, and two plow horses owned by the Hayes family, they started out for the Lac qui Parle Mission. Although abandoned in 1854, buildings still stood at the mission site, and it was as good a place as any to hide out or make a stand, whichever it would be.

It took them two days of slow travel before they got to the mission. Once there, they were heartened by what they found. Greeting them was Doctor Williamson, and just inside were Star Woman and Anton.

Anton had crossed the river on his way back after leading the settlers to safety, riding well south of the river until he joined the others at the mission.

Over a wringing of hands, tears, and handshakes, friendships were renewed and fresh ones developed. Anton's heart was filled with gladness at seeing Four Wings alive, if not well, and Star Woman flitted here and there like a hummingbird collecting a little of this and a little of that for a poultice, a remedial drink, or blankets for her son.

Anton and Tatemina talked as old friends talk, and Anton told of Star Woman and Four Wings witnessing the attack on the Lower Agency. He told of the battle of Fort Ridgely, and the disaster at Birch Coulee. The whole while Tatemina was speechless, scarcely believing what he heard. He knew it was bad. This was way beyond his imagining.

For the next two weeks, Anton and Tatemina covered the area from Big Stone Lake to Lac qui Parle, gathering settlers, and bringing them to the Lac qui Parle site for protection. The Wahpeton band of Red Iron roamed the perimeter of the old mission, ranging as far as five miles in all directions, turning away all who would do harm to the whites and mixed-bloods gathered there.

Chapter Eighteen

Little Crow's Defeat

ON SEPTEMBER 6, PRESIDENT LINCOLN appointed General John Pope to oversee the war with the Dakota. His immediate concern was to get trained army personnel involved in the campaign.

On the morning of the nineteenth, the fort was awash with soldiers redirected from Civil War duties to Minnesota to assist in solving the Indian problem. Colonel Sibley was in the final phase of organizing sixteen hundred troops for a march intended to draw the Sioux into a battle, in turn ending the conflict. His intention was to meet Little Crow and his warriors on the open plain where his men, with rifled muskets, would have a distinct advantage over the Indians' smooth bores.

They left the fort later than intended, well after daybreak, and Sibley was in a dark mood. This had been his battle, in his state, it was being fought with Indians he felt he knew better than anyone, and he was taking orders from an easterner.

The column stretched nearly four miles from front to back and he rode the whole of it sniping at anyone he took issue with.

"Straighten your cap, trooper! Keep the pace, private."

Then he turned around and did it again, driving morale into the ground.

On the third day out, they came to a place called Lone Tree Lake, and Sibley figured it to be a good place to set camp for the night, rest his men, and then continue the march the following day. In doing so, he was playing right into the hands of Little Crow and over seven hundred warriors.

* * *

Lac qui Parle
September 22

"WE WILL SURELY DRIVE THEM from our land. I have already taken five scalps and had my way with two of their women before killing them. They will leave."

The speaker was Shoonkaska, and his brag was delivered to the three who traveled with him. "It's not good that we have found no horses to steal, only white mans tools and women's things."

The whites knew Shoonkaska as White Dog. Tall, with an athletic build, he turned the heads of many Sioux maidens. Attractive to look upon, it was rumored that more than one white woman had even succumbed to his charm. He was fearless in battle, earning the respect of his brothers in arms as well as those he fought.

Lately, before the fighting, he had fallen to the bottle. With a full load of whiskey in his belly, he became sullen and bad tempered, causing trouble and raising a ruckus wherever he went. Difficult to handle, for the good of all he spent a great deal of his time in the dark hole below the main guard quarters at Fort Ridgely.

He was between stints in the hole when Little Crow led the initial raids on New Ulm and the Lower Agency, and he was in the thick of it, rejoicing in the opportunity to strike back at his antagonists, free to vent his pent up rage.

After the siege of Fort Ridgely, he broke off to roam the river valley, killing every white he came across. It didn't take long for him to find three men with similar temperaments. Between them, they killed a total of twelve settlers. It made no difference if they were men, women, or children—if they were white, they died. One of the three became a close friend of Shoonkaska and proved to be every bit as ruthless. The Indian named Mazasuta actually took gleeful pleasure in dismembering the dead.

They now waited for the wagon they'd seen two miles back. It carried close to a dozen women and children, and a single horseman rode with it.

Like shadows, two warriors edged closer to the wagon road while Shoonkaska and the other man set themselves seventy yards farther on in case the wagon was to break through the first two.

They were seven and a half miles north of the old mission where the road clung to the narrow strip of land running between the river and a thirty-foot rock wall, a perfect place for opportunists to use it to their advantage.

* * *

"Coming up to the place now." Anton spoke in a hushed tone.

Within the wagon, Tatemina pulled back the hammer on his rifle, ready for whatever this narrow passage had to offer. He sat on his knees behind the woman handling the horses, making him as inconspicuous as possible.

The two had spent the past twelve hours riding north with an empty wagon and returning with it full of families unable to seek protection on their own. Husbands and older sons had unwisely left to "kill redskins," leaving their families vulnerable, never expecting the fighting to escalate to current levels. In many cases, husbands and sons were already dead.

This was the wagon's third trip, and Anton and Tatemina knew the dangers of the area they were about to enter.

Riding slightly ahead and on the side of the road bordering the river, Anton figured to use his tomahawk in what would be a close-quarter fight if anyone jumped them. There was a stand of three cottonwoods and several low-growing willows ahead that provided the opportune place for such an act.

* * *

Mazasuta watched the man on the horse close the gap between them, and as always happened before he took another's life, his body began to tremble. It was as though every nerve ending was snapping and popping to life, sending electricity coursing through his veins. He found the sensation both pleasing and comforting, knowing he would soon enter a bat-tle to the death. Always victorious, he never considered being defeated. Looking over his shoulder to his mate and receiving the nod that signaled all was well, he returned his attention to the horseman.

Anton sensed the presence of another body, smelled the odor of death exuded by Mazasuta. As the Indian was gathering himself, Anton charged his mare forward into the opening between the cot-tonwoods catching the renegade flat-footed, splitting his head open with a single sweep from his tomahawk.

As his mate sprung from his concealed position, he was caught mid-air by the shot from Tatemina, the bullet entering the armpit below his raised right arm, ripping through the heart before exiting the far side of his body. He was dead before he hit the ground.

With the shot, Shoonkaska stepped onto the road to see what was happening, only to feel the sting and hear the residual sound left by the bullet that whizzed past his ear, followed by the rifle report sev-enty yards away.

Without thinking, he darted for cover only to realize that he had moved to the side of the road bordering the river. With the horse-man charging, he had no choice but to dive into the swift flowing water. His accomplice was already mounted and riding the opposite direction as though the devil was closing in.

Anton, unsure of where the man in the road had gone, reined his horse to a stop and scanned the water's surface.

He thought, *Nothing in sight except a bundle of roots floating to-ward the center.*

The wagon caught up with him.

"See him, Anton?"

"No . . . I wonder if you hit him. Could be the current got a hold on him and is keeping him under."

"Could be. I figure we better not hang here too long. Can never tell who else might happen along and finish what these four started."

Shoonkaska held tight to the cluster of roots, submerged, his face barely out of the water, and rode the current out of harm's way wondering what went wrong.

* * *

September 23
Sibley's Camp, Lone Tree Lake

"HEY, DAVY! C'MON, GET UP. What say we ride to the agency and dig us a few potatoes? It's just a little bit ahead."

"Are you crazy, Harry? Sibley would have our hides." Davy Brower was wide-awake, anxious for the coming day and not the least bit interested in Harry's scheme.

"Not if he don't know nothin' about it. C'mon, we can be back before the rest of the camp is even awake." Harry Crawford persisted. At nineteen, Harry was supposed to know better. He'd always been a rebel, fighting authority, and he had a way of drawing others into his schemes.

Davy answered, "That there's a pretty foolhardy plan if you ask me. I know it's only a couple of miles, and I know there ain't no Indians around, but Colonel Sibley is still here, and I don't figure to get on his bad side."

Harry persisted, "Damn, Davy. Sibley's sound asleep and won't be awake for another two hours. That gives us plenty of time to dig a few and get back here."

"Well now, fresh potatoes would taste mighty good at that. I guess there's no harm if we don't get caught."

"There's the Davy I know. Let's just ride bareback. We don't need to saddle up, just grab the bridle and reins and we're gone."

Two minutes later, they were leading their horses out of camp, avoiding the sentries Sibley had posted. When they figured they were far enough away so they couldn't be heard, they swung onto the backs of their mounts and headed toward the agency.

* * *

A QUARTER MILE AWAY, LITTLE CROW was positioning his men. Knowing that Sibley would move in a column, his plan was to allow them to string out, making it difficult to stage an adequate defense against warriors attacking the column from both sides. Knowing he was outnumbered, his strategy was to hit them hard and take the artillery out of play, and then fire from protected positions until they killed every single soldier.

From the moment Sibley left Fort Ridgely, the Sioux knew the strength of his party, and Little Crow knew it would take every warrior he could muster. Sending word upriver to where a total of two hundred sixty-nine white captives were being held under guard, he ordered most of his men with that detail to join him in the upcoming battle, leaving far fewer to guard the prisoners. The women and children were his ace cards. If things went badly he would use them as bargaining chips.

* * *

LITTLE CROW HAD DIVIDED HIS MEN into three units. One was across the road in the timber along the deep Yellow Medicine River gorge. Another unit was concealed in a line along the east side of the road. The third was hidden in the ravine opposite Sibley's right flank.

* * *

MANIPI CROUCHED NEAR HIS BROTHER.

"Two ride this way. They are whites without shirts, and their horses are without saddles. We must let them pass."

The two warriors were part of a force of twenty-five, strategically placed to close off any possibility of retreat after the action started. They had been told the column would move shortly after dawn.

Harry Crawford and Davy Brower now had their horses at a gallop, running off the road to lessen the sound of their hooves. Unknown to them, they had already passed within feet of half a dozen warriors concealed along the way.

Suddenly Davy's horse shied, nearly throwing him to the ground. An excellent horseman, he was able to maintain his position atop his mount. He saw the Indian in time to avoid a lunge, although the knife made a deep cut to his horse's flank.

"Harry! Indians!" Pulling hard on the reins, he pivoted his gelding. Davy gave a strong kick to the sides and his mount gathered himself and leaped upon the road heading back in the direction of the camp. Glancing toward Harry, Davy saw that three braves were grabbing at him while another reached for the rein.

"Indians! Defend yourselves! Indians! Here!"

The sentries on watch heard the voice, but the words didn't register. Convinced that there were no Indians within miles of the camp, their minds did not latch onto the warning screams. Then, two near simultaneous gunshots brought realization to the front and silenced the screaming.

"Everyone up! We're under attack. Everyone! Indians!"

Men scrambled to reach their weapons. Allowed to keep them close at night rather than stacking them together in centralized locations, they quickly made ready to defend the camp.

Little Crow, further along the road and hearing the shots, knew his careful planning had gone awry. Now he must react.

Riding at top speed, he alerted his warriors to the fact that they had been discovered. Soon the Army would be on them and they would have no choice except to fight in the manner they were accustomed to—ambush, retreat, ambush, retreat.

* * *

Prisoner holding area
Chippewa River

RED IRON AND THE MAJORITY of his band, along with the friendlies—Indians friendly toward the whites—from Wabasha's and John Other Day's bands, among others, made several attempts to entice Little Crow's warriors to give up the prisoners. They were ignored. After Little Crow massed his forces for the confrontation near the Yellow Medicine, things changed.

With a force greatly outnumbering those guarding the prisoners, the captives were released and moved to the deserted Lac qui

Parle Mission where a proper defense from marauding Sioux could be undertaken.

Many of the captives were taken during the first week of the war. They were dirty, near starvation, and some were sick with fever. While the men guarded them night and day, the women nursed the sick as best they could and furnished clean clothing to the women and children with the greatest needs. All used the pump to draw water and bathe their bodies.

It had been two weeks since Four Wings had been injured and he was now able to get up and walk. Star Woman did an adequate job stitching his wound closed, and her constant attention to keeping it clean allowed it to heal without any sign of infection. With the worst behind her, she could now spend her time ministering to the new arrivals, often walking among them dressing wounds or tending to the small children.

For his part, Four Wings was chomping at the bit to get back into action. He'd never before been laid up for such a long time, and he hated it.

Making him even more uncomfortable was the fact that lately, since his near death, something unnerving was finding its way into his mind and he just couldn't shake it. He began to ponder his vision more often than he thought healthy.

I looked below me, into the forest where there were seven crows dipping and swooping among the branches of a great oak. Their powerful wings carried them with ease.

He had been told they represented the seven council fires of the Sioux Nation and the power within those nations.

On the crows there appeared specks of white that revealed themselves as tricksters that pulled the feathers, one by one, from the crows.

As the old man with the turquoise eyes had said, *The specks you witnessed on the backs of the crows were the white men that move to weaken the people. I fear for Oyate, the people. Your vision is one of sadness for the Dakota Nation.*

There was little doubt this trouble with the Mdewakanton that drew in the Sisseton, Wahpeton, and Wahpekute was the start of the demise spoken of by the old man. Since the treaties, things had gotten worse, and this uprising seemed to be the crescendo.

His vision was unfolding before him, and there was nothing he could do to alter it. The old man had described most of it, but the part he hadn't been able to interpret was what bothered Four Wings.

I saw the crows lose their feathers and fall to the earth, where they shrank in size until each became a swarm of grasshoppers that flew to meet me. As they drew near they became three distinct groups, and they joined me in flight. On my right was a group of thirteen, on my left, another group of thirteen, and behind me was a third group of the same number.

Four Wings couldn't get it out of his mind.

* * *

Lone Tree Lake
September 23

COLONEL SIBLEY DASHED FROM HIS TENT and rousted the company bugler, who always slept nearby while in the field.

"Bugler, sound the call to arms, and I want it loud and clear. Stick close to me because things are about to get mighty interesting."

The bugler, Thomas Carlson, scrambled to put on his trousers, slipped into his boots, and grabbed his shirt. He'd never seen Indian combat, though he'd fought the rebels in Kansas before being sent to Minnesota. He knew what a charge was, and he loved the smell of gunpowder. The army was the best thing that ever happened to him.

Throwing his arms in his shirtsleeves, he grabbed his bugle and began to blow as ordered. Filling his lungs, he delivered three consecutive calls, each at perfect pitch and at a volume that surprised even him.

As luck would have it, Sibley, just zipping up after relieving himself, was in the only possible spot to observe a flanking maneuver by the Indians. As he watched, Little Crow raced among his men shouting orders as he rode. Unable to hear what was spoken, it was clear to Sibley through the animated gestures of the Indian and emphatic pointing of the lance he carried that he was deploying a large party into a gorge east of the military encampment.

The Indians, over a hundred of them, ran to the gorge and within moments disappeared from view.

"Marshall! Colonel Marshall!" Where is that idiot?"

The very capable Lieutenant-Colonel William R. Marshall scrambled to Sibley's side.

"Yes, sir! Right here, sir."

"Colonel, I need you to take six companies and an artillery piece. I just saw a whole bunch of Indians run into that ravine over there." He pointed to the east of the camp. "I want you to blast them with artillery and quickly follow with an all-out charge to drive them into the open. At least then we'll have a chance of taking a few out."

Snapping to attention, Marshall executed his best salute, turned on his heel, and at a dead run, yelled for his men to muster. Within five minutes, they were pulling the artillery piece into position to fire on the ravine, and his six companies of troopers were split, advancing left and right of the ravine.

When all were positioned as he felt was right, he stepped to the artillerymen.

"Men, I want two shots, and I want them in quick order. The first, about twenty yards from the end closest. The second, and I want it fast, placed about twenty yards deeper. That ought to get them running. The troopers will charge in and drive them out the other end. If you think you can reach them with exploding shells, have at it when they come out.

At his signal, they fired the first. The colonel must have spent many hours training his men, for they fired the second within thirty seconds.

The men charged the ravine screaming as though they were on fire, discharging their rifles at anything that moved. It was too much for Little Crow's men. The onslaught was just too massive for them to stand their ground, so they turned and ran.

Meanwhile, Little Crow had ordered an attack on the other flank by having his men go around the edge of Lone Tree Lake. It would have likely worked were it not for the fact that Major Robert N. McLaren, in anticipation of the move, took his men around the lake and turned back the Dakota flanking attack.

The battle lasted about two hours before the Indians turned in defeat, retreating upriver.

By the time they'd fled, someone had reached Little Crow and told him that the captives had been released and were now in the control of the friendlies.

It had been a disaster. They had lost and now there would be hell to pay. He considered taking the captives back until realizing he would have to attack his own people since it was they who protected them.

With a broken heart, he gathered his men.

"Today we fought as fools." His disappointment was deep. "Was it not possible to control the start of the battle? Could we have not waited until they were spread along the road?"

His questions were rhetorical, his mood dark.

"The soldiers will follow us. It's time to gather our families and move north and west into Dakota Territory. Some of you may wish to stay here, and if that is the case, you must disperse and live as friendlies. We have killed many whites, and they will not be easy with us. The choice is yours, but me . . . I shall leave this place. Maybe north to Canada. I will not stay here to be killed."

* * *

Lac qui Parle Mission

WORD OF THE HAPPENINGS at Lone Tree Lake reached Red Iron. Joined by Wabasha, Gabriel Renville, the son of Joseph Renville, and others, they were prepared to stand between the captives and those wishing to harm them.

Wabasha, first chief of the Mdewakanton, stood before the others.

"Let us prepare to defend this place." Turning to Red Iron he said, "Send word to your outriders to alert us if they see the army approaching."

"Yes, I will send word." He made a sign to one of his warriors who exited the conference to carry the plan to the outriders. He then turned to Wabasha, "Do you think we must shoot our brothers? I, like you, believe we must change our ways to live in concert with the whites. I will not like shooting my red brother."

Wabasha responded, "Perhaps there will be no need. We have many warriors here. It would be foolish for Little Crow to come against us in this place."

After a short time discussing the defense arrangements, they broke from their conference and began placing their warriors for defense of the mission.

Three hours later a single rider rode onto the mission grounds.

"I come with word from the battle downriver. I must speak to Red Iron."

He was led to the Wahpeton chief.

"Mazasha, I have word of the battle. The soldiers have repelled the attack. Little Crow has been defeated and will go to the upper Dakota Territory with some of his men. The others have divided, some, the worst of them, are moving west toward the Missouri. The others will take the guise of peaceable Indians and intermix with the friendlies."

Red Iron was filled with a jumble of conflicting emotions. While thinking of his people, his heart was lifted with the joy of a battle ended. While thinking of the loss of the youngest of the nation, his heart was filled with sadness. The promise they held for the Dakota Nation was now lost, and it was heartbreaking.

Setting his contemplation aside, his mind returned to the present. After showing gratitude to the warrior for the information, he went in search of Wabasha. They must now determine the next step.

"There are still renegades running throughout the valley. We can't allow the settlers to leave our care. We must find a way to get word to Sibley that the captives are safe in our hands."

"That may prove more difficult than we think. The troopers are bolstered by the defeat of their enemy. They will be filled with confidence and are likely to shoot any Indian they see." Red Iron recognized the potential of the situation. "Nevertheless, we must alert Sibley that we control the safety of the captives. If he can be convinced to come to this place, they will have the protection of the U.S. Army."

The solution proved to be close at hand. One of the captives was a mixed-blood named Joseph Campbell. The same Joseph Campbell who had visited Lawrence Taliaferro in Washington back in June of 1858. His father had been the main translator for Taliaferro, and Sibley and many of the men at Fort Ridgely knew Joseph, so it was decided he would carry the message to the army camp near Lone Tree Lake.

Readily accepting the challenge, Campbell was briefed on the situation, wished a well and safe journey, and sent on his way that very afternoon, reaching the soldier encampment the following morning.

Campbell was escorted to Sibley's tent.

"Colonel, the renegades have disbanded. I have it on good authority that most are leaving the area, however, we have two hundred sixty-nine whites who were captives of Little Crow. We have taken them to the old Lac qui Parle Mission and kept them safe. I am here to ask you to give them safe transport downriver."

Colonel Sibley, full of undeserved pride at what had been accomplished, answered with a direct statement. "I will liberate the captives at my earliest convenience. You may go back and tell your chiefs that I will come."

Sibley gloried in the victory. He left Lone Tree Lake on the twenty-fifth and leisurely marched his troops the short distance to Riggs's deserted Hazelwood Mission where he showcased his soldiers with a dress parade, in no hurry to honor the request of the friendlies holding the captives.

About noon on the second day, he marched his men a short distance from the place where the captives were being held. By that time there were nearly one hundred fifty lodges occupied by Mdewakanton loyal to chiefs Wabasha and others who had been against the outbreak from the beginning. Many had joined the uprising, and now were tired of the killing and running. They decided to mingle with the friendlies to avoid detection and the punishment they feared. Many that had participated in the Lone Tree Lake defeat were among them.

At about two o'clock on the afternoon of September 26, 1862, Colonel Henry Sibley walked through the encampment with great pomp under the accompaniment of beating drums and flying colors.

In his report to General Pope, he wrote of the encounter.

"The Indians and mixed-bloods assembled . . . in considerable numbers, and I proceeded to give them very briefly my views of the late proceedings; my determination that the guilty parties should be pursued and overtaken, if possible, and I made a demand that all the captives should be delivered to me instantly, that I might take them to my camp."

Sibley's conceit was apparent to all involved with the transfer of the captives. He had everyone on edge during the transfer, as his eyes seemed to interrogate those they rested upon. Paranoia was so great that Indian farmers who had taken the white man ways began to fear he would accuse them of being part of the uprising. It was at this point that Tatemina got word that his cousin in Mankato was nowhere to be found, and it was speculated that renegades had taken her.

* * *

"You be careful my friend. There is much danger between this place and Mankato." Anton had offered to accompany him, and he had been turned down flat. He was told that it was important that he stay with his family, especially now. There was very little trust placed in Henry Sibley, and Four Wings, now mending nicely, just might need his presence.

"Do not worry about me. I need to find out what happened to her. I will be fine."

Tatemina was once again mounted on his wonderful stallion, retrieved earlier from Riggs. With a slap of reins on the horse's flank, he left camp at a gallop. Before covering five hundred yards, he slowed to a canter. At the slower pace, he knew his mount could run for hours without tiring, and it was paramount that he reach Mankato as soon as possible.

Dusk was stealing across the prairie, the last rays of the setting sun were at his back and ahead he could see darkness approaching. He thought about the terrible mess the Dakota Nation was in. While it would have been easy to blame the arrogance of youth and lack of understanding of those involved in the outbreak, deep down he knew the cause, and it didn't lie with the Indians.

How many treaties were made and how many were broken? How many promises were made and then forgotten? From the very beginning, the white man had systematically taken everything. They had run the buffalo west, and through their treaties, they had taken Indian land and chased away the game. Streams that once ran so heavy with fish you could walk on their backs were now barren. The furbearers like mink, otter, beaver, and muskrat had disappeared.

He thought, *There is nothing left except to farm for our food.*

The rifle barrel caught him across the left temple and everything went black, the impact sending him headfirst into the stream embankment.

Chapter Nineteen

The Pardon

S IBLEY SET HIS TEMPORARY HEADQUARTERS at a place called Camp Release, downriver from Lac qui Parle, a short distance north-west of the Upper Agency. By the twenty-eighth, he had more than twelve hundred Dakota in custody, and over the next few weeks another eight hundred surrendered to the authorities. Most of these were able to establish innocence through testimony that placed them far from the battle scenes. Stephen Riggs was tasked with culling the innocent and determining those with possible ties to the battles. He was given the responsibility of identifying which Indians should stand trial.

Since the beginning of hostilities on August 18, the war had claimed the lives of over five hundred Americans and countless Dakota, although only about sixty of the latter were accounted for. While the vast majority of Indians never stood trial, over four hundred were accused of taking an active part in at least one battle. They were to stand trial during which death or imprisonment would be the verdict.

Colonel Sibley wasted no time in setting up a five-man commission to try the Indians. They were to gather the evidence and decide level of guilt, no small matter with such a large number of accused. By October 4, they had deliberated on, and disposed of only twenty-nine cases. Two weeks later, that number had grown to over one hundred twenty, a quantity much smaller than desired.

Addressing the commission members after the last case was heard on Wednesday, the fourth, Sibley made known his disappointment at how long it was taking.

"You men, good and true, know the importance of fairness, but you also are aware of the dead Americans, butchered, cruelly tortured, or burned alive, their mutilated bodies left where they died, because they were not red." Henry Hastings Sibley possessed considerable oratory skills and all were on display as he addressed the commission.

"Know also that General Pope is pushing for a conclusion to these trials. Therefore, I urge you . . . with fairness in mind . . . to recognize past deeds and install guilty verdicts upon those known to have participated in this conflict."

With nearly three hundred cases left to try, the prisoners were moved to the Lower Agency. There, in a cabin belonging to François La Bathe, the trials resumed. As the commission members became familiar with each of the battles and the particulars of each, a simple testimony that linked the defendant to the battle was often sufficient to result in a guilty verdict and the often-accompanying death penalty.

One mixed-blood named Otakle, known to the whites as Joseph Godfrey, admitted to participating in multiple battles. Offered clemency by the commission if he identified others, he became a damning witness for the prosecution, often remembering specifics of others' actions during the melee.

Eyewitnesses were brought in and testimony delivered. Indians, not understanding the severity to the proceedings, readily admitted to firing their rifles three or four times, although, no admission to hitting anything. Guilty was the verdict. If murder or rape was proven, death by hanging was the sentence.

Being so out of touch with the gravity of their predicament resulted in almost farcical exchanges with the commission:

"What goods, if any, did you take from Forbe's store?"

"Some blankets."

"Anything else?"

"Yes, some calico and cloth."

"Anything else?"

"Yes, some powder, and some lead, and some paint, and some beads."

"Anything else?"

"Yes, some flour, and some pork, and some coffee, and some rice, and some sugar, and some beans, and some tin cups, and some raisins, and some twine, and some fishhooks, and some needles, and some thread."

"Were you going to set up a grocery store on your own account?"

The Indian simply sat in the chair, nothing more being said.

There were also sad, heartrending moments when witnesses to atrocities were called to testify against, or to verify the identity of participants.

For the most part little time was spent with each Indian before finding him guilty and moving on to the next.

* * *

Lac qui Parle Mission
November 1

FOUR WINGS'S BODY WAS STRONG, and he proved to have exceptional recuperative properties, although he was quick to point out it was Star Woman's medicine that did the job.

After Colonel Sibley moved the captives, Four Wings helped take the family's belongings back to Red Iron's village. Planning for a long stay, he and Anton built a wigwam on the order of the one they shared with Dokkins and Carries Stick. Larger than the tipi they used while on the move, the wigwam was better suited for long-term shelter. They configured a separate room for Anton and Star Woman, which gave them privacy while Four Wings slept in the main space. All in all, it was a very comfortable camp that accommodated all three adults.

On Saturday Star Woman was visiting with Doctor Williamson. Williamson had come to the old mission grounds to minister to the captives, and after the invitation by Anton to share their camp, decided it would be time well spent to hang around a few days to discuss translation issues with Star Woman. They were talking about the completed translation of the Gospel of John, in the New Testament.

"Please, let us read the first verse . . . In the beginning was the Word, and the Word was with God and the Word was God. It is important that the same nuance is used in verse fourteen . . . And the word became flesh and dwelt among us. That is central to our belief and must be conveyed in the Dakota language as clearly as it comes across in English."

Williamson's limitations in speaking and reading Dakota had a way of forcing him to check, double check, and triple check every passage. Recently, a few of his Christian converts had been asking questions about these passages, and he wished to verify the correctness of the translation.

"The translation written in the Dakota Bible is accurate for the Mdewakanton dialect. Reverend Riggs has done an excellent job of following our notes in writing his Dakota dictionary. Those verses are accurately written."

Doctor Williamson evidenced relief, confirming to Star Woman that his concern for the Dakota people was sincere and deeply felt.

She asked, "Were any of your church people killed during the raiding?"

Williamson answered, "Yes, we lost an entire family when their cabin was burned. Many more did not die and they have Other Day to thank. I can't tell you how grateful I am for his presence. He, and a number of other men like your Anton and Four Wings, were responsible for saving the lives of many friendly Indians as well as countless settlers."

"Yes, they saved many lives . . . but it almost cost my son his own."

Their conversation was cut short as Four Wings entered the wigwam with an armful of fresh fish.

"Luck was with us this day. My fish trap captured a large sturgeon. We will eat well for the next couple of days. How long will you be with us, Doctor?"

"I'm afraid I must leave tomorrow morning. I plan on visiting many of my congregation at the Lower Agency before I go on to New Ulm and Mankato."

Star Woman addressed Four Wings. "I wonder how Tatemina is doing down in Mankato. It seems like he's been gone an awfully long time." She was used to having the men in her life disappear for long periods, however, this was somehow different. She couldn't explain it. She had an uncomfortable feeling about his absence.

"Hard saying. If a renegade band took his cousin, I doubt she's still alive. It's probably better for her if she isn't. Either way, I don't suppose he'll quit until he finds her." Four Wings, like most Indians, viewed death as the start of another journey.

Williamson interjected, "I'll see if I can find out anything and send word back. It's possible I'll cross paths with him along the way."

"Mother and I would be much appreciative for anything you can do, Doctor Williamson."

"I would be glad to assist in any way I can. Tatemina is a fine man, and he saved many lives," he fixed his eyes on young Four Wings, "including yours."

The three of them engaged in small talk while the fish sizzled to perfection, then they ate.

* * *

François La Bathe's Cabin
Lower Sioux Agency

"BRING IN THE NEXT ONE, CORPORAL," Colonel William H. Crooks, the ranking member of the commission, ordered.

The corporal led in a man in his sixties, short of stature, well muscled, and appearing fit for his age. His face was battered, eyes swollen nearly shut, and he was filthy. His body and clothing were coated with dirt and the right side of his head was matted with blood.

"What's happened to this man, Corporal?"

"Can't say for sure, sir. He was brought in by a relief party of troopers who say they caught him riding away from a cabin what held some dead."

"What's his name?"

"Don't know for sure, sir. He hasn't spoken a word. It's almost as though he's deaf."

"Hey, you there, you got a name?" The youngest on the commission, Lieutenant Rollin C. Olin, spoke with disdain.

The Indian stood impassively, head held high and straight, eyes swollen to mere slits, the right side of his face covered with dried blood from the eight-inch gash above his ear. There was no reaction.

"Sir . . . the men that brought him in said he called himself something like Wrong Wing, or Wrong Way, or something like that. They said he repeated it a couple of times. They didn't treat him none too gentle."

Colonel Crooks spoke toward a cordoned off area in which a half dozen witnesses stood. The building was small, so survivors who had witnessed the rage behind the killings waited at the Lower Agency until the men they were witnessing against were called in front of the commission.

"Does anyone have evidence linking this man to atrocities?"

There was a shaking of heads as those gathered mumbled among themselves. As the gavel was about to fall, two boys stepped forward, the older of them served as the spokesman.

"We seen him."

Crooks looked upon the two. "What were the circumstances under which you saw this man?"

"He's the one what had his way, and then killed our mom."

"How can you be sure? He's pretty messed up right now."

"We're sure, ain't we, Stemmi?"

The younger boy looked at the Indian, and with a grimace, pursed his lips and spit at the prisoner. "It's him all right. I'd know him anywhere."

Convinced, Colonel Crooks addressed the tattered native in front of him, "Do you have anything to say in your defense?"

The interpreter, Antoine D. Frenière, a mixed-blood, repeated the question in the Dakota language. The second interpreter, Reverend Stephen Riggs, was out of the room during the interrogation of this prisoner.

The Indian remained motionless, neither answering nor reflecting any emotion that might indicate he heard the question.

With no answer from the prisoner, the commission members briefly conversed in hushed tones.

Turning to the Indian, the colonel, as was standard practice in these proceedings, passed the verdict and punishment as one.

"This commission finds you guilty of murder and sentences you to hang by your neck until dead." With great flourish, he slammed the gavel on the bench in front of him.

"Next case!"

Tatemina, hands chained behind his back, turned, and was led from the room.

* * *

THE TRIALS CONTINUED at a record pace, sometimes completing up to forty in a single day. The commission finished its work on November 5, by which time they had tried three hundred ninety-two prisoners, three hundred seven sentenced to death, and another sixteen given prison terms.

The commission's actions were reviewed by Colonel Sibley, whereupon he approved all except one. The one exception was a case involving the brother of the well-known friend of the whites and liberator of the captives, John Other Day, who had appealed the case to the colonel, citing inconclusive evidence sufficient to convict.

The Indians in custody and not under sentence totaled about seventeen hundred men, women, and children. Sibley thought long and hard about these captives. They were guilty of no crime, nevertheless, to just cut them loose was not an option. He knew the final solution was to move every Dakota from the state.

Likely, of greater importance to him was the fact that a good deal of the success attached to his campaign was directly tied to the number of Indians that "surrendered" to him. In his mind, he had done a heroic thing. In reality those involved in the uprising, the perpetrators of the most grievous acts, were scattered before the wind. There were a few murderers mixed in with friendlies, however, in general terms those that he held were the most innocent of the lot. They wanted an end to the bloodshed as much as the whites did.

* * *

STEPHEN RIGGS AND DOCTOR WILLIAMSON were just finishing their conversation about the trials.

Riggs dumped his innermost thoughts. "I've seen men take more time choosing a pair of boots than what those men did in trying the accused. What hurts more than that, I was the one that determined if there was enough evidence to bring them to trial." Riggs was at once appalled, angry, and heartsick. "It started out as a thoughtful endeavor. After fifty or so cases, the search for justice dwindled until it became an arduous task best completed, so less and less time was spent trying to find the truth. By the end, if they were at the battle, they were guilty of murder."

"There's not much you could do about that. I suppose with so many cases it was inevitable it would take that course."

Riggs persisted, "It's just a darn shame. I know there were men that rode on those raids without the slightest intention of firing a shot. They got sucked into it by the others, the really bad ones, and once there they couldn't turn back."

"Well, Stephen . . . if you think there were unjust sentences, you have no other course than to get that information to President Lincoln, and the sooner the better."

Riggs immediately dismissed the suggestion.

Williamson continued, "You know Bishop Whipple?" Riggs had worked closely with Whipple for the last couple of years.

"Of course."

"Do you know that he is in Washington right now? He went to explain the cause of the uprising to Lincoln and push for reforms to the Indian policies."

Riggs's pulse quickened.

"No, I didn't know. I've been so tied up with this business that I'm afraid there are a lot of things I'm not aware of."

"We could telegraph Whipple of the situation. He's a very persuasive man with a strong personality. He would be perfect for pleading your case."

* * *

FROM THE BEGINNING, Pope and Sibley wished for immediate execution of the guilty. Fortunately, they both doubted they had the authority to proceed with that extreme measure. In mid-October, they sent a cable to President Lincoln requesting that power. He had not answered them.

On November 7, after whittling the number to be executed down to three hundred three, they telegraphed the names to President Lincoln and awaited his reply.

In Washington, the president, fresh off his meeting with Bishop Whipple, who impressed him greatly with his eloquence and persuasiveness, asked Pope to forward "the full and complete record of their convictions."

The executions would have to wait.

* * *

WILLIAMSON AND RIGGS WERE THANKFUL for the news that the president intended to have someone go over the transcripts of those sentenced to die. Whipple had done a superb job of conveying their fears to President Lincoln, and they were confident that the most questionable testimonies would not stand.

They were in the midst of a relaxed conversation when Williamson remembered his promise to Star Woman.

"You know that friend of Anton McAllister, the Indian named Round Wind, Tatemina, in Dakota language? Seems he left the Lac qui Parle area a couple of weeks ago on his way to Mankato. He got word that a cousin of his turned up missing so he went to find her."

"Yes, I know him. He came to our early translation sessions with Renville. A good man. I loaned him a horse at the beginning of this thing. There are lots of folks that owe their lives to him and Anton. What about him?"

"Nobody's heard from him since he left, and Star Woman is more than a little worried. She asked me if I'd ask around down here."

"No, I sure haven't seen him. Seems likely he rode straight on to Mankato. I'll keep my eyes peeled though."

* * *

New Ulm
November 9

"CLOSE IT UP BACK THERE!" Sibley barked the command. They were approaching New Ulm, and he expected trouble.

"You men, I want you riding each side of the wagon, and I want you tight together. These folks would like nothing better than to get their hands on these Indians. Your job is protect them . . . regardless of what you may think about it."

Sibley was transferring prisoners to Camp Lincoln at South Bend, just upstream from Mankato, to await execution. Although packed into open wagons and under heavy guard, he knew there was a possibility of trouble. New Ulm was overflowing with settlers come there for protection, and after two attacks on their city, the second of which burned a substantial number of the buildings, they were justifiably angry.

Although, it was possible for him to avoid the city altogether, the thought of a triumphant march was more than Sibley could resist.

They had barely set foot upon the main road through the city proper when townspeople began to mass together. The deeper they went, the more people gathered around the procession.

When they started throwing objects at the wagons Sibley knew they could be in trouble.

"Bugler, sound the trot."

The procession quickened, and the townspeople, sensing they were about to be denied justice, attacked the wagons.

"Bugler, sound the gallop." Sibley was afraid of losing control of the situation. Already there were men climbing on the wagons with clubs, swinging at any Indian they could reach.

"Clear away! Back off those wagons!" Sibley rode through the crowd, up and down the column, his men struggling to control their mounts and the angry mob while the wagon drivers urged their horses to a gallop. When they cleared the city and were a safe distance beyond the trouble, Sibley ordered a halt to assess the damage.

Several of the captives had been seriously injured, some critically, and Sibley had seen more than one civilian go to the ground during the fracas.

"There is nothing between here and Camp Lincoln. We stop for nothing. I want to see these prisoners in lockup at the earliest possible time. Now let's move out."

Camp Lincoln was just outside the town of Mankato and it had adequate facilities to imprison the Indians while providing protection for them from angry citizens. They reached the camp without incident, and the Indians were incarcerated, much to the satisfaction of Henry Sibley.

Shortly after placing the condemned prisoners in Camp Lincoln, Henry Hastings Sibley turned his command over to Stephen A. Miller, a Colonel in the Seventh Minnesota. Shortly after taking command, Colonel Miller, confronted by angry citizens threatening the camp, moved the prisoners to a more secure location in Mankato, which placed them in a large log structure easily defensible while awaiting President Lincoln's decision.

On November 25, Sibley became head of a new department created by the War Department, headquartered in St. Paul. He had been successful in bolstering his reputation, although his triumph at Lone Tree Lake, which had been given the misnomer the Battle of Wood Lake, was a result of accident more than one of battlefield strategy.

* * *

"YOU BE CAREFUL NOW, DOCTOR. I know it isn't a long ride, but it's hard telling what lies along the way." Riggs was speaking to Williamson.

"I'll be careful all right. If there were any hostiles left in this area, we would have heard about it. It's been going on a month since things settled down. I don't think there's anything to worry about."

"Ride with God."

"I always do." He reined his horse, and with a wave was on his way. He was headed for the prisoners' lockup in Mankato. He knew some of the men and felt a compelling responsibility to minister to them.

Upon reaching Mankato, he rode immediately to the large building in which the Indians were held and entered forthwith. It took him awhile to become accustomed to the dark, smoke-filled interior. After several minutes, he began to see many men seated in a haphazard manner throughout. The floor was dirt and there was the occasional small fire with men gathered closely to take advantage of the heat.

As he walked through their midst, he noticed an individual seated away from the group. He had no fire, instead wrapping himself in a tattered blanket. There was something vaguely familiar about the man so he approached him.

"Excuse me, sir. My name is Thomas Williamson. Is there anything I can do for you?"

At the sound of his voice, the man seated in front of him rose to his feet and turned.

"Doctor Williamson!"

"Tatemina?"

* * *

Red Iron's Camp

Doctor Thomas Williamson pushed his horse as never before. It was imperative he reached Star Woman, Anton, and Four Wings as soon as he could. They had to stop this nightmare.

In Red Iron's camp, he drew up in front of Anton's wigwam.

"Anton!" His voice, sharp and tinged with fear, was louder than normal.

Anton stepped out.

"Thank God you're here. We've got a huge problem, and we need to talk."

They entered together to join Star Woman and Four Wings inside the enclosure.

"Please, let us share our meal with you. You look like you have ridden hard . . . Four Wings, please tend to Doctor Williamson's horse." Star Woman didn't miss a beat, and the young man honored the request, leaving immediately to unsaddle the gelding. Using the saddle blanket as a towel, he wiped the animal down, hobbled his front legs, and placed a bucket of grain at his feet then went back inside.

Williamson was just finishing the best meal he had enjoyed in a very long time.

"We know where Tatemina is." Anton spoke to Four Wings who responded immediately.

"That means he's alive. That's good." He turned toward his mother to see sadness etched around her eyes. "There's more, isn't there?"

Williamson offered, "He's locked up with the renegades in Mankato. He says they found him guilty of murdering a white woman."

"What? That's a lie. He was with me almost the whole time. He likely saved fifty or sixty people. He would never kill a white woman."

"I'm just repeating what he told me. He said after he left here he got jumped by a group of six troopers that had just come up from Leavenworth to help the militia clean up this mess and help rebuild."

Williamson caught his breath.

"He says they bushwhacked him out of nowhere . . . laid a rifle barrel across the side of his head. Cut him open pretty badly. They were downright mean. Tied his hands together, threw a loop between them and dragged him around. He ran until he could run no more, and when he fell, they just kept on dragging."

"Those dirty bastards! Excuse me, Doctor."

"Don't worry, I feel the same. After they got tired of dragging, they decided to have a little fun just beating on him with their fists.

He'd lose consciousness, wake up to another beating, lose consciousness again . . . they wouldn't listen to him. He tried, over and over, to reason with them, but they wouldn't listen. Finally, he just shut up. Then they finally brought him in."

"How'd they figure him to be a murderer?"

"Seems there were these two German boys who identified him as the one who killed their ma."

Four Wings was appalled. "Wasn't there anyone who recognized him? All who know him know he could never do such a thing."

"Nobody saw him. After I left him, I went straight to the commanding officer to demand Tatemina's release, and was told the conviction stands. He's due to be hung with the rest." Williamson paused before continuing.

"Riggs was a translator at the trial and he never saw Tatemina. He must have been brought in while Riggs was out of the room. They were supposed to stop the trials when one of the translators was missing. It seems they were in such an all-fired hurry to get them done, they must have kept on going."

Anton stood mute, shaking his head. Star Woman seemed to be staring at nothing, and Williamson looked to be full of despair.

Four Wings said, "That's it then? There is nothing we can do?"

"The only chance is if President Lincoln gives him a pardon . . . and Riggs has already sent him a strongly worded telegram."

"What if someone were to go to see Lincoln in person? There just isn't any way that Tatemina killed an innocent white. How about this fellow, Whipple? Do you suppose he would go?"

"Doubtful. He's already been there. In fact, he's done some good it seems. It's just too early to tell. At least he got them to postpone the executions." Williamson thought for a while, and then continued, "I say we go talk to Riggs and see what he thinks. I agree with you Four Wings, there must be a way to save him."

* * *

ANTON, FOUR WINGS, DOCTOR WILLIAMSON, and Thomas Riggs were deep into a conversation that started nearly three hours earlier inside the Lower Sioux Agency.

Riggs was speaking. "It's already the fifth of December, and the president has not yet acknowledged receipt of my telegram, nor has he provided direction on what to do with the three hundred three under the death sentence. If I didn't have to stay here for translation duties, I would go to Washington myself, although, I don't know what good I could do. I wasn't witness to any of it."

Four Wings, who was slouched against the wall slightly separated from the others, jerked erect.

"I know for a fact that at the same time the boys said Tatemina killed their mother, we were holed up in a settler's cabin by the Chippewa River. That's when I was nearly killed. He saved my life."

Riggs turned to Williamson, "Thomas, do you think you can accompany this young man to Washington to meet with the president? I think it's the only way to save Tatemina's life. Henry Whipple convinced him that this whole Indian thing has been terribly mismanaged. I think there's an excellent chance that he'd listen to an eye-witness account that proves a man's innocence."

The following day, December 6, 1862, President Lincoln sent word that he approved the execution of thirty-nine from the original three hundred three. He also sent a document in his own handwriting that listed the thirty-nine by name and ordered the execution to take place on December 19. The ninth name on the list, in Lincoln's own hand, was "Ta-te-mi-na—Round Wind."

The following day Williamson and Four Wings were on a train to Washington.

* * *

COLONEL STEPHEN A. MILLER was on the edge of going into panic mode. "Good Lord, men. We have an awful lot to do if we're going to dispatch the sentence on the nineteenth. That's less than two weeks distant. I don't think we can get it done that quickly. We've got to identify those on the list, and damn near everybody listed has a counterpart with the same name. Major Brown, that is your assignment, and I need it done yesterday, so start right now. On your way, send the quartermaster in here. We're going to need some stout timbers, lots of planks, and plenty of rope." Now that he was in the thick of it, his nerves were settling, and he was back in control.

"Captain Davis, I want you to supervise the design and build of the gallows, just let the quartermaster know what you need. This is going to be some hanging. Make thirty-nine trap doors and I want them all controlled by a single rope. We cut that rope, and they all go at the same time. Got it?"

"Yes, sir."

* * *

THE TRAIN REACHED WASHINGTON on the tenth. Unfortunately, the president was too busy to give them an audience. For the next seven days they waited while he bounced from meeting to meeting, having his hands full with the ongoing Civil War between the states. The men had no alternative than to wait it out, and with every day that passed, they could feel the life of their friend coming closer to an end.

Finally, on the nineteenth, the day of the execution, they were called for the meeting with Lincoln. Thinking it was too late to be of value, they nonetheless went to see the president of the United States. If nothing else, they were determined to tell him of the terrible mistake that had been made. They were escorted into the president's private study. It was nine thirty at night, and he was in shirtsleeves.

"Gentlemen, I am so sorry I made you wait so long, it is unfortunate but unavoidable. I earlier received a telegraph message from Reverend Stephen Riggs, and more recently from my new, and very impressive friend, Henry Whipple. In it he urges me to hear you out, for the tale you have for me is worth hearing."

Doctor Williamson answered.

"Mr. President, we thank you for taking time from your very busy schedule to meet with us, however, it pains me to say we are too late. My friend, Four Wings, can prove that our friend, sentenced to hang, had nothing to do with the murder of a white woman during the Minnesota war with the Dakota."

"Whipple's message said as much. Apparently you have not heard the latest developments concerning the executions." The president had a barely perceptible twinkle in his eye. "Colonel Miller requested, and I approved, the delay of the executions until the twenty-sixth. He apparently needed more time to prepare. Quite fortuitous, wouldn't you say?"

* * *

Mankato
December 25

THE THIRTY-NINE HAD BEEN separated from the other prisoners and shackled together in leg irons. They'd been moved to a separate building where they awaited their fate. Some looked inward, some were stoic, while others were defiant. It appeared all were prepared to die.

Missionaries moved among them, blessing and listening to confessions from those whose adopted faiths required such. Some dictated letters for their families, and others whose families were near were allowed to visit during the last hours of their last night on earth.

Eventually the visitors were forced to leave, while the missionaries continued their task of tending and mending souls.

The eastern sky began to show a lightening at the horizon, and inside, a soft murmur could be heard as the Indians began their death songs. Major Brown and his men began to prepare them for the gallows that now stood in the public square. Chains were removed and their arms were bound behind their backs. The missionaries passed among them, giving last rites for those requesting them.

Brown's men placed white caps on the Indians' heads, which would be rolled down to cover their faces before they fell to their deaths, and at ten o'clock on the morning of December 26, 1862, the prisoners were led from the building to the wooden scaffold in the square.

The town square was so full of people that if one of them fainted they would not have fallen to the ground, and there were ranks of over fourteen hundred soldiers lining the scaffold to make sure there would be no trouble. As the Indians mounted the steps, they again began their death songs. The nooses were placed around their necks and the caps were rolled down. At Brown's command, a slow drum roll commenced. At the third roll, William Duley cut the rope.

So engaged were the citizens in the spectacle that they failed to notice that the total number of hanged men was thirty-eight. No one counted the men as they approached the steps, no one counted as the nooses were placed, and no one counted as thirty-eight bodies swung, and when they were cut down and brought to the mass grave prepared at the edge of town, no one noticed that one man, the thirty-ninth, was not among the dead.

* * *

FOUR WINGS AT LAST UNDERSTOOD the fullness of his vision and how closely it tied to that of Tomawka's. It was Tomawka's vision that first saw the beginning of the terrible conflict set in motion by the four young braves. Four Wings now understood that the four boulders that appeared for the grasshopper to land on represented the braves who had first started the war, the same boulders that turned to skulls.

The portion of his own vision that the old man could not interpret was now clear. The crows that fell to earth did indeed represent the Dakota Nation. *They shrank in size until each became a swarm of grasshoppers that flew to meet me. As they drew near they became three distinct groups and they joined me in flight. On my right was a group of thirteen. On my left, another group of thirteen, and behind me was a third group of the same number.*

The swarm represented Little Crow's band of renegades, the three groups of thirteen, the thirty-nine condemned men. *I looked again at each of the grasshoppers and saw they had taken the shape of whitened skulls. No sooner did I see the skulls then they vanished into a smoking nothingness. As I watched, one skull reappeared momentarily . . .* The whitened skulls referred to the death of the thirty-nine, and the reappearance of a single skull, the resurrection of one of the condemned.

Amazement and awe settled over Four Wings as he realized the specificity of his vision. It had not only foretold events that were to happen, it told of his near death experience and that the man who would save him was of the thirty-nine. *As I watched, one skull reappeared momentarily before taking the shape of a dragonfly identical to the one I was mounted on. As we flew, he was caught up in a wind vortex that sucked him high above everything.* His vision had identified the man who now rode to his right. The wind vortex . . . Round Wind, Tatemina, his friend who escaped the death of the thirty-eight.

Finally, his vision was complete. *Suddenly I joined him as we fell toward the earth.*

* * *

THREE HORSEMEN RODE toward Red Iron's encampment. They rode at a canter, legs hugging the sides of their horses, reins hanging slack, and their bodies straight and proud. Entering the camp, they walked their horses to the location that once held a wigwam, but was now bare. There the woman joined them, and the four pointed their horses west and quietly rode out of the camp.

Once on the prairie, they again brought their mounts to a canter. The men, Anton, Tatemina, and Four Wings, stretched three wide behind Star Woman as she led them toward the Missouri River and the new life that awaited them.

Epilogue

L ITTLE CROW FLED TO CANADA and was shot by a Minnesota farmer while foraging for food with his son while on his way back to St. Paul to surrender. The shooter received a reward for the killing. Many spirited warriors from Little Crow's band joined the Lakota and continued to vent their anger on white settlers and the U.S. Army.

The opening shots of the great Sioux Wars were now a memory, but the wars themselves had just begun. The broken promises and self-serving treaties made by the United States—and never honored—would continue, and the noble Indian would fight back until the war with the Sioux ended forever with the final dishonor and all out slaughter of men, women, and children by the U.S. Army at Wounded Knee, South Dakota, on December 29, 1890.

Study Aids

History of the Santee Sioux: United States Indian Policy on Trial, Roy Willard Meyer.

The Monstrous Conspiracy: Treaties and Practical Meanings to the Sioux, The Dakota War of 1862, Kenneth Carley and Cheri Register.

Radiograms of Minnesota History: Sioux versus Chippewa, Willoughby M. Babcock, Jr.

A Century of Dishonor: A Sketch of the United States Government's Dealings, Helen Hunt Jackson, Henry Benjamin Whipple, Julius Hawley Seelye, Cairns Collection of American Women Writers.

Three Score Years and Ten, Charlotte Ouisconsin Van Cleve

Kinsmen of Another Kind: Dakota-White Relations in the Upper Mississippi, Gary Clayton Anderson.

Over the Earth I Come: The Great Sioux Uprising of 1862, Duane Schultz.

The Great Sioux Uprising, C.M. Oehler.

The Dakota-Lakota-Nakota Human Rights Advocacy Coalition.

History of the Sioux War and Massacre, Isaac Heard.

Legends, Letters, and Lies: Readings about Inkpaduta and the Spirit Lake Massacre, Mary Bakeman.

Little Crow, Spokesman for the Sioux, Gary C. Anderson.

In the Footsteps of Our Ancestors: The Dakota Commemorative Marches of the 21st century, Angela Cavender Wilson.

The Autobiography of Major Lawrence Taliaferro, Lawrence Taliaferro.